FOR LOVE

&

COOKIES

A MATCHMAKERS' BOOK CLUB NOVEL

NICOLE VIDAL

COPYRIGHT

Cover design by Designs with Sass
Developmental Edit by Katherine McIntyre of Hot Tree Editing
Final Edit by Kristin Scearce of Hot Tree Editing

ISBN 978-1-961365-95-7

TABLE OF CONTENTS

KEEP IN TOUCH WITH NV

Facebook (http://fb.me/NicoleVidalAuthor)

Instagram (http://instagram.com/nicolevidal_author)

Amazon (https://www.amazon.com/Nicole-
Vidal/e/B082DJHPXP?ref_=dbs_p_ebk_r00_abau_000000)

My website (www.nicolevidal.com)

Pinterest (http://pinterest.com/NicoleVidal_Author)

Goodreads
(https://www.goodreads.com/author/show/19827329.Nicole_Vidal)

PROLOGUE

CARLY

I'm late. As the president, if you will, late isn't a good look. Not my fault, though. There was a huge multi-vehicle, multiple-casualty incident on the highway late this afternoon. Large snowfall totals aren't frequent in Southern Maine, nor this close to the first day of spring. However, this storm dropped more than the normal on our area, and some drivers weren't prepared.

I park in front of Scarlett's gorgeous waterfront home and hustle inside. The open concept living room has a wall of windows to showcase the ocean view. I shrug off my coat and greet the members. "Good evening, ladies. I apologize for my tardiness. Let's get started."

The front door whooshes open behind me. Maggie Washington and Lina Gugliotti step inside.

As they hang their coats, I call the meeting of the Matchmakers' Book Club to order. "Hello, ladies. We're glad you could make it on this snowy evening. I was expecting a small group, but eight is perfect. First, I would like to welcome our newest member, Alannah. She captured the heart of Callan Craven with a little nudge from her son, Caden, and members of our group. However, the initial helper is not here but deserves recognition. Kelsey, please thank your husband, Captain

Ramirez, for the assist in assigning Craven to the boys' basketball games instead of the girls."

Kelsey replies, "I will."

Alannah smiles and says, "Thank you. I'm excited to be here." Alannah and Callan married a few weeks ago at Clay Hill Farm. A few of the other members who know Alannah welcome her.

I continue, "For those of you who are new to our group, allow me to share our purpose. Initially, we started as a gaggle of nurses and EMTs to de-stress from the rigors of our profession with book club and girls' night in. At the onset, there were four women. Now, we have a membership of more than twice that many. Over the years, it evolved into a girl gang of epic proportions. Not only do we host events for the local children's charities, but we keep tabs on the most eligible singles in our community. Our matchmaking book club was created in good fun, and the tradition has continued for the last six years. Along with the purpose of our group, the rules for inclusion on the list have evolved. Inclusion consists of a few factors balanced against one another. First, an attractive package is a must. Also, candidates and admitted bachelors or bachelorettes must be a member of our first responder community, including police officers, firefighters, and EMTs. Most importantly, we attempt to keep the list secret until after he or she has been legally wed. Now I open the floor to all members to raise a motion or suggest additions to the list."

Willa Cappelli speaks up first. "I move to suggest two changes. First, the criteria should be expanded to include nurses and doctors. Second, I recommend changing the requirement from legally wed to engaged to allow participation in meetings. It would decrease the chance of our group being outed inadvertently. However, the honoree shouldn't be removed until he or she is legally wed."

"Interesting amendments. Let's start with expanding eligibility to nurses and doctors. All those in favor?" I ask the group. As long as these ladies don't set their sights on me, I'm fine with doctors and nurses being eligible.

Six hands rise.

"Motion carried. Regarding changing the invitation to join the group prior to marriage but not removing the honoree's name. All those in favor, please raise your hand."

Only one member fails to vote for this motion.

"The second motion is carried," I state. Rumblings of chatter start among the group.

Then Lina asks, "We need two honorees from YPD, correct?"

"Yes," I reply.

"Do they have to be men?" Kelsey wonders aloud.

I consider my answer based on the rules and state, "No. The rules indicate there must be at least one woman on each list. No reason we can't have a second."

"Perfect. I recommend Esmeralda Garcia. She joined the department in the last few months. Not only is she gorgeous but funny and new to the area. Esme, which she chooses to be called, moved here from Florida," Kelsey offers.

"She can be an option. Any other suggestions?" I ask the group.

I get no responses as far as adding to the list. "If there are no other recommendations, I move to add Officer Garcia to the YPD list and leave the second spot open."

"I second," Gladys states. She's one of the founding members and formerly worked as a caregiver for the Smithsons and assisted in matching Zack and Scarlett.

"Motion carried. Now, let's move on to our next couple. Talk among yourselves, and we'll vote on the way out. After I tally the votes, I'll reach out to the members best suited to foster our honoree." Normally, I don't participate in choosing our next honoree.

"What about Penn?" Alannah suggests after reading the list of names. If I recall correctly, Alannah and Penn are locals. Perhaps she knows more about him personally than the others in the room.

"We haven't matched an EMT or a YFD honoree yet," Willa adds to the conversation.

"True," Maggie admits. "What about Hagen? He may be a tough one to match, though. His sole focus is Lilah."

"We can handle tough. I mean, you matched my husband and me," Kelsey states with a smile.

The ladies laugh and agree.

I wrap up our meeting. "Okay. I'll set the nominees out near the door, and you can vote on your way out. We have two choices: Séamus Penn and Lachlan Hagen. Don't forget to sign up for the 5K and charity toy drive for the children's floor at York Memorial. If you have any questions about the 5K, see Maggie. For the toy drive portion, see Scarlett. The run will take place this summer. Please vote as you leave."

The group moves into our discussion of this month's book selection. We changed it up a bit and chose a book used as an outline for the *Bridgerton* series on Netflix.

Willa speaks first. "To be honest, I liked the show better. Historical fiction isn't my favorite genre."

A few of the other ladies nod in agreement.

"I was more a fan of the Duke of Hastings. Regé-Jean Page is a sight to behold," I admit.

"Yes! That man is perfection." Lina fans her face.

"His accent makes me swoon," Alannah adds.

The ladies continue chatting about this month's selection. Mostly, they focus on the show. About an hour later, they shift gears to choose the book for next month.

With the next book selected, the ladies say goodbye. It's laughable considering these women see one another frequently between meetings. Some of them are family. As the crowd dwindles, Maggie approaches me.

"Hey, Carly. I wanted to check in about the advertising budget for the 5K."

"With the storm, I left those forms at home. I'll email you."

"Great, thanks. See you next month." Maggie slips out the front door.

After thanking Scarlett for the use of her home, I leave as well.

CHAPTER ONE

EVA

Relocating will be good for me, professionally and, more importantly, personally. A year ago, I was engaged to be married. Now, not so much. I push away those thoughts and focus on the positive. My promotion is significant, and the move brings me closer to my brother and his family.

Grant chose Maine to pursue his passion as a police officer. A few years later, he met Maggie at a traffic stop when she visited her sister for the holidays. Now they have two precocious kids. One is named after our late brother, Caleb, and the other after her late grandmother, Corrinne. Our parents, Greg and Regina, downsized soon thereafter. They sold the family home and purchased a small condo, which allows them to spend time in New York as well as Maine.

I've been in York Beach about a week. It's a quaint seaside town with beaches, a small village, and even an amusement park. I took time to pack up and relax before starting my new position. Currently, I'm staying at Gen's cottage. She inherited it from her grandmother, who passed away about five years ago, and modernized the floorplan. How do I know Gen? She's my brother's sister-in-law.

I pad to the gorgeous kitchen. The cabinetry is white with matching granite with lines of black, gray, and silver for the countertops and island. With a freshly brewed cup of coffee, I step onto the lower-level deck and inhale the ocean breeze. One deep breath and I return inside. While I love the beach, it's chilly, and the sand is covered with a layer of snow from a late-season storm.

I dress comfortably in leggings and a fluffy sweater and log into my office computer since I don't have a video conference call today. My new position is based in Boston, but it's a hybrid.

Near lunch, the doorbell rings. I wrinkle my nose. Only a few people know I'm here, literally a few. Checking the peephole, I see an older gentleman on the front porch with a large bag in his hand.

I open the door. "Hello, can I help you?"

"I have a delivery for Eva Washington," he replies. He's sweet with a plaid ivy cap, which coordinates with his jacket.

"Thank you." I accept the bag and pull money from my wallet. "Have a nice day."

He tips his hat and replies, "You as well."

He's so cute! I set the bag on the island and dig into it. The card indicates it's from Maggie.

Me: Thank you. It smells amazing!

Maggie: You're welcome.

Me: Where is it from?

Maggie: My restaurant. Not mine, lol. Morgan's.

Me: Sweet. Thanks.

Maggie: See you on Friday.

Me: Looking forward to meeting some of your friends.

Spreading out my lunch in front of the gorgeous French doors, I savor the artisan sandwich and fries. Each bite melts in my mouth. Chef has some serious skills. I make a mental note to check out Morgan's soon. An image of a gorgeous man flashes through my mind. It would be a perfect first date spot. Lachlan is tall with sandy blond hair and piercing eyes as blue as the tranquil waters of Antigua. He took my breath away. We met at the YPD holiday event a little over a month ago. I drove up for a visit after my interview in Boston, and it happened to be on the same day. My brother insisted I join him at the party. To be fair, I met Lachlan's sweet daughter first. Lilah, who possesses a mass of golden ringlets atop her head, spilled her plate of decorated cookies at my feet. Instantly, tears burst from her eyes.

The problem is… I'm not interested in anything long term right now. Cody, my ex-fiancé, did a number on me. We dated for three years before he proposed. Our engagement was going well until his behavior became suspect. Instead of coming straight home after the gym at the end of the day, he shifted his schedule. He started working out in the morning, then hitting the bar with his coworkers. Coworkers—plural—wasn't exactly true. He was wining and dining one coworker, Chelsea. She was my polar opposite in every way—brunette, voluptuous, and fiery. I'm not angry with her at all. Cody failed to mention his ring was perched on my finger while dating another woman.

I should've seen the signs when he asked for my hand in marriage. He made a public show of it at a trendy bistro downtown with a photographer on hand to capture the entire thing. I'm fine with the photos, but all those strangers, no thanks. The ring was a gaudy, five-carat, pear-shaped canary diamond. It isn't me at all. I'm more of a traditional girl, and my ex didn't bother to consider me. He chose the ring to appease his mother, which is another long, tedious story. Why did he propose instead of breaking up with me? No idea.

Pulling myself out of my useless memory spiral, I return to the office and continue my workday. To push away the sour taste the memories of Cody put in my mouth, I allow myself one more moment with Lachlan in the front of my mind. My smile renewed, I make progress on my project for the soccer team and then call it a day a few hours later.

After eating and cleaning the kitchen, I lock the doors and curl up on the master balcony in front of the cozy firepit with my book.

I wake early the next morning and decide to check out the local coffee shop. It's a short walk, and it's considerably warmer than yesterday. I meander down the street and around a curve. The stretch of beach along the back of Gen's house is on my left and the Perk on my right a few blocks ahead.

The shop is cute and has a *Friends* vibe. I peruse the extensive menu before stepping up to the counter.

"Welcome to the Perk. What can I get started for you?" a young woman with gorgeous raven hair greets me. Her name tag says "Macie."

"Morning. Can I have a vanilla chai latte and strawberry cheddar scone?"

"Of course."

I pay and wait for my order. Savoring the first glorious sip of the latte, I step outside and cross the street. I decide to stroll along the beach back to the cottage instead of the sidewalk. I'll dodge the patches of remaining snow along the way.

The next few days I'm buried in campaign themes and draft ad images and have no time to explore the area more. Aside from a second trip for pastries, I haven't left the cottage. I don't need to, but tonight I'm meeting Maggie and a few others for dinner and drinks. I can't wait.

My sister-in-law indicated the dress code was casual but not loungewear casual. I opt for jeans with a V-neck royal blue sweater and booties. After locking up, I walk down the street past the Perk and search for Inn on the Blues, where I'm meeting Maggie. She assured me it was close to the cottage. I decided to take her suggestion and enjoy the balmy weather this evening.

The atmosphere here is much different than in New York City. It's laid-back and peaceful. My affinity for the ocean is soothed with each morning coffee on the deck. I didn't realize how much I missed the shore surrounded by concrete and traffic noise until moving here.

The hostess greets me as I approach, but Maggie waves me over to her table. "Thank you, but I see my party over there."

The hostess nods, and I weave my way over to my sister-in-law.

"Hey, Eva!" She stands and hugs me.

I put Maggie on the spot when we first met. I mean, my brother brought her to the hospital when our mother had a stroke. Maggie stood up for herself and Grant that day. She told me flat out that his job was a calling, and she would support him. Since then, we've grown close. "This place is amazing!"

"The food is delicious too. Not as good as Morgan's," she adds, lowering her voice, "but still worth it."

"Maggie, aren't you forgetting to introduce the rest of us?" a stunning, curvy brunette asks.

"Sorry, Caroline." She looks at me and asks, "Ready?"

"Yes."

Maggie goes around the table introducing everyone. "Caroline, Noelle, Carly, and Poppy. Caroline and Noelle are married to Auggie and Cash Morgan, respectively, and own a childcare facility. Carly is the head nurse in the emergency department at York Memorial Hospital. Poppy works for Kelly Barnett at So Elegant."

"Nice to meet you. I'm Eva." I wave and take a seat beside Maggie. It's good to put faces to the names of her friends. Four people at once isn't too bad.

They each greet me, and then we order drinks and appetizers.

"What brings you to York Beach, Eva?" Caroline asks.

"A few reasons, but mainly, my promotion transferred me from New York to Boston. Living near Grant and Maggie made sense."

"What do you do?" Carly asks. She's girl-next-door pretty, blonde, and bubbly. Interesting considering she controls an emergency room. You would think her job would increase the likelihood of sadness. There are only a few instances where a hospital visit yields a happy ending.

"I'm a graphic designer and marketing analyst."

"Sweet. We could use your assistance. Can you freelance?" Noelle asks.

A smile curls up on my face. "Yes, I can take on my own clients." I reach into my purse and hand her my card. "We should set up a meeting to talk about it."

Noelle takes the card. "Sounds perfect! I'll call you on Monday to schedule something."

"Great."

Our server delivers our appetizers and takes our dinner order. According to Maggie—while second to Morgan's—each entrée is delicious. She recommended macaroni and cheese topped with lobster.

"Speaking of advertising, I have a freelance opportunity for you. Pro bono too." Maggie turns in my direction.

I laugh. At least she's honest about using my skills for free. "Is this the same one Grant mentioned in passing hoping to lure me in?"

Maggie drops her head. "The toy drive and 5K? Yup, that's the one."

"Let me know when the next meeting is and I'll be there," I answer.

"You're the best sister-in-law ever!"

I lift my shoulder and smile. "Yes, I am."

The table laughs, and we chat until our meal arrives.

Over dinner, the ladies suggest places to visit, like the Nubble Lighthouse or Dunne's Ice Cream Shoppe. Noelle and Caroline offer recommendations for a spa and nail salon.

Carly is the one who goes there. "No man in New York, Eva?"

Maggie attempts to stop the conversation. "Nope, no guy talk."

I wave her off. "It's okay, Maggie. About a year ago, I was engaged. Soon after he proposed, his behavior started to change. Cody was cheating on me. I dumped him and his gaudy ring."

"A new job and a fresh start in the man department. Sounds wonderful," Carly offers. Perhaps there's a story there. She sounds like she may have been burned in the past as well.

"Not interested in finding a man right now. Cody made me wonder if what I want is out there."

"What are you looking for?" Carly inquires.

"I want a marriage like my parents. Cliché, I know. They have been through it all, from health issues, wealth highs and lows, and losing my brother. They still have date nights and dance in the kitchen after thirty-eight years."

"It isn't a secret to you or these ladies, but I was where you are before I met your brother. There are good men out there. Finding them is the trick," Maggie offers.

Noelle adds, "She's right. I stumbled upon Cash when my flight to my brother's wedding was delayed."

"I met Auggie at boarding school when we were kids," Caroline shares.

"We could give you plenty of examples in our social circle," Maggie adds.

"I appreciate that. For right now, it's no-strings-attached for me."

The ladies raise their glasses and toast my new job and future girls-only dinners. We chat a bit longer, and then the ladies start to leave.

"It was a pleasure meeting you, Eva," Noelle states. She's not only whip-smart, but her mane of red hair and striking green eyes make her stand out more.

I wave to her and Caroline. "You as well. I'm sure I'll see you around."

"You will," Caroline replies.

Poppy and Carly leave right after them.

"Your friends are nice, Maggie."

"This is only a small portion of the amazing ladies in this town."

"Sweet."

"The meeting for the committee is Wednesday night at six," Maggie shares.

"Where?"

"Our house."

"I'll be there. Thank you for inviting me to join you tonight."

Maggie smiles and hugs me. "You're welcome. Do you want a ride to the cottage?"

"No, thanks. I'm going to use the restroom and walk along the shore."

"Okay. See you soon."

Maggie leaves, and I weave through the tables toward the restroom. On my way out, I note the path through the bar is less crowded. When I turn the corner, I see hot, single dad Lachlan wallowing over a beer in a rear booth… alone.

CHAPTER TWO

LACHLAN

It's the right thing to do. She needs this.

"Lilah, we need to leave," I call her from the kitchen.

"I'm ready, Daddy." My sweet little girl rushes to my side. I may have been thrust into parenthood unexpectedly, but Lilah has been a joy since day one.

"A little excited?"

"A lot!" she replies with a huge smile on her face.

My heart constricts. Perhaps Noelle was right. I shake my head inwardly. Not perhaps—she is right. Noelle runs the daycare Lilah attends. She understands calls running over and the need for flexibility in pickup times for first responders without penalty, especially police officers like me. The center also has extended hours as well, which is a novelty for single parents like me who work weekends.

"Did you pack some pajamas and your slippers?"

She shoves her purple unicorn bag in my direction. "Yes. Can we go now?"

I nod tightly. She may be looking forward to tonight, but I'm not. "Yes. Let's go."

Once she's secure in the back of my SUV, I pull out of our driveway and head to the center. Her excitement increases as we get closer.

Interestingly, she left here not two hours ago. Lilah has her car seat unbuckled by the time I get to her door.

"Li, we talked about unbuckling," I said, my tone stern.

"I didn't break rules. I stay in the truck." Her tiny voice restates the rules correctly.

"You did." After assisting her with the backpack, she slides her tiny hand in mine, and we walk to the front entrance. I input the code, and the door buzzes open.

"Hi, Lilah," Casey, one of the staff members, greets her. "Ready to have a fun night in?"

"Yes!" She turns, hugs me, and rushes away.

With a deep breath, I exit the building. Aimlessly, I drive around town and find myself parked at Short Sands Beach. My affinity with the ocean led me to this small beachside town. I moved here when Lilah was about six months old. While she wasn't aware yet, she needed to be removed from our old hometown. York Beach was the right choice for us. The people here are kind and friendly. My coworkers have become a second family for us over the past four years.

Not knowing what to do with myself, I step inside the Inn on the Blues and grab a booth in the back of the bar. I can hear Smithson and Craven in my head. *"A date would be nice right about now."* Both have found their better halves, and they continually rib me to do the same. The issue is, no one around here other than my attorney understands the reality of my life before I relocated here. To be fair, no one needs to know, nor have I met anyone willing to listen to my history and not run away. I keep the truth about Lilah's mother and the reasons for moving away from her to myself. Not only does it protect Lilah, but the privacy maintains my sanity.

My daughter is my sole focus. A position my attorney can empathize with considering she was a single parent as well. I wouldn't know how to begin dating again. I haven't been on a date in over five years. I shudder to think about the last time I accepted any type of affection from a woman other than my daughter. It's longer than I care to admit.

I order the dinner special and a beer, occupying myself on my phone while I wait for it to be served. No reason for me to rush through eating, as the event runs until ten tonight. The center calls it parents' night out. The kids spend the evening at the daycare for a nominal fee. It provides parents reliable childcare. This is the first time Lilah has attended, at Noelle's urging. While Lilah goes to daycare nearly daily, Noelle recommended more activities away from me with other kids. I also signed her up for soccer, which starts in a few weeks.

The server sets my meal in front of me and leaves. Mindlessly, I dig into the plate. The food is supposedly five-star cuisine, but I'm not truly tasting it. The fact that I'm not working and my daughter is not with me is foreign. I trust Noelle and her developmental guidance, but this is more difficult than I anticipated.

"Lachlan?"

A sultry voice I've heard only once calls my name. Yet the melodic tone haunts my dreams. "Eva?"

"Hi. Are you okay?"

I tilt my head. *No. She can see how I feel?* I don't respond but rather answer her question with one of my own. "What are you doing here?"

"I live here."

Intrigue rushes through me. She has been on my mind since the moment we met. However, she was merely visiting then. "I'm sorry." I stand beside her and offer her the other side of the booth. "Where are my manners? Would you like to join me?"

When she sits, a whiff of her perfume—a mixture of flowers and vanilla—teases me. "Yes. Thank you."

"Would you like a drink?"

"No. I just finished dinner with the girls."

I finally acknowledge her words. "You didn't live here when we met, did you?" I ask to settle the disconnect in my head.

She laughs softly and sets her hand on my forearm. "No, I didn't. I was in Boston for a job interview. I added a visit with Grant and his family. My brother invited me to the party."

The heat from her touch on my skin is intense. It's as if she branded me as hers. The pull when we met was magnetic and equally intriguing. "Do you always pack a sexy dress in your luggage for a family visit?" *Way to spill your inner thoughts, Lach.*

Her flawless skin turns a light shade of crimson, but she hasn't moved her hand. "Perhaps."

Eva upped her interesting factor with her response. "Congrats on the new job."

She smiles. "Thank you. Are you going to answer my question?"

I close my eyes briefly and shake my head. "I was kind of hoping you would forget you asked."

"Sorry, no chance of that happening. If you don't want to talk about it, that's fine. You looked sad, for lack of a better word."

"Are all members of the Washington family forthright?"

She purses her lips and replies, "Yes. No reason not to be. It causes miscommunication."

I catch her blue, sea glass-colored gaze and can't help but share. "I'm not sure that is the right explanation. Tonight is the first time I've been out without Lilah and not at work."

"Oh. Why?"

"I don't trust anyone to care for her like I do."

"Fair. Most parents don't. I won't pry where her mother is, but you must have reliable support for her during the day."

"Much appreciated. I do. That's where she is now."

Eva frowns.

"The center she attends has parents' night out twice a month. The owner encouraged me to bring Lilah to have more time with her peers instead of only me."

"Makes sense. Would you join me for a stroll on the beach?"

I hesitate for a millisecond. Not sure why, though. "Yes."

I settle my bill and follow her out of the restaurant. Most women are shorter than me due to my imposing height. However, Eva stands at eye level, and the heels on her booties are not high. She's blonde and downright striking. Aside from those alluring attributes, she's smart, funny, and refreshing. Admittedly, I watch her walk in front of me, cataloging the sway of her hips. While statuesque, she has enticing curves.

We aren't on a date, but I offer her my arm before we step into the crosswalk.

"Thank you."

"You're welcome." We cross the street and stop at the benches near the edge of the parking lot. "Want to take off your shoes or risk the sand?"

"Off… despite the possible chill." With her booties in one hand, she slides her arm around mine again. We turn right and walk to the far end of the beach.

Her proximity stokes the undercurrent of magnetism between us. The last woman physically close to me was Clare, Lilah's mother. Our initial meeting was hot and explosive. Then reality set in.

I forgot how soothing physical touch and closeness is for me. Eva fits beside me. Alarm bells are sounding in my brain. If I'm honest, blood is rushing south with each unintentional brush of her hip against me.

"How is your new position different from your old one?" I ask to shift the thoughts in my mind.

"I work in graphic design and marketing. I was promoted to manager for the Northeast region."

"Good for you. Consider me clueless, but what does your job entail? Are we talking jingles and logos?"

She laughs softly. It's a sweet sound. "Yes, plus brand management and social media growth. Although, my focus is television and large-scale rebranding."

"Like?"

"Currently, designing a new logo and branding strategy for the regional soccer team is my focus. It's between my company and one other based in Los Angeles."

"Cool."

"Soccer fan?" she asks.

"Football, actually."

"You played, didn't you?"

"Yes, in high school and college. How did you guess?"

"The wistful tone in your voice leads me to believe you miss it."

She's right. "I do."

We complete one lap across the sand and turn back. As long as the water doesn't touch our feet, we should be fine as far as beating the cold.

"Given the fact that it's your first time out in over four years, I assume you don't coach or play in any adult leagues?"

I shouldn't be surprised by her observant question. "Are you suggesting I'm boring?"

"No, not at all. Your focus is Lilah, and it's admirable."

I stop, turn her to face me, and rest my hands on her upper arms. "But?"

"I'm not a parent, but taking care of yourself is equally as important as your daughter."

A ribbon of lust stretches between us in this moment. She's calling me out, and yet I want to kiss her desperately. I need to feel if her lips are as soft and silky as they appear to be. "It's easier said than done in practice."

"Perhaps. As hard as it was to drop her off earlier, how are you feeling right now?"

"You probably don't want to hear my answer."

She eliminates the remaining space between us and sets one hand on the center of my chest. There's no chance she will miss my raging erection straining toward her. Her eyes bore into mine. The desire is unmistakable. "I'm sure I do."

"I want to kiss you until you can't breathe. Then I want to explore each inch of you with my mouth until you beg for a release. Want me to stop?"

She tilts her chin up slightly before her raspy and sensual reply. "No."

"Then I'll—" My alarm pierces the bubble of our conversation. *Damn!* "I'm sorry."

"You need to go pick up Lilah," she states matter-of-factly.

"Yeah. Can I give you a lift home?"

"Not necessary but thank you."

The spell between us is broken. I would give nearly anything to have had her stop by my table thirty minutes sooner. *No, then you would know how soft her lips are and still need to leave.*

While confident her brother almost certainly taught her self-defense, stifling my inner protective alpha is difficult with her. "Turning me down wasn't truly an option." My reply is nearly a growl.

She smiles and points to the cottage on our left. "You already escorted me home, Lachlan."

My name sounds decadent falling from her lips. It never has from any other woman. I nod. "Thank you for calling me out."

"You're welcome." She presses a light kiss to my cheek and climbs the staircase. After a few steps, she looks back and says, "Good night, Lachlan."

"Sweet dreams, Eva." Without concern for appropriateness, I watch her until she's safely inside the cottage before hurrying to my SUV. I pull into the spot at the daycare facility and enter the code for the building.

"Mr. Hagen, she's been asleep for the last hour or so," Casey shares.

"Thank you." I scoop up my daughter and carry her outside. With any luck, I'll be able to transfer her to bed without waking her.

After successfully tucking Lilah into her bed, I kick myself for not asking for Eva's phone number. At least I know where she lives. I can work with an address.

I strip out of my clothes and step into the steam-filled shower. I stroke myself until I explode onto the glass door, imagining completing everything I described to Eva earlier and more.

CHAPTER THREE

EVA

I watch Lachlan hurry away while I lock the door and try to settle down. My heart is racing, and I need new panties. Who knew his frank—dirty—words would turn me on? Certainly not me. No other man has admitted his desires as honestly as Lachlan. My initial instinct is to call my bestie, Jodie, but first I strip off my clothes and attempt to relax in the walk-in Carrara shower. The master bath has it all. In addition to the rainfall showerhead, there are side jets, a heated floor, and the most luxurious part... a towel warmer.

I'm vibrating with need, and he didn't even touch me. Instead of hopping out to get my battery-operated friend, I use the showerhead set on pulse and my forefinger to release the tension he built from his words alone. I can only imagine how combustible we could be if he can back up what he said. No doubt in my mind, he'll rock my world.

Once the waves subside, I rinse off and step out of the shower. With fresh panties and a sleep set, I sit on the edge of the bed. The bedding was more luxurious than mine, so I left it.

I consider waiting until morning but call Jodie anyway. Her wife won't care. Jodie is a consummate professional by day and a doting wife by night.

"Hey, girl! You okay?"

"Yeah. No. Were you sleeping?"

"No. Keisha is, though. Give me a sec." I hear a click and then a whooshing sound. "You've been gone for two weeks. How bad is it?"

"It isn't about work. Do you remember the little girl I met at the holiday party?"

"Sure. You helped her replace her dropped cookies."

"Yeah, her. Well, her—"

"You ran into her sexy-as-sin daddy?"

I push out a harsh breath. "Sort of." I share the details of my evening with Jodie.

"Wait, you accused him of being sad and ended up needing to stroke your bean?"

"Ohmigod! Yes! His voice and his words slithered through me, and wetness pooled between my thighs. Except…."

"You aren't looking for a relationship right now?"

"Correct. I can't have a fling with this gorgeous man."

A video call request comes through. I accept.

She continues, "Why the hell not? He has obligations, including work and his daughter. So do you. Obligations, I mean. Without strings, you get to ride him as much as you want, and it won't hurt his daughter."

Tilting my head to the side, I consider her words. "I've never done it before, Jo."

"Are you ready to start a relationship with forever potential? I know you well, E. You want the white picket fence, three kids, and a dog with a man who will argue with you and then dirty you up in the bedroom."

"All true. Lachlan certainly meets the last part. Other than his hand on my arm, he didn't touch me, and I was ready to combust."

"His name sounds sexy too."

"Yeah, it matches him well. Jo…."

"Girl, you called me after taking the edge off to talk about this man. Text him and let him do the things he said he wanted to. After you're clear with him you only want a fling."

"I can't."

She purses her lips and shakes her head. "Why not?"

I drop my head. "I don't have his number. Even if I did, it's late, and I don't want to wake Lilah."

"The last time you were this riled up was with… no one. Never before has a man twisted you up so completely, and you were engaged to be married."

"Ugh! Don't remind me. Thanks. You're the best. How are things at the office?"

"The same but different. The work hasn't changed, but my lunches are boring without you."

"I miss you too. You could always video chat with me."

"Sounds perfect! I'll call you on Monday during lunch."

"It's a date."

"Get his number and surrender, sweetie. Then share every dirty detail with me."

My eyes flutter closed, imagining his hands on me again.

"Seriously, E. Call him and succumb to the orgasms he promised."

"Love you, Jo."

"Love you back. Details ASAP."

She ends the call, and I flop back onto the bed. You would think shuddering with an image of Lachlan in the shower would be enough to quell my need for the evening. Nope, not so much. I toss and turn in the bed with his words replaying in my mind until sunrise.

I hoped to be relaxed the next morning. No, Lachlan is front and center in my mind, as are Jo's words. *"Without strings, you get to ride him as much as you want."* I'm getting warm at the thought of him. A workout will serve me well. Typically, I wait until the end of the day. Today is an exception. My brother shared information about a converted rail trail close to my rental. I dress in leggings, a tank, a running hoodie complete with numerous pockets, and tie my sneakers. Turning right, I notice signs to the trailhead immediately.

I push in my earbuds and stretch before taking off in a light jog. If I recall, the trail is a four-mile loop. With a quarter done, I pick up my pace and run the rest. When I reach the starting point again, I slow to a jog and walk back toward the house. I pass it and continue to the village. I'm not ready to eat yet.

The village has a bunch of cute souvenir shops, including one with a taffy-pulling machine in the front window. The stores have shirts, blankets, hoodies, and even fudge. In short, if an item is sought after as a vacation memento, you can find it in the village. I notice a quaint restaurant for breakfast as well as Woody's pizza, a bowling alley, and an arcade on the beach. I round the corner and step into the line for the Perk, which is currently out the door. Weekend mornings are busy. I immerse myself in clearing my personal inbox on my phone while I wait.

I hear, "Are you sure, Daddy?" from behind me. "It's Barbie from the Christmas party. She has leggins like me. You said she only visiting."

Barbie? I look over my shoulder, and I'm faced with Lachlan, who is equally as gorgeous in the morning sun, and Lilah with a huge smile on her face. She waves furiously, releases his hand, and rushes forward to latch on to my leg.

"I knew it was you," she exclaims.

"Good morning, Lilah." I step out of line and guide her a few patrons back to her father. "Lachlan."

"Hello, Eva." His gaze pins to mine. Not one ounce of the heat from last night has dissipated.

I'm officially in trouble and need to buy more panties.

"Daddy, her name is Barbie."

"No, it's Eva," Lachlan corrects her.

After we shuffle forward in the line, I crouch to talk to Lilah. "Your daddy is right. My name isn't Barbie."

"You look like my doll, though." The pout on her cherublike face is impressive.

"Thank you. That's sweet of you to say."

"Welcome." She beams at me.

I rise to my full height beside Lachlan. I still feel tethered to him by a rope of sexual tension despite the intervening hours. It's downright intoxicating.

He leans closer and whispers, "I like hearing you say I'm right."

I turn my head, and our lips are a scant inch part. "Do you?"

"Yes." We move forward. Now there are only two patrons in front of us.

"What's good here?" I ask, despite having been here twice before.

"Everything, 'specially the cookies and big muffins Miss Kelsey makes," Lilah answers.

"Wow, thank you."

"Welcome."

Lachlan murmurs near the shell of my ear, "I'm partial to filled pastries."

Sweet mercy! He can turn anything sexual. "Interesting."

When we reach the front of the line, we're greeted by the same young woman behind the counter from earlier this week. "Welcome to the Perk. How can I help you today?"

"I want a chocolate chip muffin and chocolate milk, please," Lilah requests.

"Of course. What kind of coffee would you like, Mom and Dad?" Macie inquires.

I glance over at Lachlan, and he doesn't seem fazed. On the other hand, a twist of hope and fear course through me. *No. No relationships.*

I take it back. He isn't affected until...

"I don't have a mommy," Lilah corrects her.

Lachlan's face falls, and his jaw ticks. He furiously tries to hide the despair, but I saw it before he was able to force it away. Lilah's words sliced him open like a hot knife through butter.

"I'll take a vanilla latte and a chocolate croissant, please," I order to hurry this encounter along.

He rebounds and requests his breakfast. "Please add a large coffee with cream and two sugars and a chocolate croissant for me as well."

He pays for our food, and we move off to the side.

"Why don't you sit, and I'll bring our food over when it's ready?"

With a tight expression, he replies, "I'm sorry about what she said."

I shake my head and lean into him. "Don't be. I'll be over soon."

"Come on, Lilah. Let's get a table." Lachlan leads his daughter, who skips through the door, to the outdoor dining area.

I watch them go, and a beautiful, curvy brunette with an apron on approaches them and hugs Lilah. A weird sensation courses through me. Nothing for me to be jealous of. We aren't a couple, despite how it looked.

Macie calls my name and hands me the order. "I didn't mean to assume you were her parents." Discomfort is written all over her face.

"Don't worry about it."

She nods. "Have a nice day."

"You too." With our baked goods in hand, I join them outside.

"Thank you," Lilah offers when I set her food out in front of her.

"You're welcome." I take a seat on the opposite side of Lachlan and savor the first sip of my coffee.

"You don't like extra sleep on weekends?" he asks.

"Normally I have no problem with that, but it would mean I slept last night, which I didn't."

He raises an interested eyebrow in my direction, urging me to continue. When I don't, he asks, "What kept you up?"

I glance over at Lilah, who is happily engrossed in her muffin. "You and your... words."

Lachlan shifts in his chair, his knee pressing into my outer thigh. His head turns to align his mouth with my ear. The warmth of his breath on my skin raises goose bumps. "Interesting, because I was thinking of you while I painted come on my shower door. Now I have more images to use, like your pert ass in skintight leggings."

Clenching my thighs together does nothing to dull the ache building between them. "We should do something about that."

"We should, but…."

I raise a hand in weak protest. "I'm not looking for anything permanent right now. No strings," I offer.

He draws his head back and stares deeply into my eyes. Understanding crosses his face. "We should start with exchanging phone numbers. Later, we can discuss details privately." Tugging his phone from his pocket, he unlocks it and offers it to me. Ignoring the sparks from the brush of his hand is impossible.

"Daddy, I'm done." Lilah's sweet voice intrudes on my thoughts.

I save my number and send myself a text.

"Great. I'm almost finished. Want to read or color?"

"Color, please."

Lachlan assists her in pulling out a coloring book and crayons.

"Which fairy is your favorite, Lilah?" I ask after seeing the Tinkerbell coloring book.

She presses her lips into a tight line, then asks, "Two?"

"You have two favorites?"

Her head bobs up and down furiously.

"Which ones?"

"Fawn and Periwinkle."

"Interesting choices. Why those instead of the others?"

"Periwinkle because she's the frost one, and I love snow. Fawn is for animals. I want a doggy, but Daddy keeps saying no."

I can't stifle a chuckle. "I see."

"Do you have a favorite?" Lilah asks softly while coloring Silvermist's dress.

"I do. Rosetta is my choice." I share my favorite fairy to avoid the dog conversation for now. I had a dog named Archie who died a few months ago. With the move, I opted to wait on adopting a new canine friend.

"Why?" She looks up at me.

"I love flowers and gardening."

"Cool," Lilah responds and refocuses on her paper.

I return my attention to Lachlan. Something about him enraptures me. My attraction to him is off the charts. My heart is fluttering, my chest is tight, and the throbbing between my thighs won't quit.

"I'll satisfy the ache so you don't have to," Lachlan whispers, fully blocking Lilah from reading his lips.

"Too late. Well, for last night. This morning, not so much."

"You took matters into your own hands too?"

"Yes, also in the shower."

He exhales slowly. "I want to take care of this morning as soon as humanly possible."

"Yes." My reply is soft and laced with hope.

"I'll call you tonight, and we can figure out a time we're both free."

"Looking forward to it."

"Ready to go?" His question is directed at his daughter.

She shrugs. "I guess. Grocery shopping is boring."

"I know, but it needs to be done."

"Can you come, Miss Eva?"

I'm torn. This breakfast has been nice, but I'm still working through... *No strings, Eva.* "Sorry, sweetie, but I have plans in a little while with my brother."

Her face drops. "Oh. Okay. I'm ready now."

Lachlan leans in, discreetly kisses high on my cheek, and murmurs, "I'll call you tonight."

"Bye."

Lilah waves as they leave. After a soothing breath, I chuck my empty cup and the remaining trash before walking back to the cottage. Looks like I need another shower... with my vibrator this time.

CHAPTER FOUR

LACHLAN

The dating scene has changed, or at least it has for me. Never before has a woman offered me no-strings-attached sex. I wasn't looking for it either. However, if I don't taste Eva soon, I might stroke myself raw.

"Daddy?" My daughter's voice yanks me out of extremely pleasant thoughts.

"Yeah, sweetie?"

"Can we get Froot Loops instead of oatmeal?"

"Sure."

"Yay!" She happily grabs them from the shelf and puts them in the cart by her feet. "What else are we doing today?"

"What do you think about a picnic at the playground?"

"Love it! Then we need ham and cheese and chips… spicy ones."

I laugh and zoom down the aisles, filling the cart with her requests. After checking out, we stash the bags in the SUV and head home. It takes forever, but Lilah carries items inside one at a time and names them as she puts them away. Significant effort is required not to grab all the bags in one trip to speed up the process. It's cute hearing her attempt to name everything. To this day, capicola is capisoda, and prosciutto is prozoom. I correct the rest of her words but leave those alone for now.

"Lilah," I call from the living room. Our home is decidedly too large for two people. It's a colonial with four spacious bedrooms, three full bathrooms, and a dedicated office. Not to mention the massive walkout basement. However, it was in rough shape when I bought it, and the price was a steal. I renovated Lilah's room and the kitchen immediately. Then I focused on the master suite, which I finished last summer. Now the room in shambles is the living room. Not true—I just need to complete the fireplace stonework and the floor. I already finished the walls and the ceiling with exposed wooden beams. I haven't determined my next project yet. The office might be the best option.

"Yes?" She comes around the corner with two of her fairy dolls and a Barbie wearing exercise clothes. Honestly, the Barbie doll's dressed like Eva.

As if I could get her out of my mind. There's something about her that I can't explain. The world around me calms when she's near me, at least in my head. My body is a different story. Proximity to her lights me up from the inside. "Time to make our lunch and head to the playground."

She rushes into the kitchen, throws open the pantry door, and pulls out her stool. I found a foldable platform for her to stand on safely so she can help with cooking or other chores. Once it's set up, she rummages through the fridge and procures the necessary ingredients. With the right items, she sings a song Noelle taught her at school about building a sandwich.

"One bread, swipes of special sauce, two meats, one cheese, 'matoes, two meat and cheese, and one more bread. Done." She's modified it a bit today, though.

"I hope that's mine. You made a double."

"It is. Now, mine." She repeats the process while I fill the bag with waters, chips, napkins, and cookies. She washes her hands in the prep sink, dries them, and puts the stool away.

"Please go get shoes and a sweater."

She's off and running down the hall.

"Walk, please, Lilah."

"'Kay," she replies, but her footsteps don't slow.

With the tote looped around her arm, she drags it toward the garage. I know better than to thwart her attempts at independence. The Hagen stubbornness is strong in her. However, this time the bag is quite full, and she's struggling a bit more than necessary.

"Can I carry it?"

She huffs and tugs her arm out, leaving the bag on the threshold. "Fine."

During the short ride to the park, Lilah falls asleep. I know better than to wake my daughter. I pull out my phone and text Eva.

Me: Hi, beautiful. Is now later enough?

Eva: Yes.

Me: Are you free tonight?

Eva: Yes.

Me: Willing to come to my place after Lilah is asleep?

Eva: Yes. What time?

Me: 8:30.

Eva: See you tonight.

I exhale and push away thoughts of this evening to no avail. The mere notion of seeing Eva again has me at full attention and straining against my jeans. Will it always be this way? How should I know? No woman has captured my attention quite like her. To pass the time with thoughts of something other than the blonde bombshell who will be in my bed tonight, I scroll through Pinterest for renovation inspiration.

I would like built-in shelving in the office and a window seat. My research doesn't last long. After a few pins, Lilah wakes.

"Daddy, we're here?"

"Yes, you fell asleep."

"Eat first, then play?" she suggests.

I twist to face her. "Sure."

We set up on a round table under the pavilion. Lilah devours her sandwich.

"Are you starving?"

"Mmm-hmmm," she mumbles, her mouth full of food. When she finishes, she asks, "Did you miss me last night?"

I smile at her. "I did. I always do when you're gone. Did you have fun?" A light tapping sound echoes around me. I look up and see it's started to rain.

"Yes. So much! We played Lego, danced on the 'bet carpet, and watched *The Lion King.* Can I go next time too?"

It took me a minute to figure out what she meant—the alphabet carpet, where they sing the song each morning. "If you want to, you can."

She leans over and throws her arms around my waist as best she can. "Thanks, Daddy."

"You're welcome, sweet pea."

She pouts and looks at me. "Raining now."

"I'm sorry. What do you say we go home and build a fort in the basement?"

"A gigantic one?"

"Definitely."

Within fifteen minutes of our arrival, Lilah is making trips up and down the stairs with pillows, sheets, and blankets. I'm an expert fort builder with the sheer amount of practice I had as a kid. I would construct elaborate forts to avoid my brothers. They're great guys now, but then I needed solitude given our age difference. Cormac and Duncan are fraternal twins and eight years older than me. Like most siblings, especially ones with a large age gap, hanging out with the younger brother wasn't cool.

Step by step, we construct a massive fort. I crawl in with my book, and Lilah has some of her dolls and a few picture books of her own. For the next hour, we hang out in the fort. She plays and reads with minimal assistance.

"Can we leave this up till tomorrow?"

We used the incline bench as part of our fort.

"Not this time. I need to work out in the morning."

She shrugs. "Okay." We disassemble the fort, and she attempts to neatly fold the blankets and sheets. The closer we get to dinner and bedtime, the more nervous I become.

There's no question about my attraction to Eva. She's whip-smart and sexy as fuck. However, the tension between us is taut and hot. I don't want to mess it up. Not sure we could, though. A booty call makes sense for both of us. We're intensely attracted to each other. She isn't looking for a relationship, and I don't have time for one. Part of me wonders why she doesn't want to settle down. Eva is absolutely forever material. I can surmise an ex-something—husband, boyfriend, whoever—hurt her deeply, and it wasn't so long ago that she's completely over it.

My phone vibrates in my pocket.

Eva: What's your address?

Me: 18 Midnight Lane.

Eva: Thanks. See you soon.

I push away my worries. We have homemade pizza for dinner and watch *Tinkerbell and the Great Fairy Rescue*. Then I tuck Lilah into her bed. After two books, she falls asleep. I creep out of her room quiet as a ninja. Back and forth my brain hurtles between preparing something for us to eat or simply waiting to see how the evening goes. I'm out of my depth, which makes me uncomfortable, and I don't like it one bit.

At work, I know what to expect. Well, I did in my old position. With YPD, I'm a patrol officer. I hope to be able to move back to a similar role as my old department at some point.

A soft knock on the front door interrupts my thoughts. I inhale and answer it.

"Hi," she greets me but doesn't move from the front porch. I've seen this woman dressed for a cocktail party, after a workout, and for a night in. She's perfect in each scenario. Tonight, she's wearing jeans and a thin sweater over a fitted tank. The lacy strap of her bra peeks out from beneath the tank.

"Hi." Despite my reply, she doesn't move. "Would you like to come in?"

"Thank you." She steps inside, and I latch the door behind her.

"Can I take your jacket?"

She shoves her phone and keys into the pocket, then turns her back toward me and shifts her poker-straight golden hair to the side. As she does, a whiff of her perfume wafts over me. It's sophisticated and uniquely her. I set my hands on her shoulders, remove her coat, and hang it beside the door.

"We don't have to do this tonight. I can leave, or we can hang out."

I drop my head.

Her hand slides over my forearm, and she steps into me. "Why are you nervous?" she whispers. Her breath teases my skin while her body lights mine on fire.

"How can you tell?"

"You're shaking. Why?"

I scrub my free hand down my face. "I haven't dated in longer than I care to admit. Frankly, I've never had a booty call with a woman I met, then ran into twice."

"Me either, but…."

"But?" My question is barely audible.

"I've never felt tension and chemistry this intense with anyone except you."

"It isn't just me?"

"No. Ours is off the charts. We should test it out," she suggests.

Before I second-guess this again, I lift her chin up slightly and curl my fingers around the nape of her elegant neck, threading them into her silky, soft hair. One of her hands is flat against my chest while the other brackets my waist.

Our eyes lock, yet neither of us moves until she says my name.

"Lachlan."

Eliminating the small space between us, I press my lips to hers. At first, the kisses are sensual and tender. Savoring her turns addictive, and the tenor amps up exponentially. With each step toward my bedroom, heat and desire course through me. My heart is hammering as she tugs my shirt over my head.

"Damn! My imagination failed me spectacularly."

My cheeks warm at the compliment, and I kick my bedroom door closed with my bare foot. I push the skinny sweater over her shoulders and let it float to the floor. Dipping my fingers beneath the hem of the tank, I surround her rib cage and lift her into my arms. Instinctively, she hooks her ankles at the small of my back. When I push her against the door, her heated center covers my bulging length, drawing a groan from deep in my chest.

"Arms up," I direct. She complies. Then I shimmy the tank over her head. "My imagination was on point. You're stunning." Her breasts are full and the perfect size for my hands, encased in unlined, sexy black lace. I kiss and nip along her jaw and across the hollow of her collarbone. I trace the edge of the lace with the flat of my tongue. Goose bumps erupt on her skin, and a soft whimper echoes around us. Pushing away from the door, I walk over to the bed with her in my arms and sit on the edge. I drag the strap of her bra down. Exposing her aroused pink nipple, I twirl my tongue around it before sucking it into my mouth.

Eva bends her arms behind her, unclasps her bra, and threads it between us before grinding against me. Cupping her shoulders from the back, I switch breasts and meet her thrust for thrust. Swirls of pleasure build at the base of my spine.

My phone blares with a designated notification. The sound breaks the spell between us. "Fuck!" I lift my head. "That's work." I press a light kiss to her lips and set her beside me. Reluctantly, I retrieve my phone and scroll through the message. There has been an explosion at the recycling factory on the outskirts of town. Cap is calling in all available units. "I'm sorry. The last thing I want to do is cut this"—I motion between the two of us—"short. However, Cap wouldn't call unless it's absolutely necessary."

"Not your fault." She puts her bra back on, adjusts the strap and tugs the tank over it. "What about Lilah?"

She's concerned about my daughter. Not the fact that I'm walking out on one of the best... I don't even know what to call tonight—a failed booty call? Hell, I didn't get past second base. "Do you know Lia Cappelli?"

"Luca's sister, right?"

"Yeah."

"Who she is, yes, but we've never met."

I nod and continue to dress in my uniform. "Her fiancée is also a cop. He was called in as well. She's already on her way, according to her text which came in while I was listening to Cap's message."

"I should go, then."

I haul her into my arms, eliminating the space between us. "This is not how I saw tonight going."

"No? What did you foresee?" she mumbles against my neck.

"I planned to fulfill my promises from our walk." I feel her tremble in my arms, not in fear but in anticipation.

She bends to pick up her sweater, and flashes of taking her from behind invade my mind. "We'll find another time."

"Okay. Give me a second, and I'll walk you to the door."

"I'll be fine."

I reach out and grab her hand. "I insist."

She drops her head and waits.

I slip on my boots and belt. I'll come back for my weapon. In the foyer, I hold out her coat for her, and after she slides her arms in, I smooth it over her shoulders. She turns to face me, cupping my jaw with her delicate hands. With a light kiss, which leaves me yearning to finish what we started, she grabs the door handle to leave.

"Good night, Eva."

She looks back. "Night, Lachlan. Be safe."

"Always. Please text me when you get home."

She nods and steps outside. I watch until she gets into her car and pulls away. I return to my bedroom, finish dressing, and wait for Lia to arrive. Within fifteen minutes of the call, she's on my front porch.

"Thank you, Lia."

"No worries. Go. I've got Lilah."

I hustle out the door to the call. When I arrive at the scene, it's clear this is going to take all night. My phone chimes with a text as I park behind the barricade.

Eva: I'm home.

Me: Thank you.

I'm not sure what else to say. I exit my vehicle and approach the on-scene commander for instructions. He puts me on the perimeter with Finn Blake, Lia's fiancé.

The call ends near five in the morning. After a shower and coffee, I take Lilah to the center, then return home and crash.

CHAPTER FIVE

EVA

Three days have passed since our attempted booty call, and I can't get him out of my mind. We've exchanged a few texts but have no plans to see each other again. No man has ever kissed me as thoroughly and purposefully as Lachlan. I run our brief time together through my mind, and wetness pools between my thighs. Not once in the nearly four years we were together did Cody make me feel as wanted as Lachlan did from his first touch.

I wonder what else I've been missing out on. Then again, the chemistry with Lachlan is in a category of its own. The instant he kissed me, fireworks exploded in my brain. His effect on my body is shocking and welcome. I shake my lust-addled thoughts away and refresh my coffee.

Perched at my desk, dressed for a conference call, I clear my emails until my meeting.

Right on time, my boss joins the video call. "Morning, Eva. How are you?"

"I'm well. You?"

Shirley has always been disinterested in the lives of her employees outside of the office. "Let's get started. I don't want this to be longer than necessary. I've reviewed your proposal for the regional campaign. I'm pleased and believe you have a great shot of winning the bid."

"Thank you."

She continues, "I'll be forwarding you another project. This one is for an international perfume company. They're looking to increase their market presence in the United States."

Cool. "Thank you. I'll look for the details."

"Do you have anything you need to share?" Shirley asks.

"Not at this time."

"Wonderful. Please let me know if any issues arise."

"Of course."

"I nearly forgot, the in-person monthly meeting in Boston next week will not move forward. I can't swing the travel."

"No problem. Are we having a conference call instead?"

"I'll keep you informed."

Weird, but fine with me. Working from home suits me well. I don't mind her canceling one of my in-person meetings, not one bit.

"Have a great day, Shirley."

She signs off without further comment.

I bury my nose in my work until lunch. With my laptop in hand, I hustle to the kitchen and set up on the island.

Right on time—well, a day late—Jodie pops up on my screen. She pushed our lunch video to Tuesday. "Hey, girl!"

"Wow, your rental is gorgeous!"

"Yeah, it is."

"You know I'm only calling to see if you manned up."

I frown at her. "You wound me, Jo." I huff and reply, "Kind of."

She listens intently as I spill the details.

"I'm getting hot and bothered, and I'm a married woman."

I laugh. "You have been with men, though."

"True. Please don't remind Keisha."

"Me, I would never. Your wife is amazing!"

Jo smiles widely. "Yeah, she's the bomb. Anyway, what is your plan?"

"Find a time when we're both free and try again because, girl, I need him to make good on his sexual promises. My hand and vibrator are not cutting it."

"Fair. There was some news in our neck of the woods in yesterday's paper. Cody is engaged to his boss's daughter." Jo lifts the article to the camera for me to see.

"Good for him." Now he won't be trying to crawl back to me.

"Nothing? Not an inkling of what the fuck? Already?"

"No. She's the woman he cheated on me with. Plus, maybe Lachlan isn't the one for me forever—"

"But?"

"There's no comparison between Lachlan and Cody. If how I feel with Lachlan and we aren't a couple is closer to normal, then to hell with Cody. I'm holding out for incredible sex plus the picket fence."

"Proud of you, girl!"

"Me too."

She laughs. "Same time Thursday?"

"I'll see you then. Miss you, Jo."

She blows me a kiss. "Same, lovely. Bye."

I close the laptop, refill my water, and step out onto the rear deck. The sunshine feels wonderful. Spring has arrived, and I'm excited. After soaking in some Vitamin D for ten minutes, I retreat to the office to review my new project. As I climb, I get a text from Maggie.

Maggie: Don't forget the meeting tomorrow. 6 pm.

Me: I'll be there.

Maggie: Great.

The requirement list for the new project is extensive, so I print it and pull out my favorite tool of all, a highlighter. An hour later, I have a cursory understanding of their request and jot down a note to schedule an initial meeting with their project lead. It'll likely be either quite early or late given the contact is in England. If I recall correctly, they are five hours ahead. I plow through the remainder of my workday and change to exercise.

I stretch, lock up the cottage, and take off jogging toward the trail. There's no taking it easy today. My brain has been rewinding my evening with Lachlan in my mind continuously. Each caress of his rough hands filters through my mind. Shivers cascade over me as my feet pound the pavement. The sheer bliss of his mouth on mine is unmatched. I haven't been able to sleep without taking the edge off nightly since his kiss set my body on fire. I can't imagine how I would feel if we had enough time to…

The next thing I know, I'm back within a quarter mile of the beginning of the loop. Recalling skilled, feverish kisses that make you question every single one before helps a four-mile run pass quickly. I slow to a light jog and then a fast walk until I reach the parking lot.

"Hey, sis!" Grant states, stepping out of his car.

"Hey! Fancy seeing you here. Don't you have a treadmill in your basement?"

My brother laughs. "We do, but—"

"Outside is better. I know and agree."

We stretch together—him at the beginning of his run and me at the end.

"See you tomorrow, right?"

I nod. "I'll be there."

He waves and takes off down the gravel trail. I meander along the sidewalk and let myself into the cottage. After a long scalding shower, I prepare dinner and curl up on the deck. Halfway through my meal, I get a text.

Lachlan: How was your day?

Flutters erupt low in my belly. *No. I'm not ready to try again.* Yet Lachlan does the relationship things without being asked or being in one either.

Me: Good and yours?

Lachlan: Painfully slow at the desk but otherwise fine.

Me: Any chance you're free this weekend?

Lachlan: Unfortunately not.

Me: Okay.

A video call request comes through. I accept it despite my wet hair and disheveled appearance.

"Hi, beautiful."

His words. "Hi."

"Don't misunderstand my unavailability. I want to see you again. We're explosive together, at least we were as far as we went. I don't like to leave things unfinished."

"I completely agree."

"Daddy," I hear Lilah call in the background.

Lachlan turns away from the screen. "Coming, Lilah." He returns his attention to me. "Can I call you again later?"

"Sure."

He ends the call. I finish my dinner and enjoy the sound of the waves crashing against the beach below.

Over an hour later, I head inside, lock up, and climb to the massive, gorgeous master bedroom. Maggie shared that a huge tree fell through the roof, and Gen had to repair the upper floor. She went all out. The windows are floor-to-ceiling, and the furnishings and decor amplify the dove gray wall color and flooring. The French doors to the balcony spanning the length of the house are spectacular. The balcony is perfectly appointed with rattan furniture and a firepit. She thought of everything to make the master suite an oasis in addition to the stellar ocean views.

A little past eight, my phone rings with a video call request. The sheer idea that it might be Lachlan causes butterflies to take flight. *No!* I'm not ready. *Am I?*

"Hey," I answer the call.

"Hi." After a slight pause, he asks, "You okay?"

"Yeah."

He shakes his head. "You recall my profession, right?"

My eyes close briefly. "Yes. I'm not ready to share yet with anyone."

"Fair. Then I won't press. Let's talk about something else."

"Such as?"

"How are you liking York Beach so far?"

"It's quaint and cute. The Perk is amazing, and I'll spend more money in there than I should."

He laughs. It's deep and hearty. "Kelsey is a magician with flour and eggs."

"Don't forget the lattes."

"Never. How does it compare to living in the Big Apple?"

"The slower pace is growing on me. The ability to get massive amounts of rice and wonton soup or perfect pizza at two in the morning may be a challenge to give up, but the change is nice."

"I agree."

"You were in New York City?"

"No, Chicago. Same concept, though. I might challenge your opinion about pizza. Deep dish is the only way to go."

"We shall see about the pizza. Why did you pick York Beach?"

"For Lilah."

I hear the sadness in his voice as if he lost something with the move but gained peace of mind for her in return. "What did you give up?"

"Your brother taught you well."

"Not really. Hearing subtle cues is a gift I've always had."

He continues, "I was a K-9 officer in Chicago, but there wasn't an opening here. It isn't part of the department."

Yet he chose the location for his daughter. Putting Lilah first pushes Lachlan higher on the relationship material ladder. "What was your partner's name?"

"Miranda."

I laugh softly. "That's cute. A sweet name plus the law enforcement undertone. It works."

"Thanks. We should figure out a time we're both free. I have promises to fulfill."

The loss of his K-9 partner was difficult, as noted by his quick change of subject and denials of Lilah's request for a puppy. Losing Archie was sad, but I imagine leaving Miranda behind was immensely harder. My body heats up from his words alone. "Can't wait. Are you free next weekend?"

"As of right now, Friday evening I'm free. Saturday morning Lilah will have her second soccer session. Not sure how that's going to go. I'm working on Sunday."

"Soccer is fun."

"Did you play?" he asks.

"Yeah, through high school. Volunteering to coach might help her stick with it. You miss organized sports, right?"

"True, but I know nothing about soccer."

"Fair. You could learn. We're getting off topic."

"What is the topic again?" His tone is playful but laced with lust.

"Having enough time alone for you to finish exploring me," I supply.

"Not possible."

I wrinkle my nose and frown. "What do you mean?"

"I will never be done exploring you."

Sweet mercy! I get caught in the memory of his mouth on my skin again. He's dangerous to my focus.

"Eva, did I lose you?"

"No, I'm here," I manage.

"Please share."

"I've never met a man like you. You're an amazing father and a nice guy, but your words are forthright and make me hot. Your mouth is dangerous to my panties. It's nearly pointless to wear them when I know we're going to talk."

"Is that a problem?"

"No. Not used to it is all."

"Who have you been dating?"

I shake my head inwardly. "We aren't dating."

"I know. You were quite clear. However, if we're tangling up the sheets, you'll know exactly what I plan to do to your gorgeous body and for how long. So, next Friday at my place?"

I fan myself with my free hand and clench my thighs together. "Yes, when?"

"Six thirty."

"I'll see you then."

"Picture me when you take the edge off before snuggling beneath your sheets." His words send shivers skating down my spine. "I'll be thinking of you and planning for the next time I see you. Good night, Eva."

Swallowing hard, I reply, "Night, Lachlan."

The instant the call ends, I throw the blanket back, rummage through the night table for my vibrator, and strip off my clothes.

CHAPTER SIX

LACHLAN

My brain is working as hard as my body during my weight session first thing the next morning. Eva is in the forefront of my mind. Not even stroking myself to orgasm before turning in last night was enough to keep her out of my dreams.

"Daddy, the buckle is stuck," Lilah calls from her bedroom.

"Bring it out here, sweet pea."

"'Kay."

She bounces into the kitchen with one shoe on and the other in her hand. I set her on the island, and she thrusts the offending shoe in my direction. "See!"

"Look." I turn the shoe toward her and point.

"Twisted," she explains.

"Yup." I untwist it and let her buckle the shoe. "Ready to go?"

"Yes, I can't wait to see my new friend."

"Who is your new friend?"

"Her name is Isla. She has black hair and blue eyes. She came last week for the first time."

"Oh, cool." I check her bag for all the necessities, including her lunch, spare clothes, and her stuffy for naptime. Lately, she hasn't been napping—the park was an exception—but Noelle indicated it's best to be prepared with all the accoutrements in case she chooses to.

I enter the code and usher Lilah into the center.

"Morning, Mr. Hagen," Lisa from the infant room greets me as we walk through to the preschool room.

"Morning," I reply.

Lilah throws her bag on the floor, hangs her coat, and then pulls out her lunch box. "Bye, Daddy," she states and hugs me.

"Bye. Don't forget we're going out after school tonight."

"I 'member, to Uncle Grant's house." Technically, Grant isn't really her uncle, but it's easier for her.

I nod tightly. "Yes."

"I'm excited to see Caleb and Cor'n." Caleb and Corrinne are Grant's kids. Lilah has trouble saying her name.

"Good. Have a great day."

"You too," she replies, rushing over to hug another girl who I assume is Isla. She meets my daughter's description, anyway.

I hustle to my truck and drive to the precinct. Unfortunately, I won't have time to stop for a pastry this morning. With a minute to spare, I line up at roll call.

"Cutting it close," Davis whispers as I fall in line beside him.

"I know."

Cap steps in front of the group. "I'll keep this brief. Your assignments are posted on the door. Please sign up for the toy drive and 5K. The funds help defray the costs of the Blue and White Gala tickets for the scholarship recipients. Hagen and Garcia, please see me in my office when we finish here."

"Roger," Garcia replies from the other side of the room.

"Yes, Cap," I reply.

"Caught," Davis mumbles.

"I wasn't late."

"You're about to find out."

"Grow up, Davis." Davis was with the department before I arrived. He's a decent guy but doesn't take the job as seriously as I believe he should.

He chuckles.

"Any questions?" Cap asks from the front. With none posed, he continues, "Dismissed."

I pass through the break room for coffee on my way to Cap's office. Not sure what he needs, but I have no cause for concern. After the first sip, I round the corner as Garcia is leaving.

"Garcia," I greet her.

"Hagen," she replies and walks down the hall in the opposite direction. She joined the YPD in the last six months as a patrol officer fresh out of the academy. While younger than me, she's older than other coworkers. She's solid and adept at easing tensions with the Latino community.

"Hagen, come in. Please shut the door," Cap instructs as I knock on the doorframe.

I comply, then take a seat.

He continues, "How are you? My wife said she saw you and Lilah on Saturday morning."

"We're well. Kelsey gave similar sentiments about you and your children."

"We are. Thank you. When you joined this department, it was for a position beneath your skill set to provide stability in a new location for Lilah."

"Yes, sir." A slight note of concern is in my voice.

"Nothing to be worried about. You may not know this, but I trained K-9s while I was in the military. I understand how difficult it was for you to choose your daughter over your passion."

Difficult? No. Disheartening, sure… but I don't dare correct him. I tilt my head in question as he continues, "For the last three years, I have petitioned the city for an expanded budget to include the addition of a K-9. My request was granted. Do you believe there's an officer under my command who may want to be her handler?"

I'm speechless. My old department wasn't overly friendly, but they weren't rude either. Yet my fellow officers and my chain of command here, including Captain Ramirez, are family. "I don't know what to say. Yes, I want to take on the challenge. How would it work?"

"I thought you would. Your credentials are up to date, correct?"

Excitement bubbles within me. "Yes." I maintained them, hoping an opportunity would present itself eventually.

"Excellent. Your initial meeting and training session is next Wednesday. Her name is Roxie." He consults the sheet in front of him. "She's about a year old, dark-haired German shepherd. Until then, please see the guys in the garage and make sure a department vehicle is properly prepared for your new partner. Also, create a list of the necessary items to outfit Roxie and provide it to me as soon as possible. I want to make sure they are on-site before she arrives. Check the equipment locker as well. Though I doubt you'll find anything useful, as it's been nearly a decade since we had a K-9 officer."

"Thanks, Cap."

He nods. "Your schedule will change a bit as well. You would be more likely to be called in. Kelsey asked that I offer her as an option to watch Lilah, if necessary."

"Thank you. I'll be sure to add Kelsey. Lia Cappelli is the only person on my list at the moment."

"Good. Do you have any questions?" Cap asks.

"No. Thank you for the opportunity to return to my preferred role."

Cap smiles and nods curtly. "It was always in the plans. Took longer than I would have liked. Here is her file, which includes her training program and commands."

"Thank you."

"Dismissed."

I hurry out of his office with Roxie's file in hand and head straight to the maintenance garage. On the way, I pull out my phone and scroll to her number. Eva is the first and only person I want to share this news with, but as she reminded me last night, we aren't dating. I wonder how firm she is on "no strings attached." I clear the screen and talk to the maintenance officer about a department vehicle.

The remainder of the day passes quickly until I'm escorting Lilah to the truck after school.

"Daddy?"

"Yes?"

"Can we eat before seeing Caleb and Cor'n?"

"Of course." I don't make a habit of drive-thru dinners or allowing Lilah to have dinner in the truck. However, tonight is an exception.

After grabbing her food, I park off to the side. I pull down the center console, put in her nuggets and fries, and set her chocolate milk in the cupholder in the door. "Good?"

"Yes. Nuggies are the best," she states while biting into one with a flourish.

I laugh, pull out of the spot, and drive to the Washingtons'. When I round the truck to assist Lilah, Eva parks behind me. *What is she doing here?* Then again, Grant is her brother. Still, though....

"Lachlan?"

A ribbon of sexual tension stretches between us. Resisting the urge to kiss her the moment she's close to me is significantly harder than I anticipate, especially with the reminder about dating on my mind. "Nice to see you again."

"You too."

Lilah wiggles to the ground and immediately hugs her. "Hi, Barbie. I mean Miss Eva."

"Hello, Lilah. How was school today?"

Lilah grabs Eva's hand and spills the entirety of her day as fast as she can.

"Wow. Sounds fun and busy," Eva replies after listening intently to my daughter. Lilah has never taken to a woman like she has with Eva. The fact that Eva hasn't shied away makes me consider long-term options despite our discussion to the contrary. Arguably, I haven't given any woman a chance.

"It was. Daddy, it's time."

"Yes, let's go inside so you can play with Caleb and Corrinne. Did you know Miss Eva is their aunt?"

"Really?"

Eva looks at my daughter. "Yes, that's true."

"Cool," Lilah replies and rushes inside the instant Maggie opens the door wide enough.

"Did you two come together?" Maggie asks innocently.

Eva instantly replies, "No." Yet the faint flush of pink in her cheeks leads me to believe the question hit her the same way as it affected me with a reminder of how our night together should've been.

"We arrived at nearly the same time, and Lilah co-opted her ear," I offer.

"Oh, well. You two are going to be spending tons of hours together."

"We are?" Eva asks.

"Yes. Come in, and I'll explain."

Once the door closes, Caleb and Corrinne hurry out of the playroom into the living room.

"Yay! Lilah is here!" Caleb exclaims. The kids hug each other, and Caleb guides Lilah away.

Once the kids are playing, Maggie offers us drinks as her husband enters the kitchen.

Before saying anything, he presses a kiss to his wife's temple. "Hey, Hagen. Sis." He hugs Eva and then bro hugs me.

"As I was saying, you two are the only people who haven't backed out of the planning for this event. Well, to be fair, Scarlett and Smithson are working the toy drive aspect, but the race side is on you."

"Okay," Eva states with a smidge of hesitation in her voice.

At first, I worry if it's about spending excess time with me, but my concerns are stifled after her next statement.

"Please tell me you have a template or set of must-dos because marketing is more my wheelhouse. I've never planned a 5K." Her question is directed at Maggie.

Maggie swipes a stack of papers from the island and hands them to Eva. "This is from Noelle Morgan. The Morgan Family Foundation hosts a 5K in New York City."

"Wait, the Noelle I met at dinner chairs this event?" Eva asks. "I ran it a few times while I lived there."

"Yes and no. Sam, her brother-in-law, was in charge before Noelle married Cash. However, she provided the framework we started with."

"Okay. How far are you into this pile?"

"About a third of the way. I pared it down for our purposes," Maggie replies.

"The major items such as the route and permits have been secured?" I ask.

Maggie turns to me. "Yes. You and Eva need to handle the registration website, collecting donations, marketing, and volunteer coordination."

Eva sets her hand on my forearm. "I'm in if you are."

The warmth of her skin on mine temporarily short-circuits my thoughts, and a reminder of her breasts filling my hands flashes through my mind. "We'll find the time. Can we use Craven to round up some high schoolers for community service credit?"

Washington replies, "That's a great idea. Do you have his number?"

"Yeah—"

Crash!

Maggie and I take off running toward the playroom. At the threshold, we both exhale sharply. Legos in every color and shape imaginable litter the carpeted floor.

"Sorry, Mama." Caleb looks up at her with a sad expression on his sweet, pudgy face.

"It's okay. We wanted to make sure no one was hurt. Can the three of you put the Legos back in the buckets?"

"Yes," Corrinne answers.

Lilah nods in agreement.

"When you guys are done, we can go home," I share with my daughter.

She frowns but then answers, "Okay."

I have no doubt she will slow down their progress cleaning up the mess to stay longer. Maggie and I retreat to the kitchen, where Eva is laughing at something her brother said. The sound is glorious and soothes me. It certainly isn't a hardship for me to spend more time with her. Finding it is another story. Although I have most evenings free, Lilah will be present. I continue thinking it through. Probably wise to not be alone, at least to get these tasks done.

Almost an hour and some discussion later, Eva and I agree to meet on Friday evening at my house to start the registration website. I plan to speak with Craven at work by then as well. I drag Lilah away from the playroom and usher her to the truck.

"Eva, hold on a sec," I call to her as she walks toward her car.

She pauses and turns back.

I buckle Lilah in and move beside Eva near the rear of my truck. "Can we talk more when you get home?"

"Is that enough time for you to get Lilah settled?"

I shake my head. "Probably not."

"I'll text you, and then you can call me when you're done."

"Sounds good." I lean closer as if no one else is around. "If we didn't have an audience, I would kiss you breathless and ruin the panties you're wearing."

Her gaze meets mine, and she sighs softly. "I wish we were alone right now as well."

"I'll talk to you soon." I escort her to the driver's side of her car despite the fact that we're in her brother's driveway. When I return to my truck, I note Maggie watching us from the doorway as well.

She waves, and I wave back before hopping into the driver's seat of my truck. The good news is Lilah is sound asleep in the truck before we arrive at home. The bad news is the same. Unlike for parents' night out, she's not wearing pajamas. Instead of considering how to change her clothes without waking her, I slip off her shoes before lifting her out of her car seat. Scooping her up, I carry her straight to her bedroom and slide her beneath her covers.

Once I change out of my uniform, I shuffle to the kitchen for dinner. While I stopped for Lilah, I didn't get anything for myself. I'm starving. After rummaging in my fridge, I find leftover chicken from dinner a few days ago. I chop up some vegetables, sauté them in a pan, and add the chicken to warm it. Halfway through cooking, I realize I didn't hear my phone. A bit worried, I check and find it on silent. A text from Eva stares right back at me.

Eva: I'm home. Call when you're set.

Her response to my statement about kissing her is still on my mind. It makes me wonder again why she insists on a fling instead of dating. I resolve to simply ask her. It can't hurt.

After inhaling my dinner, I clean the kitchen, check on Lilah, and dial Eva.

CHAPTER SEVEN

EVA

While my dating history isn't extensive, Lachlan certainly tops the list. We aren't dating, I remind myself. Yet his words pulse through me. He's forthright about what he wants, and I can't say I would be opposed to the same thing. I tug my phone from my purse as I arrive at the cottage and text him.

Me: I'm home. Call when you're set.

I lock up and climb to the master suite. Then I text Jo.

Me: Am I crazy wanting to try dating again?

Jo: No. It's been over a year.

Me: What if...

Jo: No what-ifs. Lachlan isn't Cody. Only Cody is Cody.

Me: I'll think about it.

Jo: As you should.

I consider Jo's words while I change. Lachlan's descriptive candor keeps me on the edge of need even when we aren't within touching distance. The moment he's close enough for me to touch, heat pools between my thighs. Add in his desire to kiss me, and I would melt like ice on a hot summer day. Before I tug on fresh clothes including panties, I set my vibrator on pulse and flick my clit until I shatter with self-induced pleasure. Then I dress and wait for his call.

Waiting for him is different. With Cody, all communication was on me. Scheduling was on me. Intimate—

The phone ringing pulls me out of my spiraling thoughts.

I answer the video request. "Hi, again."

"Hi. Before we chat about the race planning, I need to ask you a few questions. You don't have to answer, but… why don't you want to date me? Before you respond, I need to share something with you, which is a departure for me. I keep my life—both good and bad—private. This morning something amazing happened at work. As soon as I absorbed the information, I pulled out my phone call you."

He wants to date me? I'm flattered and intrigued. "You didn't call me until now," I accuse.

"I know. Your reminder of our relationship status came to mind. Is it me or all men?"

My eyes close briefly. "Neither. It's me."

He shakes his head furiously. "There is absolutely nothing wrong with you. You're smart, funny, comfortable in your own skin, and sexy as sin. I learned those attributes in one perfect evening stroll on the beach. Each time we're together, I learn something else I like about you."

"You may believe that, but Cody… not so much."

"Who is Cody, and where can I find him?"

"Why?"

"He needs some lessons in how to treat an amazing woman."

My heart constricts in my chest. "He's probably off with Chelsea, his new fiancée."

Fury blooms on his face. "He cheated on you?"

"Yeah. I'm not sure how long or whether it was before or after he proposed, but he was sleeping with our regional boss's daughter. She's wearing the gaudy canary diamond ring he gave to me."

"Does she know that?"

I shake my head. "Don't care. The kicker is I would never select an ostentatious ring. It boils down to me wanting to avoid being hurt again or at least admitting I suck at judging people's character."

"It isn't about how you judge character. It's how others judge yours. Cody assumed you would be fine with his infidelity. He was wrong. Rightfully so."

"Thank you. Still terrified to make another mistake."

"Isn't that what living is for? Making mistakes and fixing them, or at least learning from them."

I shrug.

"I won't hurt you."

His words cut straight to the heart of my worries. In the short time we've known each other, I believe Lachlan is honest and trustworthy. He's a devoted, doting father and hot as hell. His kisses make me pliant and weak in the knees. "I'm scared." My admission surprises me.

"Me, too, but for different reasons. What do you say to starting slow? We're going to be together anyway, so perhaps we should see if we like each other."

"Liking you isn't an issue. It's a fact. The rapid nature of me coming to that conclusion is part of my hesitance. I fell hard and fast for Cody. To be honest, I like your daughter too."

"Lilah is pretty great. She takes after her father." He winks at me.

I smile. "How slow are we talking?"

Hope graces his gorgeous face and chiseled jaw. "Whatever pace you need to say yes."

He might be perfect. "Except…."

"Except what?"

"Slow would require me to forget how your hands and mouth on my skin stir up my emotions and make me feel."

"Which is?" His voice low and gravelly.

"Desired."

"Glad to hear I was conveying my feelings accurately. You were engaged and never experienced that before?"

His answer isn't sexual at all, but I'm going to need fresh panties again. *Is this normal?* I drop my head before replying, "Not like I do with you." When I lift my gaze, a devilish smile grows on his face.

"Interesting."

"How so?"

"I feel the same thing about you."

"I want you, but what about Lilah?" The pull of him is more than I've known before with anyone else.

"What about her? I haven't dated since she was born. It isn't as if I hid her existence from you. You met her first."

"Not what I meant. Do you plan to tell her, or are we sneaking around?"

"Sneaking around sounds terrible. We'll share with her eventually. Perhaps we should go on an actual date. Then worry about Lilah."

"Okay."

He tilts his head. "Yes, you'll go out with me?"

"Yes to going slowly and a date."

"Sweet. Next Friday night?"

"Yes, Lachlan."

"I love how my name sounds when you say it."

"Noted. Are you still willing to share what happened at work?"

A huge smile widens on his face. "I'm getting a new partner."

I wrinkle my nose. "Wait, a K-9 partner?"

"Yeah. Cap has been working on adding one to the budget for the last few years, which I didn't know until today."

"That's fantastic! How excited are you?"

"Over the top. Shifting to patrol was difficult for me."

He put Lilah over his career. Would I be able to handle it if he chooses to put me over his career? Isn't that what every woman wants? Undeniable chemistry, good communication, laughter, and incredible sex? "Congratulations! How does getting a new K-9 partner work exactly?"

"I'm meeting Roxie next Wednesday for a training session and handoff. Over the next week, I'm equipping a vehicle properly and ordering the necessary items like a vest, crate, etc. with the maintenance guys."

"Cool."

"How is your big project going for the soccer team?"

He remembers? "Not too bad. My boss did her intermediary review and had positive things to say. Plus, she assigned me an international perfume campaign."

"Good for you. Do you like marketing?"

I shake my head. "I actually prefer behind-the-scenes work like data analytics for websites and customer focus groups. However, in college, I learned I'm also equally talented at creating full branding packages that sell well. Not sure how the two correlate, but my current position is more the latter."

"You're fascinating."

"As are you." I politely stifle a yawn.

"Want to turn in?"

"No, I like talking to you."

His cobalt eyes meet mine again. "I enjoy it as well. However, you're tired, and my daughter will be up sooner than I would like."

I nod tightly, knowing he's right. "Good night, Lachlan."

"Sweet dreams, Eva."

When the last sound I hear is his soulful voice, sexy dreams of him are inevitable. I silence my phone, plug it in, and snuggle beneath the duvet until morning.

Waking to the sound of the doorbell, I know I've overslept. With a glance at my phone, I realize I never set my alarm. *Crap!* I pull on an oversized sweater and open the door, but no one is there. Instead, I find a tray with a cup of coffee and a bag from the Perk on the stoop.

Given my lateness, I accept the unexpected gift and close the door. I'm hesitant to eat the filled pastry until I find a note.

Good morning, beautiful,
I hope this arrives before you eat breakfast. I'll call you.
Lachlan

A grin grows on my face as I take a sip of cool coffee. He clearly pays attention. He remembered the soccer team project and my order from the Perk. I bite into the pastry and hustle toward the office. I log in and return to the bedroom. I wash my face and brush before plucking my phone off the charger and returning to my desk. Thankfully, I'm only fifteen minutes late.

Instead of tackling my work, I send a text to Lachlan.

Me: Thank you for breakfast.

Lachlan: You're welcome. Talk tonight.

With a huge smile on my face and warmth cascading over me, I dig into my work for the day. Rather than waiting for the end of the day, I tug on my sneakers at lunch when Jo cancels with a promise to call in the afternoon and get a quick run in on the treadmill in the basement. Like Grant, I would prefer to exercise outside. However, I need to get rid of some excess tension. Sexual tension, but tension nonetheless.

I realize our date isn't until next week, but I'm excited, nervous, and terrified all at once. It's a weird feeling. Perhaps it's the men in New York City or simply who Lachlan is, but I like the fact that he has manners and takes care of me, and I like his suggestive words. A lot. I rinse off quickly and plop back down in my chair.

Near three, I submit my final boards for the soccer team campaign to the review committee and do a happy dance around the desk. Then Jo calls.

"Hey, girl. Sorry I had to skip lunch."

"No problem. Everything okay?"

"Yeah, Keisha is having some issues at her job. I needed to calm her and smooth out her pitch to keep her cool and collected."

"Understood. Your wife ranks over me, hands down."

"Thanks. Did you say yes?"

"I said yes to taking it slow."

"YAASS, girl! So happy for you."

"He sent me breakfast this morning," I offer as evidence.

"Oooohh. He's an acts of service guy."

I shake my head. "Probably." His dirty innuendos suggest otherwise, but I don't share with Jo.

"Let the man take care of you. You deserve a good one."

"In my head I know you're right. However—"

"Your heart is freaked out," she offers.

"It's scary how well you see me."

"Perhaps. Go slow but give him a chance."

"I plan to let them in."

"Them?" she questions.

"Yeah, he has a daughter."

"You've met her?"

I smile and share my meet-cute with Lilah.

"That's sweet."

An email pops into my inbox with a red exclamation point attached. *Great!*

"Eva? Did I lose you?"

"No, I'm here, but I need to go. Shirley sent an urgent email. Lunch next week?"

"Deal. Later."

I end the call and read my boss's request. With her issue handled for the time being, I empty the rest of my inbox and pad to the kitchen to make dinner.

I throw together a chicken quesadilla and Spanish rice. With my plate in hand, I curl up on the back deck to enjoy my dinner and the peaceful sounds of the ocean below.

About an hour later, a black-and-white dog scampers up the staircase and lies beside me. He's cuddly and doesn't appear to care that I'm not his owner.

"Charley?" I hear a young voice shout.

"He's up here," I answer.

A minute or so later, James crests the top of the stairs. "Hi, Miss Eva. Sorry about him. He thinks this is his home."

I frown. "Hello, James."

"Before my mom moved in with us, she stayed here. Charley was her dog, and then I kind of stole him," he shares.

"Makes sense."

"Come on, Charley. Time to eat."

The dog's ears perk up, and he sets his front paws on the deck and dutifully walks to the stairs.

"Good night, Miss Eva."

"Bye, James."

Rather than wait out on the porch, I wash my dishes and climb to the bedroom. The house is gorgeous, but if I didn't need food, I could live in the master suite. Near nine, my phone alerts me with a video chat request.

"Hi, Lachlan." He looks delicious, and I can't even see his entire body. Not that I need to right now. The YPD shirt he's wearing is taut over his broad chest. I've seen him dressed in casual clothes and his uniform and, well… hawt! Given how adamant our parents were against Grant becoming a cop, it's intriguing that I find myself desperately attracted to one with the potential of a future. *Scary.* I wonder how my parents will handle the situation. Grant became a cop after our older brother was killed in a random shooting in the city.

"How was your day, beautiful?"

I've never been a woman to swoon at pet names, but when he uses them, swoon I do. "Pretty good. I sent off the soccer team campaign and started boards for the perfume pitch. Yours?"

"Great! I was able to locate the equipment I need for Roxie and the house. I'm waiting on the maintenance guys to finish the department SUV."

"That was fast."

"Yeah, they started as soon as I left the garage yesterday. Do you happen to be free for lunch tomorrow?"

"I can be. I was considering working through it to finish my day earlier for our meeting."

I can almost see the wheels in his brain turning. "Hmm. Okay, never mind." I frown, and he continues, "I had the day off, but I'm going in early to handle some things, and I have an appointment with Alannah late morning."

"Feel free to stop by if you can. I'll be here. If not, what time do you want me to come?"

His eyes widen, and he tilts his head. "Last week and as frequently as possible."

I tug my lower lip between my teeth. "Do the ones I achieve on my own count?"

"No. When?"

"Last night after I texted you."

"I want to drive over there right now."

"No can do."

"No, they don't. I want to provide all your pleasure, Eva. Your lips and skin are incredibly soft. I need to mark each supple, flawless inch."

Holy hell! "Well, you should know I don't normally kiss on the first date."

He scowls.

"However," I keep going, "we've already kissed and then some. Perhaps I could make an exception for you."

"I approve of your train of thought."

I giggle softly. "What time would you like me to arrive tomorrow night?"

"You can keep trying to choose your words more carefully, sweetheart. However, my mind and body have been in overdrive since I learned how you feel and taste while topless and writhing against me."

Silence passes between us for a long minute. *I'm going to need more panties if he keeps this up.*

"Nothing to add?"

I manage to shake my head.

"Can you hold out until then?" he asks.

No! "I'll certainly try not to take matters into my own hands. Is tomorrow appropriate?"

"Probably not, but I don't know how I'll manage to make it another week, especially with you close enough for me to caress and kiss senseless."

I may not make it if he keeps sharing his thoughts with me. "I'll see you tomorrow, Lachlan."

"You're welcome to visit any time after five. Sweet dreams, Eva."

Dirty, sexy dreams is more likely. "I'll see you then. Night, Lachlan." I end the video chat and flop to my side on the bed. After changing my clothes again, I slip beneath the sheets and dream of him being able to fulfill his evening stroll promises.

CHAPTER EIGHT

LACHLAN

After tossing and turning until four in the morning with thoughts of Eva pleasuring herself in my head, I give up on sleep. Tugging on a shirt and shorts, I shuffle to my basement gym and pace through a drop set workout before Lilah wakes.

After I finish my protein shake and prepare her lunch for school, she pads into the kitchen with her favorite unicorn stuffy tucked under her arm.

"Morning, sweetie. Want to eat first today?"

She silently nods and takes her seat at the table. I heat up mini pancakes and sausage for her in the microwave and join her with the rest of my breakfast.

"Everything okay?" I ask as she digs into her food but says nothing.

My daughter shrugs and pushes her breakfast around on her plate.

"Lilah, please share what's bothering you."

"I need to find a mommy."

Whoa! My mind is spinning with possibilities. Where are these questions coming from? Why now? "What do you mean?"

"Miss Casey said we're going to host a tea, and we can invite our moms. I don't have one to bring."

My heart shatters into a million tiny pieces for her. Explaining the situation with her mother isn't palatable for a four-year-old. "Oh, Lilah. Do you remember Miss Alannah?"

"Red hair?" Lilah asks between bites.

Alannah is statuesque with strawberry blonde hair and a killer three-point shot. She's my lawyer and, most importantly, my friend. "Yes. She said she would go with you to tea, right? She joined you last year."

"Okay. I forgot."

"We can invite her over the weekend."

She nods and carries her plate to the sink. "I get dressed now."

"Please remember to brush."

"I will," she replies and walks away.

Scrubbing my hand down my face, I inhale sharply. If meeting Clare means I have Lilah, I would do it again. Shaking my anger and sadness about her mother away, I clean the dishes and finish preparing for the day.

After dropping Lilah at the center, I drive to the precinct. Before heading in, I text Eva. No matter how crappy I feel, she brightens my mood.

Me: Good morning, sweetheart.

I pocket my phone and catch up to Garcia and Davis walking in. "Morning," I state.

"Morning," Garcia replies.

"You're on time today," Davis points out the obvious.

I glare at him. "Haven't been late without permission yet."

When Cap finishes the meeting, I grab a seat in the conference room and go over Roxie's file again, studying the commands and her history. It's impressive. She's trained for tracking and protection as well as detection.

"You're off today," Cap states, peering into the room.

"I know. My appointment with Alannah is at ten. I decided to review the file here instead of at home. It didn't make sense after driving Lilah to the center."

"Understood. Is everything in order for next week?"

"Should be. The maintenance guys stated the vehicle will be ready in time. The ordered items will arrive on Monday."

"Perfect." He nods and leaves as quickly as he came.

My phone vibrates in my pocket. I pull it out, and the preview puts a smile on my face when I see who it's from.

Eva: Morning. Looking forward to dinner.

Me: Me too. See you tonight.

A little over an hour later, I close the file and change into jeans and a Henley in the locker room before driving to Alannah's office. She has a family and transactional practice on the outskirts of town. When I arrive, the outer door of the office is locked. I knock and wait.

A flustered Alannah rushes down the hall to greet me. "Hi, Lachlan. Sorry I'm late. My assistant is on vacation, and the morning got away from me."

"No problem. I've only been here a minute." I extend my arms to take her files and bag while she opens the door.

She lets us inside. "Would you like coffee or water?"

"No, thanks. I'm sure you don't have anything good to share."

Alannah assisted me with the custody arrangements for Lilah with Clare's court-appointed guardian and her attorney.

"I'm not sure how you'll feel about the news. Clare, through her guardian, has petitioned to be released to a less-intensive care facility. It's more like assisted living."

"Meaning what? She has someone monitoring her medications, but otherwise she's free, if you will?"

"Yes."

"Okay. Good for her."

Alannah continues, "She wants to see Lilah."

I'm on my feet and pacing the length of her office in an instant. "No. Absolutely not!" I close my eyes, grip the back of my neck, and take a deep breath. "I'm sorry. She terminated her parental rights at the recommendation of her guardian and medical team. Right?"

"Yes."

"Then I don't understand how she can ask to see my daughter."

Alannah rises from her chair and keeps up with me as I walk. "She can ask."

"Do I have to allow it? The timing is interesting."

"How so?"

"This morning, Lilah was worried about the Mothers and Special Friends Tea at school."

"I'll go," Alannah states.

"I appreciate that, and I reminded Lilah, but I think she's looking for the kind of mom who lives with us. Not the strong female influence, which you and the other women in her life have provided for her."

"I see. What brought this about?"

"Seeing the Washingtons together at home as a family on Wednesday." I purposely don't mention Eva.

"Any potential women I should know about?"

Eva with a gorgeous smile on her face appears in my mind. I shrug, hoping Alannah will move on without an answer. I'm not ready to divulge the potential between Eva and me with anyone yet.

She takes my silence as confirmation. "I won't push you to share who, but you deserve to be happy. The smile on your face would lead me to believe it's possible with this woman."

More like probable. "Thanks. How is married life?" Until Craven and Alannah became a couple, we would commiserate about our single parenthood at least once a month. Yet despite her beauty and brains, there simply wasn't an intense attraction on a dating level. We're just friends with similar parenting paths.

She smiles. "Pretty fabulous. Take it from someone who was in your shoes, and don't wait until Lilah is in high school like I did with Caden."

"Noted."

"We should refocus, though. You do not have to allow Clare to visit."

"Okay. How do I satisfy her request without subjecting my daughter to the potential trauma of meeting her mother for the first time at four and having to explain her condition?" Clare disclosed her diagnosis of dissociative identity disorder when she was pregnant with Lilah. It's a rare condition. The alter I met indicated her name was Chloe Jones. She was outgoing and vivacious. Her no-holds-barred take on life was refreshing. We learned of the pregnancy three months later. The beginning months were fine, but then she started acting strangely. I took her to the hospital during one of her delusional episodes. With a social worker present, she gave consent and shared her diagnosis with me. Later I learned her parents ignored her symptoms, which started in childhood. They wrote them off as attention deficit hyperactivity disorder. By the time she was properly diagnosed at twenty, her parents had disowned her.

"What are you comfortable with?" Alannah asks.

"Nothing. Clare has had three different alters in her life that I'm aware of. How can I protect Lilah? I'm glad Clare's received necessary treatment and made progress, but I don't want to traumatize my daughter for her mother's change of heart."

"Okay. I'll respond with a flat no."

"Thank you," I grumble.

"Please understand, it won't be the end. Consider what you're willing to give to appease her."

"I shouldn't have to, Alannah. I'm sure it was a difficult decision, but she was informed of the possibilities with her condition, the gravity of signing those papers, and had legal counsel present. Frankly, she put my daughter ahead of herself for the first and only time."

"I'm here for you and will do what you request. Please know, I agree with you personally and would do the same, but it may not be enough for her to stop seeking more."

"I'm hearing you, but I don't appreciate Clare forcing me into this position. One where I need to balance my daughter's well-being against her mother's informed choices."

"I understand."

"I know you do." Alannah chose her son Caden by selecting a different college and seeking assistance from family so she could pursue her collegiate basketball career and then law degree after tragedy killed her parents and Caden's father. "Please share when you get a response."

"I will. Are you going back to the precinct?"

"No. I have lunch plans."

Alannah smiles. "Have fun."

I let myself out of her office and hurry to my truck. Before pulling out of the spot, I text Eva.

Me: Up for some company? I promise to be quiet and not bother you.

Eva: Yes. Hmmm, is that possible?

Me: Maybe. See you soon.

Like I have many times before, I compartmentalize my life and lock away my emotions about Clare. With a smile on my face, I knock on Eva's door.

"Coming," I hear her call out.

Not yet you aren't. Everything she says revs me up regardless of her intended meaning.

The door swings open, and I'm met with Eva clad in leggings and a fitted, threadbare V-neck, which barely masks her full, perfect breasts encased in a lacy bra. "Hey."

She motions for me to enter the cottage. The moment the door latches, I set my mouth on hers and devour her like I wanted to on Wednesday evening. Each swipe of my tongue is met with hers. She tastes like coffee and chocolate. I crouch, cup her backside, and lift her into my arms. Her ass is a work of art. She pulls my lower lip between her teeth and releases it slowly. Containing a groan is impossible.

"Like that, huh?" she murmurs.

"Apparently." I take a few steps into the living room and set her on the top of the back of the couch. "Time to lose this. It isn't hiding anything anyway." I lift the shirt over her head and unclasp her bra.

"Was that a complaint?" She pulls her arms from the straps and allows it to float to the hardwood floor.

"No. Hell no." I reply, then latch on to her, sucking her taut nipple into my mouth. At the same time, I roll the other between my thumb and index finger.

"Oh God!"

I release her briefly to respond, "Nope, not God. Lachlan."

She laughs and scores my biceps with her fingernails. I alternate between my mouth and fingers on her breasts. The soft mewls spilling from her lips urge me to continue. Setting her on the floor, I slip my hands beneath the waistband of her leggings and shimmy them over her hips toward the floor. She doesn't cover herself up or try to hide, and I love it. I haven't been with anyone since Clare. Before that, I was choosy, which meant I had one girlfriend through high school and college. I hook one side of her panties, but she stops me.

I'm taken aback until she says, "No more nakedness over here without less clothes over there," she demands.

Without hesitation, I grip my shirt behind my head and drag it forward.

"So hot how guys do that!"

I shake my head, pop the button of my jeans, and push them to the floor before kicking them to the side.

"That part of my imagination was on point," she mumbles with her gaze cast on my length straining against the fabric of my boxer briefs.

I tilt my head in question. "You mean before you nearly came in my lap."

She inhales sharply, her breasts rising, and exhales slowly.

"Too much?"

"No. Yes, before you brought me close to orgasm at your house. Perhaps we should finish what we started?"

Without another word, I drop to my knees on the floor before her. I slide the flat of my tongue along her thigh and drag her black lace panties down. I'm surprised to find her waxed nearly bare. She catches my reaction.

"Just because it's been too long since a man has seen me naked doesn't mean I let myself go."

I chuckle, and she does as well. Instead of speaking with words, I set each thigh on a shoulder and lick her from back to front. Searching for purchase, she claws at the top of the couch. With an intoxicating rhythm, I savor her and bring her to the edge of ecstasy.

"Don't... sweet mercy." Her words don't make sense. Perfect, I want her to be lost in the sensations I cause in her body. I continue tasting her until she's attempting to scramble away.

Looking up at her, her skin flush and her body on the edge of splintering, I make a choice. Setting her feet on the floor, I gather her in my arms and ask, "Bedroom?"

"Upstairs, top floor," she manages. "I can walk."

I kiss her hard, refuse to put her down, and start climbing. Once successfully upstairs, I lower her to the plush duvet and reposition myself between her thighs. "Where was I?" I spear her with my tongue, and she arches off the bed. "Found it," I state.

She laughs softly and looks directly at me. Her half-lidded eyes meet mine while I tease her relentlessly with my tongue.

"Lachlan...."

I replace my tongue with two fingers in her throbbing core and suck her clit into my mouth. Her inner walls pulse, and I know she's close to splintering with bliss. I press my hand to her lower abdomen to keep her from squirming away. Seconds later, she shatters, coating my fingers with her come.

"You good?"

Eva attempts to speak more than once before mumbling, "That's never happened before."

I nearly growl. "I like knowing I'm the first."

She smirks and says, "Time to lose the boxers."

"Yes, ma'am."

She laughs and sits up. Her attention is pinned on me.

"Any chance you have condoms?"

Her lips tighten into a flat line. "No. It's no problem." She kneels on the plush carpet before me and draws her tongue along my hard, pulsing shaft.

"Baby, you don't—"

"I want to." Before I can protest more, she takes me deep into her hot mouth while sucking hard.

I freeze stock-still and revel in the sensations coursing through me. Her mouth is insane. This woman is a force of nature when she decides she wants something. Her hands grip my ass and urge me to move. I may have found a woman compatible with me inside and outside the bedroom. Yet I don't share that with her. I gather her hair and comply. The moment her sapphire eyes meet mine when I thrust forward, I erupt down her throat.

Once I finish shuddering, I withdraw and tug her to her feet. I kiss her breathless, and we fall on top of her bed. Rolling to our sides, we tangle our legs and kiss more.

"As much as I want to stay here naked with you for the rest of the afternoon, I need to get back to work. Still willing to have me over tonight?"

"Why wouldn't I?"

She shakes her head. "I didn't mean it like it came out." She buries her face in my chest.

"I'll allow the use of *came* in this instance as nonsexual."

"Much appreciated. I meant to start the website."

"Of course. Any time after five. Do you have food allergies or absolute dislikes?"

"No."

"Perfect. Why don't you grab your robe, then clean up. We'll collect our clothes while I head toward the door."

"Sounds good."

She slips on her robe while I tug on my boxers. I follow her downstairs to our pile of clothes in the living room and pull on my jeans and pick my shirt up from the floor. In the time I've completed the task, Eva is wearing the leggings sans panties and the V-neck only.

"Not fair, gorgeous."

"What?" She looks down at her body.

"Making me leave when you're bare beneath your clothes."

"You don't have to go, but I need to get back to work."

"Are you sure I won't distract you?"

"You'll distract me whether you're in the same room as me or not."

"You think about me when I'm gone, beautiful?"

"Yes, more than I should admit to you."

"It's only fair. I do too."

My words cause her shoulders to drop.

"Please tell me how to make you believe Cody was an asshole, and I'm not him."

She steps closer and wraps her arms around me. "You're as close to Cody's opposite as possible. Not purposely, but you are. You're honest with your feelings, you show up when you say you will, and how you care for Lilah is what I would look for in a man to have children with."

"Is that something you want? Children?"

"Yes, the movie happily-ever-after marriage, one like my parents and grandparents had. I want a doting husband, a few kids, a dog, and a white picket fence. Not literally, but I want a partner in all things and someone who'll muss me up in the bedroom. Don't get me wrong, tough times are inevitable, but my man will never give up on our marriage or family."

It takes a lot to make me pause, but this certainly does. "You singlehandedly spelled out what I'm looking for as well. However, Lilah's mother is a complication to what our future could look like." I mean mine and Eva's future but probably didn't convey it well.

"Alannah didn't have good news?"

I drop my head. "No, she didn't."

"You hid it well."

"I've had a lot of practice."

"I know we said slow, but please don't hide things from me. It puts you in the same category as Cody, and you're nothing like him."

I close my eyes and process her statement. "Until I met you, only Alannah and Cap knew my personal business. To be fair, Alannah is aware as my attorney and fellow single-parent compatriot. Cap knows only to the extent it would impact my job. Meaning he recognizes I'm a single parent who moved here from Chicago but not why we moved."

"I understand needing someone to talk to, truly. I have my bestie, Jodie. If something is wrong, I would appreciate it if you tell me. Perhaps right now, so soon, you don't want to provide all the details. Fine, but at least share that there's an issue. It'll go a long way to keep me from thinking you're shutting me out."

"I will. I'm going to go. I'll see you later for dinner and to work on the registration website." I haul her against me and kiss her hard. My brain is swimming with thoughts and feelings. Emotions I've never felt before which should force me to slow down. The truth is, I want to speed up despite the potential pitfalls in doing so. Being with Eva is incredible, and we barely know each other. Yet no one has ever understood me like her. No one before her made me want to share our entire story.

CHAPTER NINE

EVA

Dinner last night was fun and easy. Lilah was surprised to see me at her house. "Daddy doesn't have people over here. You're different." I wasn't sure what to make of her statement. We dined on pesto chicken with pasta and sundried tomatoes, which Lilah ate as well.

She colored for a bit before Lachlan put her to bed near seven. We made great progress on the registration site. Lachlan didn't share anything more about Lilah's mother except to say he would when we had enough time.

Now, the next morning, I'm rushing out the door to soccer for my niece and nephew. According to Maggie, soccer for little kids here is first thing on Saturday mornings. I pull into a spot at the park and search for Maggie. Instead, I hear my name.

"Morning, Miss Eva."

Lilah? I turn and see Lachlan and Lilah advancing toward me. He did mention soccer. It's been less than a day, and my body is still humming at the sight of him. Broad shoulders and powerful thighs encased in athletic pants. *Damn!* Clenching my legs together at this moment is not a great plan, but I do it anyway to stave off my reaction to him. "Hi, Lilah. Good morning, Lachlan."

He steps as close as he can and brings his mouth near my ear. "Hey, gorgeous. I see we're on the same page."

I reply in a whisper, "Yes, we are. The small taste wasn't enough."

He raises an eyebrow and adds space between us. "Agreed, but slow, remember?"

I grumble, "Yes, I recall my request."

Lachlan reminds me of a cinnamon roll hero from one of my romance novels. The type of hero who is a good guy but has many layers. Lachlan certainly has plenty and a filthy, dirty vocabulary, which he can back up. I intend to dig into his gooey, melty center. In doing so, I hope to find out if the rest of his bedroom skills are as heavenly as the small sample I've already experienced.

"Miss Eva, why you here?" Lilah interrupts—sort of.

She disrupts my train of thought, at least.

"I came to watch Caleb and Corrinne play soccer this morning."

Delight grows on her face. "Really?"

"Yeah."

She grabs our hands and hustles the two of us toward the pitch. I glance over at Lachlan, who has shock written on his gorgeous face.

"What?" I mouth.

"Noelle was right, and I'm kicking myself," he replies softly.

"Don't be too hard on yourself. I'm sure your reasons are valid."

He drops his head in acknowledgment. "They were, but seeing my daughter blossom because she's spending time with people aside from me, well…. I'll be back. I'm going to check her in."

"Okay." I return Lilah's wave and join Maggie on the sidelines.

"Morning. Did you two come here together?" she probes.

"No, I ran into them in the parking lot."

Maggie nods, but I get the sense that she doesn't believe me. I don't blame her. Our chemistry is obvious.

"You two would make a cute couple. How is the 5K coming along?"

I shrug. "We almost finished the registration website last night. We plan to check for bugs tomorrow evening and open to registrants on Monday."

"Good for you. I would still be trying to log in," Maggie states.

Lachlan approaches after leaving Lilah with her coach. He stands beside me and greets my sister-in-law, "Morning, Maggie."

"Hagen. I heard you've made progress on the 5K."

"Yes, Eva is a whiz with the website-building program."

"I'm sure she is."

We watch the kids go through fun drills to teach basic soccer skills. I don't recall the early days of soccer being this much fun for me. I stuck it out, though. Lilah's team is facing Caleb's team today. Midway through their scrimmage, Lilah scores a goal. Her arms fly into the air, and she jumps up and down. She's so excited. It's sweet to see. Someday my kid will seek my approval and praise.

"Daddy! I did it!" She runs to the sideline.

Lachlan smiles. "I saw. Keep going."

She waves and hurries back into the huddle. When his hands drop to his sides, his fingers curl around mine briefly before he unhooks them and crosses his arms over his chest. We continue watching until the final whistle. Caleb and Lilah rush over to the sideline together while Maggie gathers up Corrinne.

"Daddy, soccer is awesome!" Lilah exclaims. "Miss Eva, did you see my goal?"

"I did. It was perfect!"

"Why do you call my aunt 'miss'?" Caleb asks.

"'Cause she's not my aunt, and it's p'lite," Lilah replies with an emphasis on the *P* sound.

"Oh," Caleb answers.

"Thanks for watching him," Maggie states, rejoining the group with Corrinne. Caleb and Lilah offer her a high five, and she obliges.

"No problem," I reply.

"Time to go, guys. We need to shop before our afternoon trip to the park with the Morgans."

Immediately, Caleb hugs Lilah, who then hugs Corrinne. "Ready, Mama."

"See you later." Maggie waves and walks off with her kids.

"Ready, Li?"

Lilah shakes her head. "Miss Eva?" she calls me.

"Yes?"

"Are you free for lunch?"

I look from her to Lachlan, who drops his head. I don't want to say yes unless he's fine with me spending time with her.

"Yes, I'm free."

"Daddy, can she come to ice cream?"

"Fine with me, sweet pea."

"Wanna come with us?" Lilah invites me officially.

"I would love to."

Lilah throws her arms around my thigh and squeezes. "Yay!" She looks up at her father. "Need to change, though."

Lachlan smirks at her. "Okay, let's go home first."

"Would you like to join us or meet us at Dunne's?" he asks me.

"I'll join you, if you don't mind."

"Not at all." His devilish thoughts are painted on his face. After checking who is around, he inches closer to me. "It'll give me the opportunity to kiss you thoroughly."

"Is that allowed?" I ask.

He frowns. "Why not?"

I tilt my head in Lilah's direction.

"I have my ways."

"I know all about your ways."

Lachlan winks at me and whispers, "We've barely scratched the surface of me sharing with you."

Just like that, I need to change as well. After a deep, settling breath, I say, "I'll follow you."

Lilah takes my hand and her father's and leads us toward the parking lot. "Where's your car?"

"Over there." I point.

"It's red," she observes.

"Yeah, it is." We stop at the driver's side door.

Lachlan reaches around me to open it. A shiver cascades through me when his hand brushes the small of my back.

Lilah continues, "Is that your favorite color?"

"No. It's purple."

"Really? Mine too. I wonder what else we like the same?"

"We can talk about it after you change," I suggest.

Lilah nods furiously. Her springy curls bounce in the high ponytail atop her head. Lachlan has skills with fixing her hair.

I sit in the seat, and he closes the door. Watching them walk to his SUV is necessary for me to control the feelings running through me. I'm conflicted. Part of me wants to be with them as much as possible except... we're taking this slowly. He's potent, and he barely touched me this morning. Then again, flashes of yesterday have been in the forefront of my mind on repeat. I barely accomplished my afternoon tasks.

I follow Lachlan to his house. He parks in front of the garage. Lilah scurries to the front door, where they wait for me to join them.

"Make yourself at home. It won't take long." He pauses in the living room, thinking better of his statement. "I'll be right there, Lilah."

Lilah rushes past me and disappears down the hall. "'Kay!" she replies.

Lachlan twines our fingers and leads me into a room in the front of the house. His mouth is on mine in an instant. Heat slithers along my spine while our tongues tangle. This man's kiss makes me weak. Yet I feel powerful and fulfilled at the same time.

As quickly as it started, he pulls away. "I'll be back in a bit. We'll continue this later."

My only response is to bring my fingers to my lips and nod once. *Holy hell!* I've never been this unsteady before from a kiss.

Once he slips out the door, I take in the massive room. It has a desk and a chair and a few shelves with books. His office, I guess, or at least eventually it'll be an office. A picture of Lilah is on the desk and another lone photo across the room on a shelf. When I look closer, I see three young boys. Perusing the book titles, I notice he enjoys thrillers and suspense novels. I love reading as well. However, I sprinkle in a romance every third book or so.

Lightly, he raps his knuckles on the doorframe. "Hey, sweetheart."

"You don't have to knock in your own home."

"I do. It reminds Lilah to do the same for me."

"Good point."

He moves beside me and slides his arm around me, setting his palm on my hip. "You didn't have to stay in here."

"I was judging your reading material."

"Oh. Did I pass?"

"Yes, actually. I've read most of those plus others."

"Something else we have in common."

"Else?" I wonder what he means.

"Aside from books, we both have an affinity to the ocean."

"How can you tell that about me?"

He offers me a megawatt smile. "Only a woman who loves the ocean would willingly carry her shoes and risk getting her formfitting jeans wet in the early spring to feel the sand under her feet no matter how cold the sand or water may be. Plus, when we talk, I can usually hear the ocean. Whether you're outside or have the windows open, I'm not sure, but if given the choice, you prefer the smells, sounds, and feelings of the ocean."

Speechless. No man has ever seen me as well or as soon as Lachlan. This between us feels terrifying, but the fall will be worth it, right?

"Still with me, Eva?"

"Yeah." I meet his gaze and wonder how long I'll be able to hold on to my slow progress request. Each time I'm with him, he burrows his way deeper and deeper under my skin.

He presses a sweet kiss to my head and leads me out into the kitchen. "Lilah is playing with her fairies in the playroom. Would you like a drink?"

"Lemonade? Iced tea? Water?" I wonder out loud.

"I have all three," he replies while pulling two glasses from the cabinet to the right of the sink.

"Lemonade, please."

His kitchen is spectacular. It has dark gray, almost charcoal-colored, cabinetry with granite countertops and a massive island. The double oven and refrigerator are certainly meant for a large family or a man who likes to eat or both. Yet he doesn't seem like a person who entertains people often. Lilah admitted as much. Although it's more likely because he prefers to keep to himself rather than having an aversion to company.

He sets a glass down and leans against the island facing me. "Interested in answering some questions?"

"Like?"

"Basic getting-to-know-you stuff. For example, how do you take your coffee?"

"Same as you—cream and two sugars for a large. I have grown to like the vanilla latte at the Perk too. I prefer sweet over savory scones if given the choice. I recall filled pastries are your go-to option."

He cants his head and glances behind him before he murmurs near the shell of my ear, "I want to fill—"

A wail comes from down the hall. "Daaaaddyyyy!"

Lachlan is fast when he hears her cry. I consider following him but decide against it. Lilah didn't sound as if she was in pain, merely that she needed Lachlan's attention.

He returns quickly. "Crisis averted. She decapitated Zarina. I popped her head back on."

I giggle softly.

"Your laugh is soothing."

"Thank you. Can I ask a tough question? You don't need to answer immediately."

"Okay." Trepidation is obvious in his voice.

"How much or how little should I interact with Lilah? I don't want to overstep. I was going to follow you, but... I need to know about her mother and other women you've...."

He visibly relaxes. "First, I haven't dated anyone since Lilah was born, which I thought I shared with you already. Our history with Clare isn't easy, and Lilah isn't aware of any of the information. Are you free tonight?"

Clare. A streak of something races through me. Jealousy? Perhaps. Although it would be for time more than anything else. I would never choose for him not to meet her because then Lilah wouldn't be in his life. "Yes."

"We can talk about her after Lilah goes to sleep."

"I can work with that."

"Have you been to the Nubble yet?" he asks.

I shake my head. "Want to visit before we get our ice cream?"

"Sure."

He closes the limited space between us, kisses me lightly, then pulls away. "Any more and I'll drag you to my bedroom."

Yes, please! I nod tightly.

He leaves the kitchen, and within ten minutes, they appear ready to leave.

"Miss Eva, are you coming to the lighthouse too?"

"I am. Is that okay with you?"

"Sure. I can share you with Daddy."

"What do you mean, sweet pea?" Lachlan asks.

"Miss Eva is my friend. She can be yours too."

I chuckle softly.

"Oh, of course," Lachlan replies, stifling a laugh of his own. "I'll be right back."

"Have you ever been to the lighthouse?" Lilah asks.

"No. I moved to the area recently."

"Where did you live 'fore?"

"In New York City," I reply.

"Do you miss it?" Lilah wonders.

"Maybe a little, but only because I have some friends back there. I love being near my brother and his family as well as the beach here."

Her eyes widen, and she smiles. "I love the beach!"

Lachlan returns with a hoodie draped over his arm. "It gets breezy up there. You may need this." He extends it in my direction.

"Thank you. What about you?"

"I'll be fine." He winks at me and turns to Lilah. "Ready to go?"

"Yes!" she shouts. "Ice cream is awesome."

We step into the garage, and Lilah waits by the rear door. I grab the passenger door handle, but Lachlan stops me.

He leans in and whispers, "I'll get your door every single time… even in my garage."

I drop my hand and wait. His chivalry is foreign to me. None of the men I've dated before opened my door, shifted me to the inside of the sidewalk, or offered his arm to cross the street. Only him. What the hell else have I been missing?

Once Lilah is secure in the back seat, Lachlan reaches around me and unlatches the passenger door. I take a seat, and he closes the door before rounding the back of the SUV. The drive to the Nubble is quiet as far as words between Lachlan and me. However, he threads his fingers with mine in my lap out of Lilah's view. She's blissfully unaware because her fairies are currently on an adventure to find lost treasure.

At the top of the winding road, Lachlan pulls into a small parking lot. Straight ahead is the stately lighthouse. It's beautiful. I tug on his borrowed hoodie the moment my feet hit the pavement. It's cozy, warm, and smells delicious like him. We wander closer to the majestic building. We just arrived, and I could sit up here for hours listening to the waves crash on the jagged rocks separating the mainland from the island where it sits.

"How do you like it?" Lilah asks.

"It's beautiful here."

Lilah agrees and takes a seat on one of the engraved benches. Lachlan and I stand in silence behind her, our fingers discreetly linked. Cody shied away from sharing our relationship with the world until his proposal. Despite the relatively short time we've known each other, Lachlan seems content with telling everyone who may glance our way. I'm not sure how sharing is slow, but I can get behind being his.

We absorb the soothing waves and salty breeze for nearly an hour before Lilah requests coffee Oreo ice cream.

"Coffee Oreo this time?" Lachlan asks her.

She smiles, grabs our hands, and leads us to the parking lot. The drive is short.

"What kind are you having, Miss Eva?" Lilah asks me.

"I have to check the flavor list, but my favorite is chocolate chocolate chip."

"Huh, Daddy gets the chocolate extreme every time."

I glance over at him, and he drops his head in acknowledgment of her statement.

With our spoils in hand, we take a seat at one of the green tables. Once Lilah is poised with her spoon, Lachlan sits beside me and promptly rests his hand on my thigh. His touch, even an innocuous one, sends tingles of awareness zipping through me. With a quick look in my direction, he digs into his dish. Lilah and I follow suit and enjoy as well.

After a few bites, Lilah asks, "Isn't it the best?"

"Yeah, it is." My response is more for the overall day and Lachlan's hands on me. However, his sweet daughter doesn't need to know his touch twists my stomach and other places into knots of longing. No, it's him. Only him. Our connection has been strong since the moment we met. Each passing day, it grows more.

"You okay?" He leans toward me.

"Absolutely." I turn to look at him to bolster my response.

Could they be my movie ending? It's probable. The only thing stopping me is me and my fear of being hurt again. I have to believe him when he said he wouldn't hurt me, right?

We clean up the table and head back to their home.

CHAPTER TEN

LACHLAN

"When we get home, I have some exciting news to share with you, Lilah."

She looks at me as I buckle her into her booster seat. She shrugs. "'Kay."

Eva wrinkles her nose but says nothing. She already knows about Roxie. I need to prepare my daughter as well.

Once we're inside, Lilah races to her room to put her bag and shoes away. "I'm ready," she declares when she returns to the kitchen.

I laugh. "Give me a few minutes."

My sweet daughter plops down in the middle of the tufted ottoman. I pull out chicken to defrost for dinner, then guide Eva to the living room, which is nearly complete. I've been sneaking in work here and there whenever I can. I need to touch up the mortar on the stone fireplace and finish painting the floor returns.

I sit in front of Lilah with Eva beside me. "Before we moved here, I had a dog," I share. Eva nods in understanding.

"You did?"

"Yes. She was a special dog."

"What's her name?"

"Miranda was my K-9 partner at work."

"You had a police dog?" Lilah's eyes pop open, and joy appears on her face.

"I did, but when we moved here, there wasn't a position at work with a dog until now." She's too young to realize I made the choice for her—at least I hope she is.

"A doggy?"

"I'm getting a new K-9 partner named Roxie next week."

Lilah launches herself off the ottoman into my arms. "Can I pet her and love her?"

Her excitement is sweet to watch.

"Yes, but there will be rules for her."

Lilah frowns. "Like?"

"She needs to stay in her crate at night. She'll go to work with me every day. Plus, any others I deem necessary."

"Okay… but she lives with us?"

"Yes."

"I'm excited!"

"Me, too, sweet pea." *More than I could ever express.* Cap was right, and I'm grateful he saw my discomfort. I miss training and working with a K-9 partner. Yet I would do it all over again for Lilah.

"When?"

"Probably Wednesday," I reply. Unless there's a major issue, I foresee the trainer leaving her with me.

"Yay! Can I play until dinner?"

"Sure."

Lilah kisses my cheek, scrambles to the floor, and takes off toward her bedroom.

"Walk, please, or you're—"

Thud.

Uncontrollable wails come from behind us. For the second time, Lilah slid into the corner of the island. This one appears worse. I leap over the back of the couch and hustle beside her.

Eva follows, circles the island, and asks, "First aid kit?"

"Daaaddy! It hurts." Tears are streaming down her cheeks between sobs. One of her tiny hands is covered in blood, the other clutching my shirt.

"Bottom drawer of the island," I direct Eva. "I know, sweet pea."

Eva grabs the kit and hands me some gauze from inside.

"Ice pack in the freezer on the door, bottom bin," I shout louder than I intend.

Without hesitation, Eva brings it over to me with another gauze. She crouches beside us and attempts to soothe Lilah by stroking her forearm. Slowly, her grip on my shirt loosens, and my daughter reaches for Eva.

"My head hurts," she whines.

"Will you move your hand away so I can look at it?" My voice is shaky. I've seen many horrible things on the job, and maintaining my composure is necessary. However, when the injured person is my daughter, being emotionless rarely kicks in.

Slowly, Lilah lifts her hand from her face. Eva shifts beside me. She hands me a fresh gauze and takes a wet cloth to clean it. The blood has slowed a bit, but the cut along her hairline probably needs stitches.

"Sweet pea, we need to see a doctor about the cut on your head."

"No, I'm fine."

I drop my head.

Eva intercedes on my behalf. "He's right. It's a good idea to have someone with special skills check out the cut."

"I'll go if you come with me," Lilah negotiates.

Eva's cerulean eyes meet mine, and I agree almost imperceptibly.

"Deal. Why don't we sit you up a little more?" Eva suggests.

Lilah twists and leans against the island.

Eva assesses Lilah and determines she's okay for the moment. Then she points at me. "Where can I find a clean shirt for you?"

I appreciate that she knows I don't want to leave Lilah's side to get a fresh shirt. "In the tall bureau in my bedroom along the far wall near the closet. My wallet and keys are in the foyer."

Eva stands but doesn't move. It takes me too long to realize she's waiting for me to direct her. As far as Lilah knows, Eva isn't aware of the location of my bedroom.

"The master is to the right of the main entry," I state, and she steps away.

"Daddy?"

"Hmmmm."

"I'm gonna be okay."

"Yes, you are."

My daughter sets her clean hand on my face. "No, I'm tellin' you."

"Why?"

"You look sad."

I exhale sharply. "I won't lie to you. I'm a little worried, but you're going to be fine."

Eva returns with a fresh shirt. After setting it down, she sits beside Lilah, but she's watching me. I strip off the bloodied shirt and tug on the clean one. As much as she tried to mask her feelings, Eva failed miserably. Despite the circumstances, I'll allow the ogling.

"Ready to stand up?" I ask with an outstretched hand.

"Yes," Lilah answers. She takes my hand, and Eva helps her stand from the floor.

Once my daughter is secure on her feet, I offer Eva assistance as well. I whisper for only her to hear, "Thank you. You're amazing with her."

"You're welcome. We should go. That new gauze is nearly full again."

I close my eyes for a moment. I've never had help with Lilah before. Eva jumped right in. It's... nice.

"Lachlan."

I open my eyes to meet hers when my name falls from her pouty lips.

"She will be fine."

I carefully lift Lilah and carry her to the garage. "Would you mind sitting in the back with her, or would you prefer to drive?"

"Already willing to let me drive your SUV?"

"You're quickly proving yourself to be everything I ever wanted for myself and my daughter."

Eva is stunned silent and wordlessly climbs into the back seat beside Lilah. When I glance into the rearview mirror before exiting the garage, I see my daughter take Eva's hand in hers. My heart bursts. Lilah may care about Eva as much as I do. I could fall for this woman and build a life with her. Am I willing to let her in completely given Clare's recent attempt to reenter my daughter's life? *Yes. No. Damn!*

My thoughts carry me the entire ride to the emergency room. When I attempt to carry Lilah, she asks for Eva instead. She obliges and hoists Lilah into her arms. She looks as if she belongs in Eva's arms. I wouldn't wish for these circumstances, but without a doubt, Eva could handle being part of our family. *Can I allow her into the deepest cavern in my heart and my daughter's? I want to. Is wanting enough?*

Thankfully, York Memorial has a pediatric area, which is serendipitously empty right now.

"Hagen, how can I help you?" Janet, the nurse manning the desk, asks. Her son attends the same daycare as Lilah.

"Lilah hit her head on the corner of the island. She has a goose egg and decent-size cut along her hairline."

"Okay. Follow me." Janet escorts us to an exam room.

Eva settles Lilah on the bed, but my daughter refuses to release her hand. While I answer the questions about how the injury occurred and provide our insurance information, I link my fingers with Eva's. When Janet finishes, she indicates a nurse will be in shortly. While we wait, I switch out the gauze on Lilah's head with one I stashed in my pocket.

Soon thereafter, a nurse enters the room.

"I know you. You married Uncle Zack," Lilah states matter-of-factly. Technically, Smithson isn't her uncle either, but she started calling him that during dance rehearsals for his wedding. Scarlett wanted her bridal party to tango during their first dance. As one of the few members of the bridal party, I obliged. Lilah was present for each one.

"Hagen," Scarlett greets me.

"Hey. I thought you worked weekdays?"

"I do. I'm covering for a coworker." Scarlett turns her attention to Eva. "Washington's sister, right?"

"Yes. Eva. Nice to see you again."

"You as well. Hello, Lilah. I see you bumped your head," Scarlett addresses her.

"I runnin' in the house when he told me to walk so I won't get hurt." She points at me.

Scarlett effectively stifles a laugh. "Okay. Perhaps he has a point?" Lilah lifts her shoulder. "Can I take a look?"

With gloved hands, Scarlett lifts the bandage. "Ouch! How badly does it hurt on a scale from one to ten? Ten being the worst thing ever and one being no big deal."

"Six."

Scarlett continues, "The bump is called a hematoma. It's temporary and will go away over the next few days. The cut needs to be cleaned to avoid infection." She turns her attention to me. "I recommend a consultation with a plastic surgeon to determine if stitches are necessary. My inclination is to use a butterfly because it's along her hairline and isn't overly long or deep. Dr. Templeton may have a different opinion."

"Sure. Please request the consultation," I reply.

"Give me a few minutes, and I'll be back to clean out her wound."

"Thank you," I say before she slips out the door.

Before Scarlett returns, Dr. Templeton arrives. It was quick, but I'll take any small favor the universe wishes to provide. She's a petite woman with a mass of curly dark hair tied in a low ponytail at the base of her neck. She's chatting up Lilah to put her at ease while inspecting the wound.

"How did you hurt yourself?"

"I ran in the house."

"I see. Well, the good news is I wouldn't suggest stitches. Nurse Scarlett can place a special bandage on it to help it closed."

"No needle?"

Dr. Templeton smiles down at my daughter. "No needle." Turning in my direction, she adds, "I'll make a note in her chart. You should be out of here soon."

"Thank you," I offer, and Dr. Templeton leaves.

"I promise no more running in the house, Daddy."

"Thanks, sweet pea." Relief ripples through me.

Scarlett returns with supplies.

"Is it going to hurt?" Lilah asks Scarlett.

"It shouldn't, but you will need to lie on your side facing me."

Lilah is tough. She can handle this. As if she heard my inner thoughts, Eva threads her fingers between mine.

Lilah complies. Scarlett cleans and bandages the cut. "I brought stickers and a lollipop for you."

"Thanks." Lilah accepts it graciously.

"I'll be back with her discharge paperwork in ten minutes."

"Much appreciated."

She slips out the door again.

I ask Lilah, "Do you want that now?"

My daughter shakes her head. "No. Can we get Woody's on the way home?"

"Sure. We can introduce Eva to good local pizza."

"You're staying for dinner?" Lilah asks her.

"I would like to."

"Yay! Me too."

While I need to share how Lilah and I got to this point, I'm not worried about my daughter accepting Eva as part of our life anymore. With paperwork in hand, I escort my ladies to the SUV. *My... sounds perfect!*

"Any no-go pizza toppings?" I ask Eva.

"Do you not like pizza, Miss Eva?"

"I'm from New York. You and your dad are from Chicago. They have different styles of pizza."

"There's more than one kind?" Lilah wonders aloud.

Eva laughs softly. "Yes, there is. New York pizza has a noticeably thinner crust, while Chicago pizza is known as deep dish with a thicker crust."

"Oh. What is Woody's?" Her question directed at me.

"They lean more toward New York style," I reply.

Eva answers my question about toppings. "Not a fan of anchovies, pineapple, or olives. Otherwise, go crazy."

"What's 'chovies?" Lilah asks from the back seat as I place our order by phone.

Eva turns to face her over the center console to answer her. "Slimy, salty fish." As she does, her perfume, or shampoo, wafts toward me. She's delectable.

"Yuck!"

Eva laughs again. "My thoughts exactly, Lilah," she replies, then retakes her seat facing forward.

I can't help myself, and I reach over the center console and thread my fingers in hers. I pull in front of the pizza shop, hop out, and pick up our dinner.

Lilah directs Eva to the plates while I get the drinks once we arrive at the house. We dine on the pizza, and Eva seems to enjoy it.

"No complaints about this pizza?" I ask.

"No complaints. It's middle of the road as far as crust thickness," she replies.

"Fair," I admit.

"Can I go to sleep now? I'm tired," Lilah asks.

"Sure," I reply. "I'll clean up when I come back out."

Eva nods.

"Night, Miss Eva."

"Good night, Lilah."

My gaze pins to Eva's before I disappear down the hall.

CHAPTER ELEVEN

EVA

While I wait, I clean our dishes and set them to dry despite Lachlan's promise to wash them himself. I wrap the leftover pizza and store it in the fridge. Twenty minutes later, I tiptoe down the hall and find Lachlan sound asleep beside Lilah atop her purple unicorn bedding. The room is fit for the princess she is. The huge, muscled man curled up in the corner of a bed, which is decidedly too small, with his massive hand on his daughter's back makes my heart constrict. I sigh and wonder if I could fit in with them long term.

Pushing the train of thought away, I recall seeing paper in his office, and I grab a piece and scrawl a note to Lachlan. I slip out the front door, locking it behind me. When I arrive home, I'm keyed up. Instead of turning in, I read on the master suite balcony.

Four hours later, my phone wakes me.

Lachlan: I'm sorry.

Me: Nothing to be sorry for.

Lachlan: We didn't get a chance to talk.

Me: Are you free Tuesday for talking and the site?

Lachlan: Sure. Sweet dreams, gorgeous.

Me: Good night, Lachlan.

I gather my book and cup before snuggling beneath the luxurious sheets, wishing I wasn't alone. It's way too soon. We haven't been able to fit in an actual date yet. I suppose lunch was a date, but not really. Lunch was a partial fulfillment of our evening stroll promises.

The next morning, I take to the trail again, slightly hopeful to run into Lachlan and Lilah at the Perk when I finish. However, I wasn't lucky in that respect. Then I wonder if he mentioned his plans for today, but don't recall. After showering, I putter around the cottage. The laundry won't wash itself.

The remainder of the weekend and Monday have passed in a blur. Shirley was on a rampage all the way from Washington, DC. My inbox was jammed with unnecessary emails from over the weekend. Not one contains an action item for me to handle, simply her musings and suggestions for the perfume account. Lachlan and I have exchanged texts but nothing else. Honestly, I miss him and Lilah.

I stroll into the Perk before my meeting on Tuesday morning.

"Hi, I'm Eva. Kelsey, right?" She's a stunning brunette with curves I would kill for.

"Yes."

"Nice to see you again."

"What can I get for you?"

I place my order and shift to the side. She serves the next person in line before preparing both orders. The young girl who helped me the first day emerges from the kitchen and offers Kelsey help.

With my vanilla latte and filled croissant in hand, Kelsey approaches me. "Here's your order. How are things going with the 5K planning?"

At first, I'm taken aback by her knowledge of my involvement, but then I realize it's a police department event. She's the captain's wife and friends with Maggie. Of course she knows all the details. "Pretty well. Lachlan and I have nearly completed the registration website, which should go live tomorrow. We're working on the volunteers and race day items next."

"He's a great guy, and Lilah is the sweetest."

I tilt my head at her odd statement. "Yes, they are. Thank you for the coffee. Bye, Kelsey."

She waves and says, "Have a great day," with a huge smile on her face.

Weird. I shake off her opinion about Lachlan and drive to the daycare center to meet Noelle and Caroline. Parking at the side of the building, I take the structure in. It's cute. The building is painted with bright, bold colors. The playground in the rear is expansive. As instructed, I ring the doorbell, and a young woman answers through the intercom.

"Good morning. How can I help you?"

"Morning. Eva Washington. I have a meeting with Mrs. Morgan."

"Which one?"

"Both," I reply. The door buzzes, and I enter the building.

"Morning. I'm Casey. Please follow me."

The center appears to be separated into four distinct areas with a bank of offices along the far side of the building.

"Miss Eva?" A sweet little voice I've grown accustomed to hearing surrounds me. "What are you doing here?"

"Hi, Lilah. How is your head?"

"Better. We stayed home for two whole days. Watched movies, colored, ate popcorn. Built a huge fort in the basement."

Part of me is torn. Why didn't he call? I would've happily joined them on Sunday. His texts didn't indicate he was staying in with Lilah. My stomach twists in knots wondering if I overstepped on Saturday. "Sounds wonderful. I'm glad you're feeling better."

"Miss Washington, right this way," Casey interrupts. "Why don't you go work on your project, Lilah?"

"'Kay, Miss Casey. See you later, Miss Eva."

"Bye, Lilah."

Casey escorts me to the offices and knocks on the door.

"Come in," a voice from inside answers.

"Mrs. Morgan, your ten o'clock is here."

"Perfect."

I step into the office. "Morning, Noelle. How are you?" Her red mane flowing over her shoulders in soft waves catches the sunlight filtering through her window. She's beautiful and a savvy businesswoman.

"I'm well, and yourself?"

I would've said amazing until Lilah shared the rest of her weekend with me. "Same. Thank you."

"Caro will be in momentarily. Her appointment outside of the office ran over," Noelle informs me.

"No problem. Thank you for sharing the 5K planning steps with Maggie. The guide has been quite helpful to me and Lachlan."

"Lachlan?" She ponders the name a moment. "Oh, Hagen." She smiles. "Now I know who you mean. Lilah's dad, right?"

"Yes."

"You're working together on it?" Noelle asks as Caroline rushes into the office before I get the opportunity to answer her.

"Sorry I'm late. The grandmother had a bunch of questions."

"No problem. We should get started, though," Noelle suggests.

Caroline pulls a chair alongside Noelle. Then I begin asking about their needs.

"What is it you're looking for?"

Caroline speaks first. "Up until now we've been relying on word of mouth, which has been fantastic. However, most people aren't aware of the individualized education plans I create for students through high school. Also, we're looking to either expand this location or add a second one in the next year."

"Congratulations. Who handles your web presence and advertising right now?"

Noelle takes this question. "We have a basic website but no traffic monitoring or analytics. As Caro mentioned, we haven't done any print or web ads."

"I can certainly create a comprehensive plan to amp up each of those avenues. Once I see where you are, I can determine which will give you the best increase in traffic. Of course, you can pick and choose which option is best for your company."

"How would that work?" Caroline asks.

"I would review your current website and traffic for the last year, your mission statement, and how Caroline's individualized plans can be advertised in the school system. That sounds terrible. What I mean is—"

Caroline raises her hand. "I understand. You want parents and caregivers to learn about my services but not seem icky."

"Exactly. I would likely start with the administrators and counselors rather than a public ad campaign," I offer.

Both women smile.

"Excellent. What do you need from us?" Noelle inquires.

"Tell me how your process works on both sides of the business," I ask.

For more than the next hour, we delve deep into how their business works, and my mind spins with possibilities to expand their reach and profit margins.

With a huge smile on my face, I exit the office and make my way toward the exit.

"Miss Eva, you're still here?" Lilah asks as I pass her classroom.

I crouch. "I'm leaving now. My meeting with Miss Noelle and Miss Caroline is finished."

"'Kay. See you later." She throws her arms around my neck and gives me a hug.

"Bye, Lilah."

When I stand, I note Caroline watching my exchange with Lilah. I expect her to question me, but she doesn't. I wave to her and exit the building. Without another thought, I pull out my phone and text Lachlan.

Me: Can you talk?

I buckle my seat belt and pull out of the spot. As I drive toward the cottage, my phone rings with a video call request. I answer but don't move my phone from the cupholder.

"Hi. Sorry, I'm driving now. Please don't take offense if I don't look at you, though I would prefer to."

He laughs. "Your profile is gorgeous too."

I can't help but frown.

"Did I say something wrong? You're beautiful, Eva."

I shake my head. "Thank you. It isn't that. I had a meeting with Noelle and Caroline earlier today and saw Lilah."

"Okay." His response is laced with concern.

"She mentioned you were home for two whole days, but… you know what, never mind. I'm overreacting. They hired me, and I wanted to share with you."

"Congrats! I want to hear about your business wins, but… please tell me what you think you don't have a right to feel."

I park in front of the cottage and lift my phone to eye level. *Damn, he's hot!* "You didn't mention you were going to be home all day on Sunday."

"I figured you would need time alone since we monopolized your entire Saturday unexpectedly." His answer is straightforward and unwavering.

"Okay."

"Honestly, I would like to spend every possible minute with you regardless of the quick timeline. You bring sunshine and brightness to my life, and it scares me. Our explosive chemistry only makes us more intriguing. How you cared for Lilah… I've never had a woman step up for her. Her mother… I've never allowed it, but you're sneaking past every barrier I have around my little family."

"The two of you are doing the same to me."

"Are we still on for finishing the site tonight and talking about Clare?"

"Yes. What time would you like me?"

He pushes out a breath. "Always."

My eyes drift closed briefly while I acknowledge my response to his words. Butterflies flutter in my low belly, and my chest tightens. "I'll be there by six."

"See you then."

I end the call and settle into my desk chair. With the new client form filled out, I set it aside. Yet something tells me not to file it with the home office. Near lunch, I get a message from Jo indicating she's swamped and can't talk. We agree to try again on Thursday, and I push through the rest of my work for the day.

Before I'm ready to finish up for the day, I receive an email from Joseph Cavallaro, the marketing consultant for the regional soccer team. Attached is an invitation to a gala in three weeks, where they'll announce their choice for the new logo. Joy spreads across my face. Immediately, I message Maggie.

Me: Hey. I need a dress for a work thing. Does Kelly have a storefront, or do I need to make an appointment?

Maggie: Both. It's around the corner from the Perk.

Me: Okay. I'll find the number. Thanks.

Maggie: Bringing a date?

Me: Considering it.

Maggie: Good for you.

I smile and set my phone aside. I met Kelly when Maggie and Grant got married at their engagement party. Kelly is Maggie's sister and a sought-after couture designer and costumer. Maggie organized a private shopping experience for my mother and me so we could be part of the wedding.

Shutting down my computer, I step into the bedroom and change into comfier clothes. With ten minutes to spare, I park in front of Lachlan's home. The front door swings open before I knock.

"Hi, Miss Eva." Lilah hugs me close.

"Should you be answering the door by yourself, sweetie?"

Lilah frowns. "I was watchin' in the window for you."

"Where's your—"

Lachlan appears to my left from the master bedroom, his hair damp from a shower. "Lilah, you know you're not supposed to open the door without me."

"But it's Miss Eva. You said no strangers. She's not a stranger," Lilah replies with an impressive eye roll for someone her age.

I artfully stifle a laugh because it'll only encourage her.

"Fair point. Going forward… no one except Miss Eva or Miss Lia."

"'Kay, Daddy." Lilah scampers down the hall toward her room.

Before I can greet him, Lachlan links our hands, hauls me out of sight, and kisses me breathless. Lust and pleasure zing through me. I could easily surrender to kissing this man every single day. *Wait, what?* Ignoring my inner thoughts, I melt into him and accept the overwhelming bliss from his mouth on mine.

He adds a sliver of space between us and whispers, "Hi, sweetheart."

"Hi."

"I'm sorry about Saturday and not calling on Sunday."

"Don't worry about it. I can see your side." I crane my neck and press a soft kiss to his lips.

His hand threads into my hair, and he angles my head for better access. As his lips are about to meet mine again, Lilah calls him.

"Daddy."

Lachlan presses a sweet kiss to my forehead and walks toward his daughter's voice. "What's up?"

"I'm hungry."

He laughs. "What about you, Eva?"

I followed a short distance behind. "Starving. What's on the menu?"

"Nuggies and fries," Lilah states with emphasis on the nuggies.

Lachlan flashes one of his gorgeous, megawatt smiles at his daughter. "You're having nuggies. We're having burgers with balsamic onions and Swiss with seasoned fries."

Lilah lifts one shoulder. "Okay."

"Lilah, can you set the table for three, please?"

"As long as Miss Eva sits next to me," she replies.

Lachlan looks over at me and winks. "Sure."

"How can I help?" I ask after washing my hands.

"Can you toast the rolls and put the nuggets in the air fryer for Lilah?"

"No problem." I busy myself with my tasks and discreetly watch Lilah pull out a stool and get the items she needs for dinner.

Initially, she only grabs two plates and starts to climb down again.

"What about me?" I whisper.

She giggles softly. "I have special fairy plates. These are for you and Daddy."

"What was I thinking? Of course you do."

The smile on Lachlan's face during my exchange with Lilah is different than ones I've seen before. It's content and, dare I say, hopeful.

I move to the fridge and search for the rolls. When I turn back, I bump into Lachlan. His arm immediately curls around my waist and steadies me. After a discreet check on Lilah, he kisses my temple and redirects me.

Warmth cascades through me. I didn't realize how much I prefer physical touch until him. Cody wasn't affectionate unless he wanted sex. To be honest, I should've taken his lack of attention to me as a warning of things to come. Yet with Lachlan, I crave his touch more than ever before.

I'm lost in my thoughts until I feel him nearby. His warmth and cologne, a mix of cedar and vanilla, surround me. I don't know what brand cologne it is—hell, it could be his shampoo or detergent. Either way, he smells delicious. With his front pressed against my back, he brings his mouth near my ear. His cool breath raises goose bumps on my skin.

"You okay?"

All I can do is nod. Each time he's close to me, tingles spread across my entire body. *Are we how a relationship should feel? If so, I'm in.*

Fifteen minutes later, we take seats at the table with me between them and devour our dinner.

CHAPTER TWELVE

LACHLAN

In an effort to make progress on the website, I break my movie rule for Lilah. She's allowed to watch movies on weekends only. She's settled on the couch ready for bed with her fairies, specifically *Tinkerbell and the Great Fairy Rescue*. Eva and I are huddled together at the dining table troubleshooting the website before opening it up. The race is in three months. I've spent the last thirty minutes mesmerized by her checking and rechecking things on the administrative side of the site.

"Are you going to run?" Eva asks.

"Will I be able to if we're coordinating it?"

She shrugs. "Good point. Either way, can you go to the site and try to register from your phone?"

"Sure." I pull out my phone and head to the link she sent me. Within a few minutes, I'm confirmed to run. The confirmation came to both my email and the administrative email she set up.

"It's perfect! Do you want to do the honors?" she asks.

I raise an eyebrow. "For?"

"Making the site live."

"We should do it together."

"Okay." She takes my hand, sets it on the mouse, and covers it with hers as best she can.

Click.

I lean closer and murmur, "I would like to click something else... repeatedly."

Her gaze zips to Lilah, who is completely engrossed in her movie despite seeing it at least a hundred times. "I'm looking forward to time alone with you too." Innuendo and intentions zigzag between us with few words and hidden caresses. "Where are we going?"

"I made a reservation at Morgan's for six thirty. It'll give me enough time to drop off Lilah and pick you up."

She wrinkles her nose. It's downright adorable. "I can meet you there."

"Absolutely not. It's our first official date. It may be a little later than it should have been, but we're doing it right."

She inhales sharply before replying, "Okay."

"Daddy, the fairies were rescued," Lilah's sweet voice filters in our direction.

"Okay, sweet pea. Time to brush and hop into bed," I reply.

Lilah rises from the couch and gathers her fairies. "Miss Eva, will you read a story to me before bed?"

"I would love to. Go brush. I'll be right there."

Her eyes light up. She replies, "Thanks," and walks away. At the corner of the hallway, she drops two fairies. After picking them up, she disappears.

"Are you sure about this?" she asks me.

"Are you?" I draw her into my arms. She rests her head against my shoulder.

"Yes, but we haven't talked about Clare yet."

"Does it matter?"

She shakes her head against me, then meets my gaze. "You're an exceptional father. Whatever the reason her mother isn't in the picture I'm sure was a difficult choice. All I need is information and how you want me to handle Clare and my relationship with Lilah. The rest will work itself out."

I exhale audibly and nod. Pressing a kiss to her head, I lead Eva into Lilah's room.

"I have these two," Lilah says when we step into the room. "Daddy, I want Miss Eva to read." She's in her bed against the headboard.

"Is it okay if I listen too?"

She raises her index finger to her lips as if she's considering saying no. Then, after thinking about it, she answers, "Yes. Miss Eva, you need to sit here." She pats on the edge of her bed. For the next ten minutes, we dive into Tinkerbell's world again. The book is about the Pixie Hollow Games, the fairy version of the Olympics.

When I finish, Lilah claps and asks, "Daddy, can Miss Eva read to me every night?"

From your lips, sweet pea. "When she's here at bedtime, definitely."

Lilah throws her arms around Eva and hugs her tightly.

Eva rises and steps toward the door. "Good night, Lilah."

"Night," my daughter replies with a huge smile on her face.

She slips out the door while I tuck Lilah in.

"Miss Eva is awesome! Do you think she will come to tea?" Lilah whispers while hugging me.

She is awesome and could be everything I ever wanted. "You can invite her if you want. Sweet dreams," I offer before leaving her room.

Eva is gazing out the French doors toward our darkened backyard. I slide my arms around her from behind, clasping them at her waist. Her hands rest atop mine, and she leans into me. "Ready to talk?"

"I am. Are you?"

"I never thought I would find someone willing to listen. No, not true. I never let anyone close enough to have this conversation." With a kiss to the nape of her neck, I link our hands and lead her into the sitting room off the master bedroom. I settle on the couch with my back toward the arm facing her. Eva is cross-legged, and my hands rest on her knees.

I pinch the bridge of my nose and breathe deeply before sharing. "Clare has dissociative identity disorder. It was officially diagnosed when she was twenty. I learned when she was pregnant."

"I'm sorry."

I press my lips into a tight line and continue, "I met one of her alters named Chloe. Chloe was outgoing and vivacious. She realized she was pregnant about three months after we met. Up until about twenty weeks, she was fine. Then she started acting strangely. I took her to the hospital during one of her delusional episodes. With a social worker present, she gave consent and shared her diagnosis with me. Later, I learned her parents ignored her symptoms, which started in childhood. They wrote them off as attention deficit hyperactivity disorder."

"Okay. She knew she had this condition but wasn't treating it?"

"Yes."

"How did you get to now?"

"Soon after Lilah was born, her medical team informed her she needed intensive inpatient care to handle her condition coupled with postpartum depression. Voluntarily, Clare petitioned the court to terminate her parental rights. With her diagnosis, the court appointed a guardian and an attorney for Clare. She followed through and put Lilah ahead of herself."

"Now she's changed her mind, almost five years later. Can she do that? "

"It would appear so. Through her court-appointed guardian, she reached out to Alannah, requesting to see Lilah. I declined. I'm sure she'll come up with something else."

"Oh. I mean can she have her rights restored?"

"Legally, she can petition to do so. Will she be successful? I don't know. I hope not."

"Can she be cured?"

"Unfortunately, no. However, from my research, she can learn to control her behaviors over time with therapy after determining the cause of her first break. Before you ask, I don't know what triggered her first break or anything about her treatment other than she vowed to seek help. I moved Lilah away to protect her."

"She's the luckiest little girl on the planet to have you as her dad."

"You have no idea what your words mean to me."

"I do and I'm sincere. Any reason for me to distance myself from her?"

Containing my distaste for her words is nearly impossible. "No, not at all." I pitch forward, wrap my hands around her rib cage, and lower her onto the couch while hovering over her. "Before I kiss you senseless, Lilah asked me if she could invite you to the Mothers and Special Friends Tea at her school before I left her room."

"I would love to go."

"Really? It isn't too fast for you?"

"No, but it isn't about me. If she feels comfortable, then I'm there."

Without further hesitation, I kiss her deeply and thoroughly. Her soft, delicate hands dip beneath the hem of my shirt. She lightly drags her perfectly manicured fingernails along my back as I savor the curve of her jaw, the hollow of her collarbone, and down as low as her V-neck sweater will allow. Frustrated by the limitation of her sweater, I rock onto my heels and draw her to sitting. In seconds, I lift her shirt off and free her full breasts from her lacy bra. She wastes no time ridding me of my shirt as well.

Her eyes meet mine, and I would swear she can hear my thoughts. Eva is smart, witty, gorgeous, and more importantly, willing to be there for

Lilah. I can't ask for much more from a woman I'm dating. The bigger question is can we survive Clare lurking in the distance for the rest of our lives? Will Clare make her run?

I lower her to the microfiber cushions and draw her jeans and panties down her legs. Casting them aside, I caress her with my gaze from head to toe before covering her with my body. Our hands roam freely. Her long, elegant fingers move in sync around my length as I curl mine in her heated center.

"Eva."

"Lachlan."

She stops stroking me briefly to push my shorts out of the way. Then her soft hand surrounds me again and falls back into rhythm. In minutes, she convulses around my fingers, and I explode into her hand.

Our gazes meet and hold until our breathing calms. I lean down and kiss her plump lips before withdrawing from her core. She does the same, and we clean up in the bathroom.

"I should go," Eva states once she's dressed. "You have a huge day tomorrow."

I nod tightly and escort her to the door. "Sweet dreams, beautiful."

"Good night, Lachlan. I'll see you after work." After a deep kiss, she disappears.

I wake before my alarm the next morning. Noting I have enough time, I slip on workout clothes and head into the basement. Forty-five minutes later, I climb the stairs and check on Lilah. She's still fast asleep. After a quick shower and partially dressing, I step back into the kitchen.

Lilah joins me shortly thereafter, still rubbing the sleep from her eyes. "Morning," she grumbles like a moody teenager.

"Want pancakes or cereal?"

"Cereal. I'll get the bowl and spoon."

I nod and grab the rest of the items she needs. Halfway through the bowl, my phone chimes.

Eva: Good morning. Good luck with Roxie today.

I can't contain the smile her thoughtful text brings to my face.

"Daddy, is that from Miss Eva?"

I arch an eyebrow at her. "Why do you think that?"

"You only smile at me and her like that," Lilah replies and immediately scoops another spoonful into her mouth.

"Yes, the message is from Eva."

"Can we call her? I want to ask her about the tea."

"You'll see her for dinner tonight," I answer.

"Okay."

I type out my reply and hurry Lilah along. I'm ecstatic and nervous about today.

Me: Thank you, sweetheart. Dinner?

Eva: I'll be there.

Less than thirty minutes later, I strap Lilah into her car seat.

"Are you excited about today, Daddy?"

"Yes, I am." *More than you know.*

"Me too. Please come pick me up as soon as possible. I can't wait to meet Roxie."

I grin at her. "I will."

With drop-off complete, I drive to the precinct and settle my nerves before heading inside for roll call.

On the way, I run into Smithson. "You're awfully happy this morning. What's up?" he comments.

"I'm getting a new partner today."

Smithson laughs. "That usually isn't a good day."

"It is when it's a K-9."

"Sweet. Congrats, man! You've been waiting since you moved here, right?"

"Yes. Thanks. How was the rest of Scarlett's weekend shift?"

Smithson frowns at me. "You saw Scarlett?"

She didn't tell him because she can't. "Yes, Lilah hit her head on Saturday. Scarlett put her right at ease."

"Is she okay?"

"Yeah. She's fine now. Plus, I'm fairly certain she won't run in the house anymore."

"Glad to hear it. Good luck today."

"Thanks."

We bro hug, and he walks in the opposite direction to the detective unit. Before I can line up, Cap pulls me aside.

"Morning. Captain Snow is early. She's waiting for you in the training area out back," he informs me.

"Great. Thanks." I take a deep breath and hustle to the rear of the building.

"Captain Snow," I greet her.

"Officer Hagen. Morning. I apologize for my unexpected early arrival." She's short and fit with dark hair wound in a tight bun high atop her head.

"No problem. I'm ready to get started whenever you are."

"Excellent. I trust you've studied the commands for Roxie."

"Yes, ma'am."

She waves me off. "Megan or Snow is fine."

"Hagen works for me."

She leads me to her vehicle and unlocks the back. Roxie sits perfectly still with her eyes cast outward at us.

"Go ahead," Snow urges.

"Roxie, *hier.*"

Her ears perk up, and she jumps out of the truck and promptly sits beside me.

"How long since you've had a partner, Hagen?"

"Nearly five years," I answer.

"Mind if I ask why?"

"I moved for my daughter, and there wasn't a K-9 spot here for me."

Snow drops her head. "I understand. I'm a single parent as well." She hands me a tennis ball. "She's at ease with you."

I show Roxie the ball and say, *"Bring,"* which is the English pronunciation for the command to fetch as I throw the ball out to my far right. Within seconds, she gets the ball, runs back, and sits, facing me. *"Aus,"* I command with an extended hand, and she sets the ball in my hand. I praise her by saying, *"So ist brav."*

"How long did you have your previous partner?" Snow asks.

Before I answer, I give Roxie a few more commands, and she readily responds. "Miranda was with me for nearly three years. She was injured on the job and retired." I spend the next hour working with Roxie as Snow looks on.

"When Captain Ramirez indicated you had skills, I was skeptical."

"Thanks." A hint of disbelief lingers in my voice.

She smiles and shakes her head. "The higher-ups are usually wrong about handlers and their skills."

"Cap trained K-9s while he was in the military. He adopted his last partner after Bear was injured on the job."

Snow nods curtly. "Now it makes more sense. He knows what to look for. I'm set if you are."

"We're perfect."

"It was a pleasure to meet you. Take care of my girl." Snow offers her hand, and I take it.

"Thank you. You as well. Roxie is in good hands."

Captain Snow leaves, and I work with Roxie for a few hours outside before introducing her to the noisy bullpen. With her walking with me stride for stride, we move toward the building. Snow did a great job with her early training. Roxie heels before I instruct her at the door.

I praise her, and we head inside. Overall, my coworkers are receptive and heed me when I share that she is working and not a pet. At least that's true outside my home. With a light knock at Cap's door, he waves us in.

"Thank you for knowing how much I missed this part of my life."

Cap rises from his chair and approaches. "Despite adopting Bear after he retired and when Kelsey added Knox, I miss the training aspect as well as the companionship. May I?"

I appreciate his acknowledgment of my role as her handler despite his previous work with K-9s and me being his subordinate. "Of course."

Cap extends his hand in front of Roxie before petting her.

"We're going to be out and about training."

"Okay. Thanks for the heads-up. Good luck," Cap answers.

I nod and settle into the department SUV set up for my girl. I introduce Roxie to the area and practice commands with her until the end of shift. After parking in the lot, I remove Roxie's gear. Ideally, it will mark when she's working and when she's off duty. I intend to use English commands at home and German commands at work to ease switching between the two for Roxie. I send a text to Eva when I park at the daycare.

Me: I'm picking up Lilah now. Can you meet us at the house?

Eva: Definitely.

"Roxie, stay," I command and exit the SUV. After inputting the code, I greet Casey as Lilah crashes into me.

"Is she here?"

With a huge smile, I reply, "Yes."

Lilah rushes away, grabs her backpack and sweater, and returns almost immediately. "I'm ready."

"Okay."

Glee is plastered on my daughter's face. I'm sure mine looked the same when Cap told me about Roxie as well.

"She's pretty," Lilah states as we get close to our truck.

"Yeah, she is." I unlock the rear door and set my daughter on her feet. "Don't move."

She nods and stands perfectly still. I open the passenger door and set one hand on Roxie. "Put yours out in front of her with your fingers down."

Lilah does as I ask over the center console, and Roxie sniffs her fingers. "Good girl, Roxie." I turn my gaze to Lilah. "Now you can pet her."

The sweetest giggle echoes in my truck when Roxie snuggles into Lilah's hand. "Daddy, she's amazing!"

"She is. Ready to go home? Eva is meeting us there."

Lilah hops into her seat and attempts to buckle herself. "Is it okay for me to ask her before dinner?"

"Sure." I close the passenger door, check her buckle, then round the truck. Part of me feels guilty for giving Eva a heads-up about the tea. The other part knows without a shred of doubt that she'll play it off as if it's a surprise. For that, I'm grateful and hopeful for our future. What woman willingly attends a Mother's Day event with her boyfriend's daughter?

Boyfriend? I laugh inwardly. We haven't been on a date yet. Though it's soon—very soon.

Eva's waiting for us when we arrive. "Were you waiting for my call?" I ask her after parking in the garage. Before allowing her to answer, I discreetly block her with my body and kiss her out of Lilah's view.

She wrinkles her nose. "Hi. What if I was?"

"Are you more excited to meet Roxie or see me?"

Eva taps her finger on her lips.

"You shouldn't need to think about it." I eliminate the remaining space between us. "I give you earth-shattering orgasms."

"I had no intention of saying Roxie. In fact, memories of last night have been replaying in my head all day long. To be fair, you get earth-shattering ones as well."

"True, very true. I accept your answer. Want to meet my new partner?"

"Absolutely," she replies.

When I open the passenger door, Roxie isn't there. I find her in the footwell in the back seat, her head resting on Lilah's lap.

"Daddy, she's awesome! Hi, Miss Eva," Lilah manages between giggles.

I smile at her and instruct Eva the same way I did for Lilah. My new partner takes to Eva as quickly as she did to Lilah.

"Let's go inside. I need to give Roxie a tour."

"Can we make dinner?" Eva asks.

"Can you cook?"

She stares at me with slight disapproval on her face. "I'm not terrible at it."

"I didn't mean to offend you. Also, I didn't invite you over to cook for us."

"Okay. I want to."

"Fine with me."

"Can I help?" Lilah asks.

"Definitely," Eva answers. "Let's get started."

I watch them enter the house and take over the kitchen as if they've been making dinner together forever, not for the first time. I escort Roxie out through the garage and walk the perimeter of my property. The backyard is partially fenced, but she needs to know the far boundary. Once we're finished with the yard, I guide her to the house and indicate the exits on all sides before joining my ladies inside.

CHAPTER THIRTEEN

EVA

The sheer joy on Lachlan's face is wonderful to see. I didn't know him before when he had a K-9 partner. However, he's a tad less grumpy about work today. I can only credit the gorgeous shepherd who walks beside him while he's on duty and even when he's not.

"Do you put your bag away somewhere, or does your dad do it?"

Lilah shakes her head adamantly. "I do it myself. I'm a big girl. Only babies need help with their unicorn bags."

"I see. Well, go ahead. I'll wait." In under ten minutes, Lilah returns to the kitchen, barefoot and with her lunch box clutched in her hand.

She puts her lunch box in a cubby, then washes her hands. "Ready," she informs me.

"Well, it looks like your dad chose spaghetti with meatballs and garlic bread. Have you helped with that before?"

She lifts her shoulders and wrinkles her nose. "I don't think so."

"No problem. Why don't you bring your stool to the sink? We'll start with the water in the pot."

"Water comes out over the stove," Lilah shares.

I turn and notice the pot filler. "Nice, much easier. Okay, stool over there, then."

Once the pot is on the stove and set to boil, Lilah climbs down and pulls out a pan for the meatballs and sauce. With meatballs in the pan, Lilah pours the sauce over them a bit too fast, and it splatters everywhere.

"Oh no!" She's on the verge of tears. It makes sense. She doesn't know how I'll react.

"Don't worry. It's cleanable. Let's start the bread and then come back and clean this up."

"Deal."

I set the broiler to preheat. We work together to get the ingredients out. "Do you have shredded cheese?"

"For bread?"

"You've never had cheesy bread?"

Lilah's eyes widen, and she shakes her head left to right.

"Well, you will today if you have the cheese."

"Like for pizza?" she asks.

"Exactly."

"We always have pizza stuff." She hops off the stool and pulls shredded mozzarella from the fridge.

Interesting. "Perfect." Together we slice the loaf of bread lengthwise. "Can you spread butter on both sides?"

"Yes," she replies and starts slathering butter on the bread.

I break the spaghetti into the boiling water and stir the sauce and meatballs. When I turn back, Lilah is nearly finished with the butter.

"Nice job!" I raise my hand for a high five, and she complies.

"Thanks. Now what?"

We finish the bread and put it into the oven. After a cursory clean around the stove and nearby counter, I check the pasta. Determining it's perfect al dente, I turn off the burner and strain it in the sink.

"Can you set the table while I finish this?" I ask Lilah. Making dinner with her feels seamless. I could get used to it.

"Yep."

After checking on the meatballs, I lower the heat. Pulling the bread out, I set it on the counter. When I turn to search for a bread knife, I find Lachlan watching us from the living room with an indiscernible look on his face. He's changed from his uniform into shorts and a Chicago Bears T-shirt. I catch his gaze and mouth, "You okay?"

He nods tightly and commands Roxie to lie down and stay near the edge of the dining room rug.

"Daddy, Miss Eva knows how to make cheesy bread." The excitement in Lilah's voice is super cute.

"Really?"

"I know, right?" Lilah replies and sounds like a teenager.

Lachlan enters the kitchen and stands beside me. "What can I do?"

"If you could cut the bread, I can plate dinner."

"You were a server?" he asks.

"Yeah, how can you tell?"

He laughs softly. "You said plate dinner, not serve or dish out."

"Fair. You too?"

"Yeah, during high school, but it was short-lived. You?"

"No. I was a server at my parents' restaurant from the time I could carry a tray."

"What kind of restaurant?"

"It was called EggStop. My dad is an exceptional omelet maker. They were open until two and served breakfast all day. They sold it about two years ago now."

I carry the plates to the dining table and set them down. Lilah follows with the bread while Lachlan brings drinks.

"This is amazing!" Lilah exclaims, biting a cheesy breadstick in half.

I smile. "Glad you like it."

"Will you teach me next time?" Lachlan requests.

"Sure."

"Can I ask now, Daddy?"

Lachlan links his hand with mine under the table out of sight. "Go ahead, sweet pea."

Lilah twists in her chair to fully face me. "Miss Eva…." She takes a few beats to gather her words. It's sweet. I have an idea what she's going to ask. A sheen of sadness casts between us. She's nervous, and for that, I'm sad for her.

I reach over with my free hand and cover hers with mine.

She takes a deep breath and says, "There's a tea for special friends at school. Will you come with me?"

"I would love to."

Lilah pops out of her chair, circles the table even though she was beside me, and throws her arms around me. "Thank you, thank you."

Oh my heart. "You're welcome."

"Daddy knows the day and stuff."

"Okay. I'll ask him."

The rest of dinner passes quickly. Once the kitchen is clean, Lilah asks if she can read to Roxie.

"Sure. Why don't you get two books?" Lachlan asks her.

She pops out of her chair, her excitement evident.

"Please walk, Li," Lachlan commands.

"I will. I like Nurse Scarlett better at dance class than the 'ospital."

"Thank you."

I whip my gaze from her to him. "Dance class? I need details immediately."

Lachlan smiles as Lilah skips away. "When Smithson and Scarlett got married last year, she wanted the wedding party to participate in their first dance."

"So you learned a choreographed dance for her?" I ask with intrigue laced in my words.

"The tango."

Jealousy streaks through me, and I didn't even know him yet. Who was his partner? I tamp down my reaction and reply, "Awesome. Maybe you can teach me sometime."

He glances over toward the hallway and leans closer. "I'll do anything you want that allows me to touch each inch of your gorgeous body."

Most of the time his words are sexual, but then he throws in a sweet one, and I melt more. Before the prickles of awareness dissipate fully, Lilah returns, dressed in her pajamas with two books tucked under her arm. She curls up on the floor with Roxie and starts to read.

"Miss Eva, will you tuck me in now? I'm tired," Lilah asks almost an hour later.

"Sure."

Lilah wraps her tiny arms around Roxie. "She's soft and fluffy." With a hug and a kiss on her head, she rises and does the same with Lachlan.

Once she releases him, he stands.

"I only want Miss Eva tonight, Daddy. Okay?"

My gaze meets his, and I agree with a slight dip of my head.

"Of course. Good night, sweet pea."

Lilah takes my hand in hers and leads me to her room. She slips beneath her unicorn bedding and pats the spot beside her. "Are you sure about the tea?"

"Yes. Why wouldn't I be?"

"Daddy doesn't have friends who are girls except Miss Lia. But she isn't the same as you. She has Mr. Finn. He works with Daddy. I like you lots. Daddy likes you. The tea isn't for a little while. I don't want you to leave me too."

Oh, Lilah. My heart twists into a knot, and a lump forms in my throat. "I have a secret to share with you."

She perks up slightly.

"I like you lots too. I'll be at the tea, Lilah. I promise."

She wraps her arms around my waist and pulls me close. The tension in her little body evaporates the longer I hug her. "Thank you."

"Good night."

When I turn into the hallway, I run into a wall of muscle. He's ninja-like. I didn't hear him approach Lilah's room. Without hesitation, he grips my nape and kisses me hard and deep. We kiss down the hall, across the living room, and into his bedroom. The last thing I want to do is stop him, but... I pull back slightly.

"Were you worried about her or me?"

He draws me flush against him, dipping his head onto my shoulder. "Both," he replies, his lips against the exposed skin.

"We can't mess whatever this is up." I motion between us. I'm not sure we can be what I want us to be, but either way, I refuse to let Lilah down.

"We won't." Within a second, his lips are back on mine, and I snake my fingers beneath the hem of his shirt and glide my palms over the ripples and ridges of his abs.

A ringtone I've heard once before halts my progress. He presses a lingering kiss to my forehead and leaves the room.

"I need to go into work. Will you watch Lilah, or would you like me to call Lia?"

"I'll stay. While you change, I'll grab my bag from my car."

He kisses me lightly. "Thank you."

"You're welcome."

When I return inside, Lachlan is securing Roxie's vest.

"The code to the alarm is 5813. I'll turn it on when I leave."

I nod. "Can you share the reason for the call?" I'm not sure of the protocol here.

"A missing kid. Roxie is a dual-purpose K-9. However, she excels at tracking and protection."

"Good luck," I murmur and kiss him lightly.

"Roxie, *hier*."

Roxie moves beside him and follows as he exits into the garage. With a quick look back, he arms the security system and disappears.

I take a deep breath and set my laptop up on the ottoman. Without Lachlan nearby, I feel chilly. After padding to his bedroom, I locate a Chicago Bears hoodie folded neatly in his closet. Nice. Tugging it over my head, I'm immediately warmer in a Lachlan-scented hug but from his clothes.

I check my phone and reply to the text from earlier.

Maggie: How are things going with the site?

Me: The site is up and running. The signs and ads will start tomorrow.

Maggie: Awesome! What about Hagen?

Me: What about him?

Maggie: You two have been spending lots of time together.

Me: No comment.

I scowl inwardly as I press Send, considering I'm in his house alone, wearing his clothes.

Maggie: I'm just saying, you two make a gorgeous couple.

Me: No comment. Love you.

Maggie: Love you back.

Over the next hour, I answer a few emails in my inbox but schedule them to be sent in the morning. Then I message Callan Craven about scheduling a meeting to discuss community service hours for the high school students at the 5K. Lachlan gave him a heads-up but didn't finalize anything.

His response is nearly immediate, and I plan a dinner with him and Alannah next Wednesday night at the cottage.

With those tasks complete, I verify my sign order for the race will be available tomorrow morning and shut down. I walk down the hallway to Lilah's room and check on her. She's blissfully in dreamland. Hoping to find a guest room, I check down the hall. There are two more bedrooms, but they are devoid of furniture. For a moment, I consider sleeping on the couch but quickly dismiss the idea because I would have to locate pillows and blankets to be warm.

Once I wrap my head around the idea, I grab my book, pad to Lachlan's bedroom, and snuggle beneath his cozy, warm comforter.

CHAPTER FOURTEEN

LACHLAN

Despite the reason that I'm leaving Eva with Lilah, it feels right. Lilah's words nearly broke me when I was eavesdropping in the hall. I was equally worried about both. However, I had no idea why Lilah wanted only Eva until I heard her sweet voice. Not only am I significantly attached to Eva, but my daughter is as well.

I push my thoughts away and pull up to the trailhead near Mount Agamenticus. The missing boy lives in the neighborhood at the base. I exit my SUV and open the passenger door.

"We've got this, Roxie. Right?" I don't expect an answer, but she pushes her nose against my shoulder. "Roxie, *hier*." She hops out of the vehicle and heels beside me. We hustle to the command center.

"Hagen." Cap waves me over.

"Cap."

"I realize you've had her for less than a day, but she's our best chance of finding Chase Littleton before it's too late. He's seven, diabetic, and overdue for a blood sugar check by three hours. Mom was held over at work, and Dad was late getting home. Teenage babysitter left him gated in his room near seven this evening. He managed to climb the gate and slip out the back door. The trail cam picked him up one hundred yards to our west just before eight."

Anger bubbles in my chest toward the babysitter, but I push it away. "Okay. Has anyone entered the trails?"

"Yes, Gugliotti, Davis, Garcia, and Montgomery entered about ten minutes ago. They plan to check the lodge at the top of Summit Staircase. It's a trail his mother indicated they walked numerous times."

"Understood. Do we have an article of his for Roxie?"

Cap indicates a zippered blue hoodie to his right. "What else do you need?"

"Nothing." I scoop up the hoodie. "Roxie, *such*," which means track. She sniffs the article and takes off down the First Hills trail to the left, away from the lodge.

"*Langsam*." Slow. "*So ist brav*." Good.

My only reason for commanding Roxie's pace is it's pitch-black. The single ray of my flashlight only illuminates so far ahead. She veers off the path toward the restrooms.

"Chase. Chase," I call out and then clear both sides of the building. No luck. Although Roxie turned in this direction, Chase may have as well.

"Hagen, status," Cap calls over the radio.

"Restroom empty. Continuing down Big A trail toward the barn."

"Roger," Cap replies.

I offer Roxie the hoodie again, and she continues along the path. When we get to the fork, I hear over the radio, "Officer Montgomery to command. Lodge is empty. I repeat, lodge is empty. Please advise as to bearing."

Cap replies, "Acknowledged, Montgomery. Two of you continue east on the Big A trail, and the other two take Summit Staircase to Hairpin Trail." The Big A trail is a large loop. The lodge they searched is to the east, and the barn is to the west.

"Roger," Montgomery answers.

Rather than get disheartened, I follow Roxie along the west leg of Big A trail toward the barn. As we approach the area where the Fisher trail intersects with Big A, Roxie pauses, then advances down the Big A trail. After about two hundred yards, Roxie turns back and starts to run. It's impossible for me to keep up with her.

"Roxie, *halt*!"

Instantly, she stops but remains in her alert stance rather than sitting.

When I catch up, I give her a command meaning go slow. "Roxie, *lauf langsam*."

She continues toward the barn quickly but not quite a run. When we reach the entrance, she alerts at the door, then attempts to scratch her way in. "*Bleib*." Stay. I shine the light inside, but I don't hear anything. "Chase," I call out but don't receive an answer. "Roxie, *geh rein voran, langsam*." Go inside, search, slow.

Roxie barrels through the door. She lies flat on her belly near the stall door in the rear of the barn as if she could squeeze beneath the door. She can't.

"Chase," I call again. No response. I approach and shine my flashlight into the stall. Chase is curled into a ball in the rear corner. Relief passes over me as I open the stall. My nerves kick up when he doesn't respond. Then I command, "Roxie, *pass auf.*" Guard.

Roxie enters the stall and positions herself to protect Chase. I approach slowly. "Chase." With no answer, I check for a pulse with my heart in my throat.

"Hagen to command."

"Go for command," Cap responds.

"I've located Chase in the barn off Big A trail. Request immediate medical assistance. He's alive, but his pulse is weak. His breathing is labored, and he appears to be sleeping."

"Roger. Penn and Ransom are en route," Cap replies.

"Roger." I remain crouched beside Chase with my hands on his tiny wrist.

After what seems like forever, but the equivalent of how long it takes Penn and Ransom to hike here with their gear, I hear Penn call out, "Hagen."

"Penn. Last stall on the right," I reply.

Séamus Penn is a local and overall nice guy. He's big and burly. His stature would scare some if not balanced out by his teddy bear demeanor. Grumpy bear is more accurate. Lacey Ransom is his friend and partner. She's girl-next-door pretty with mahogany hair. They enter the stall, and I order Roxie to move.

"Roxie, *so ist brav. Hier*." Good. Come. She complies and heels at my side. "*Blieb*." Stay.

Penn does a quick exam while Lacey preps an IV. Given his known diabetes diagnosis, Penn pricks his finger and measures his glucose level. "His blood sugar is 200," Penn states. "How he made it here is unfathomable."

Lacey loads a syringe with a dose of insulin and feeds it into the IV. "Let's get him on the backboard and out of here." Once he's secured to the backboard, they shoulder their gear, and we begin the trek back to the command post.

When we exit the trailhead, two weary parents rush toward us. Frankly, I block out most of what they're saying because they aren't speaking to me. Penn and Ransom load Chase into the ambulance, followed by his parents, and speed away.

"Well done, Hagen," Cap states as I approach.

"It was her." I stroke Roxie's head. "Other than a moment of urgency where she was confident of the trail, she followed commands perfectly."

"I'm glad it went well. Throwing her into the deep end on day one would not have been my preference," Cap acknowledges.

"I agree but understand your call completely. I would've done the same in your shoes."

"Go home. I don't expect to see you before noon tomorrow. You can write your report then," he orders.

"Night, Cap." I pat Roxie on the head. "Roxie, *hier.*" She dutifully follows me to the SUV.

Once I park in my garage, I remove her uniform and praise her a bit more. Any search where Roxie would be required that turns out well is phenomenal. For her to assist and work well so soon is exceptional.

I enter the house, silence the alarm, and turn it back on before checking on Lilah. She's fine, I'm sure, but I look in on her each night before I turn in. Tonight is different. I work hard to protect her and make sure she's safe, but so did Chase's parents. There's only me. To be fair, Eva has been present, but we're new. While I trust she won't stop seeing Lilah if we don't work out, the worry is there. Roxie follows me. She moves to the edge of Lilah's bed, checks on her, and lies down on the floor. Despite my statements to the contrary, tonight's case makes me consider allowing Roxie to stay with Lilah. Instead of deciding right now, I turn toward my bathroom, stripping out of my uniform as I go.

In my head, I knew Eva would be in my bed because she wasn't on the couch or Lilah's room. There also isn't anywhere else for her to sleep. The guest rooms are bare. Seeing her in my king-size bed is a different story. Her long blonde hair is fanned out on one of my pillows, and my ultra-soft sheets are twisted around her sexy, toned legs. If that isn't enough, she's only wearing lace bikini panties and one of my YPD shirts, which I can see because she's facing away from the door. The shirt is taut around her waist with my name emblazoned on the back. *She belongs here.*

Before I start feeling creepy about watching her sleep, I lock my weapon in the strongbox, shower, and tug on some boxer briefs. Initially, it concerned me when she didn't wake when I arrived. Thinking about it more fully, I'm extremely quiet, and it also means she feels safe here. Safe enough to sleep without worry. *Mine.*

As much as I don't want to disturb her, startling her by climbing into my bed with her isn't an option either. I sit on the edge, drag my fingertips along her forearm, and whisper her name. "Eva."

She shifts and smiles up at me. "You're here." Pushing up, her lips meet mine. After a sweet kiss, one I could get used to each time I come home, she asks, "Did you find the child?"

"Yeah, Roxie was amazing, especially for her first case. Chase will be fine."

"Happy to hear it." She skims her lips across mine again lightly. "Which side is yours?"

I grin at her. Also, I'm glad she has no intention of leaving. "I sleep in the middle. Closer to the door works for me."

Eva swaps the pillows, giving me the cold one, not the one she was using, untangles the sheets, and shifts to the far side of the bed.

I snuggle beneath the covers and tuck her against me. "Thank you for staying," I mumble into her hair, which smells like vanilla.

"You're welcome."

I consider sharing that I like having her in our home but decide it's early. Despite Lilah's growing attachment to Eva—hell, mine too—it's too soon to share my feelings out loud. *Right? Yes.* I press a kiss to her nape and murmur, "Good night, sweetheart."

"Night, Lachlan."

It may have been only for a few hours, but it was the best sleep I've ever had. There's only one difference... Eva snuggled in my arms. I feel the moment she wakes and realizes where she is.

"Morning, gorgeous."

She turns her head to look at me but fails. Instead, she twists in my arms, intertwining her legs with mine. "How are we handling this with Lilah?"

"The truth. You stayed over because I had to go into work," I offer.

She wrinkles her nose, which is cute but also means she has an opinion. "Okay, I'm fine with that part, but shouldn't I be on the couch instead of in your bed?"

"No." My answer is emphatic and unwavering. I may not say it out loud yet, but I want her here with us.

Her head drops in understanding, but she says nothing else on the subject. "We should get moving before she wakes up. Plus, doesn't Roxie need be released from her kennel?"

"I caved... sort of."

"You let her sleep with Lilah?"

"Her protective instincts are off the charts, so instead of sleeping on her floor, I left Roxie in her room."

"It makes sense, but you may not be able to wiggle out of it going forward."

"Probably not, but it was worth it to know Roxie was watching over her. I slept with you in my arms instead."

Emotions neither of us want to acknowledge play out on her face. She's as terrified as I am. She told me herself. How do we get over it… together?

"Do you have an extra toothbrush?"

I laugh softly. "Yeah, under the sink. Breakfast?"

"Coffee too."

I kiss the tip of her nose and then her lips. "Coffee goes without saying."

She pads to the bathroom, and honestly, I watch her go. The hem of my shirt leaves the lower quarter of her ass exposed. The dirty thoughts in my head need to wait for another time. I tug on a shirt and shorts, then join her in the bathroom. Once she's dressed, we head toward the kitchen.

"Willing to start the coffee while I wake Lilah and Roxie?"

"Sure," she replies.

I pad down the hallway and find Roxie with her head on Lilah's bed. My daughter is wide awake and petting her.

"Morning, Daddy. Roxie's fur is soooo soft."

I smile at my daughter. "Morning. Yeah, it is. Why don't you get up and get dressed for school?"

"Okay."

"Roxie, come."

Lilah pouts, but Roxie dutifully follows me out of her room. I accept a cup of coffee and a kiss from Eva. Then I let Roxie into the backyard. While I wait for her to run around, I watch Eva and Lilah. My daughter has a huge smile on her face and hugs Eva after finding her in the kitchen first thing in the morning. *She fits with us.*

"Daddy, you didn't say Miss Eva was here," Lilah accuses while I feed Roxie.

"Next time I will. I had to go into work last night, and Eva offered to stay."

"Instead of Miss Lia?" Lilah asks.

"Exactly."

She smiles and tilts her head in Eva's direction. "'Kay."

"Pancakes or eggs?" I ask her.

"Eggs, please. Miss Eva, will you eat with us?"

"Of course."

"Lilah, can you set the table?" I request.

"Sure."

Eva sidles beside me. "How can I help?"

"Can you make her lunch? She has a peanut butter and jelly sandwich, cookies, and pretzels."

"Just point me in the direction of the snacks. Wait, do you need one?"

I kiss her without thinking and indicate where the snacks are. If Lilah saw the kiss, she didn't mention anything. "No, not today."

She frowns, then gets to work. While I cook, Eva makes lunch for Lilah and starts a second coffee for each of us. Somehow, she seems to know where her lunch box is. Then I realize she guided Lilah to putting it away properly while I was training with Roxie.

"Time to eat," I announce.

Once we polish off our food, Lilah clears her plate and gets ready to leave. "Daddy, why aren't you dressed in your uniform?"

"I'm going in later because I worked really late last night."

"Oh. 'Kay." She rounds the island and hugs Eva. "Have a good day."

"You, too, Lilah."

"Will you be here this afternoon?"

"Not sure yet."

Seemingly satisfied, she rushes to the door leading toward the garage. Usually getting Lilah out the door is a feat most days.

"Is there something extra fun going on at school today?" I ask my daughter.

Lilah smiles. "It's Isla's birthday."

"I see. Give me a second, and we'll leave."

She shrugs.

"Roxie, crate." Without hesitation, Roxie saunters to her kennel, and I lock it. Stepping into the kitchen, I stand as close to Eva as possible and whisper, "I would prefer to kiss you breathless right now."

"Same. We should talk about that."

"Kissing?"

Eva laughs softly. "Boundaries."

"We will. Have a great day. Just set the alarm when you leave." She nods, and I walk away before Lilah grows more impatient.

I pull onto our street and drive toward the center.

"Daddy?"

"Yeah?"

"Is Miss Eva your girlfriend?"

"I haven't officially asked her, but I would like her to be. Would you be okay with that?"

"She's pretty and funny and reads with me."

She's brilliant, comfortable in her own skin, sexy as fuck, and calms me to my core. "All of those things are true."

"Plus, she makes you happy. You never smiled except at me before you met Miss Eva."

Children are more perceptive than most adults give them credit for. Aside from overhearing her share similar sentiments with Eva, she's right. Eva makes me happy. Happier than I've been before relationship-wise. "Also true, sweet pea." I park at the center and escort her to the door.

Entering the center, Lilah rushes to her room and unpacks. "Bye. Love you."

I've been dismissed, and surprisingly, I'm okay with it. When I reach the house, I let Roxie out of her kennel. Before I can decide whether to lift or run, my phone rings.

"Good morning, Hagen."

"Cap. Is everything all right?"

"Yes. News of Roxie's assistance in the search last night has been the topic of conversation. The newspaper is looking to talk to you, and Chase has asked to meet Roxie. Can you come in?"

"Sure. I'll be there within the hour."

I dress in my uniform and drive to the precinct. When we arrive, we're met with applause in the squad room. I knock on the doorframe of Cap's office, and he waves us in.

"That was quick," he states.

The details aren't important. Truthfully, I didn't want to exercise, and my house felt empty without Lilah and Eva. To be fair, Eva's absence hit harder than Lilah's today. This morning was seamless. We moved around the kitchen as if we have been for years. She fits with us, plain and simple.

"Linda Smithers has been calling from the local paper. Ideally, you can talk to her over the phone. We can have Craven snap a few pictures outside and send them to her to avoid her coming here."

"That would be preferrable. While last night was a win, Roxie is young. I don't want to overexpose her." *Or me.*

"I understand. However, Roxie is a novelty in this area right now. It'll wear off."

I grumble inwardly and take Linda's number from him when Craven appears in the doorway.

"You wanted to see me, Cap," he states.

He shares his plans, and Craven and I head outside with Roxie. Thirty minutes and too many photos later, we sit to narrow them down.

"How is the 5K planning coming along? You're working with Eva Washington?"

"Good. You are aware of our meeting next week, right? At least, I'm pretty sure that's when it is."

Craven smirks at me. "Eva is controlling your schedule like Alannah controls mine?"

I glare at him. *Yes, kind of, and I don't mind one bit.* "For this, yeah."

"You like her," he states.

"Yeah, I do. How can you tell?"

"The instant I mentioned her name, the tension radiating off your body due to the reporter and photos decreased, which I surmise has more to do with Lilah's mother than the actual photos. Plus, the smile on your face is an obvious tell. How does Lilah feel about her?"

I shake my head. He isn't wrong about the press coverage. I'm not a fan. It was a wrinkle I hadn't considered when Cap offered me a K-9 partner. The court paperwork is redacted. Clare doesn't know where we live. "She asked if Eva was my girlfriend this morning."

"Is she?" Craven asks.

"Our first date is tomorrow, actually."

"Good for you. You deserve to be happy."

"Thanks."

Craven points to the third and fourth images. "I would use one of these two."

"I agree. Thanks for the assist."

"No problem. See you on Wednesday for dinner. I'll bring the contact list for the juniors and seniors and the community service form you need to complete."

"Sounds good."

Before I head inside to call the reporter, I text Eva.

Me: Free for dinner?

Eva: Maybe. The perfume company pushed up the deadline to Monday.

Me: You've got this! Let me know either way.

Eva: I will.

I feel as if I lost something when she said she may not be available tonight. I'm getting used to having her in my space to the point that when she can't be there, I miss her. *Damn! I'm falling for her.*

With the realization fresh in my mind, I head inside and get the call with the reporter out of the way. Once that's complete, I draft my report and send it to Cap for approval.

I drop by his office to get an update on Chase. "Is he still at York Memorial?"

"Let me check with Mrs. Smithson." While Cap calls, I sit and command Roxie to lie down.

"I understand. We can schedule a visit at a later time." He ends the call and turns his attention to me. "Mr. and Mrs. Littleton have decided to push off the visit. The press coverage is a lot for their family."

I drop my head. "I understand. I'll be outside with Roxie. Let me know if you find any errors in the report."

"Will do."

I exit Cap's office and train with Roxie until the end of shift. When I park at the daycare, my phone chimes with a text.

Eva: I'm not going to be able to make dinner tonight.

I'm disappointed. I was looking forward to seeing her. I feel better after her next text.

Eva: I'm choosing to work now instead of rescheduling tomorrow.

Me: I'm looking forward to having you to myself.

Eva: Me too. I'll call you later.

When we arrive home, I take off Roxie's vest and let her run around in the backyard with Lilah. She spills the details of her day and Miss Kelsey's yummy cupcakes for Isla's birthday.

After an easy dinner and a fairy book, I tuck Lilah into her bed.

"Good night, sweet pea."

"Night, Daddy. Are you going to talk to Miss Eva?"

"Yes." *Why?*

"Can you say good night to her for me?"

"Of course. I love you."

"I love you too."

With my latest book and a cup of coffee in hand, I take a seat on my expansive back deck by the firepit, waiting for Eva's call.

Near ten, I get concerned and video call her instead.

"Hi, Lachlan."

"Hey, gorgeous. Still working?"

"Yeah, why?"

"It's almost ten," I inform her.

"I'm on a roll. Sorry I didn't call you earlier."

"No problem. I was worried. Lilah asked me to say good night to you for her."

"Awww. That's sweet of her. Please say good morning for me."

"I will. You should get some sleep. I need you rested for tomorrow."

"For dinner?" She raises her eyebrows suggestively.

I shake my head. "No, for after dinner. I haven't completed my initial exploration of your flawless, soft skin."

She pauses briefly and then asks, "What is the required attire for Morgan's?"

"Any one of your sexy dresses will be perfect."

Her skin turns bright red. "How do you know I have more than one sexy dress, as you put it?"

"It's a hunch. Although there's nothing wrong with wearing the emerald one you wore to the holiday party again."

"I'll consider it. Thank you for worrying about me."

"Can't help myself. I'll pick you up tomorrow night for our date. Sweet dreams, Eva."

"Looking forward to it. Good night, Lachlan."

I end the call and turn in, hoping to speed time until I have her to myself.

CHAPTER FIFTEEN

EVA

Despite the late night, I drag myself out of bed and into my office with coffee before seven the next morning. For whatever reason, the perfume company has pushed up the deadline to Monday rather than two weeks. I send a short email to Noelle and Caroline to set up a meeting to discuss my findings before returning my attention to the boards for the perfume ad. Ideally, I can finish these today, only leaving a cursory review before submitting them over the weekend. Working on the weekends is not something I do often, in fact never, but given the timeline change, I need to.

About an hour later, my doorbell rings. I check the peephole and find my gorgeous man standing there. I love that—*my*.

I open the door. "Hi."

"Good morning, sweetheart." He slides his hand around my neck and kisses me boneless. His mouth makes me gooey inside, and I'm not ashamed to admit it.

The little taste of him is merely a tease, but I'll take whatever I can get.

He pulls away and hands me the tray in his other hand. "I wanted to kiss you and make sure you eat breakfast. I'll see you tonight."

"Thank you," I reply and steal another before he rushes away.

He flashes me his signature grin, and then he's gone. I watch him hurry to his SUV where Roxie is sitting in the front seat, her eyes trained on Lachlan.

I sigh at the first sip of the latte and hustle back into the office. Each bite of the brie and raspberry scone pushes me to work harder. Not really, but it helps. I'm focused and diligent until my phone rings near noon.

"Hi, Mom."

"How are you? How's the new place? Your promotion?"

"The cottage is gorgeous. The ocean outside my back door is a wonderful way to start each day. The job is the same, just a different title and a little more money. How are you and Dad?"

"We're fine. How are you doing outside of work? Have you been able to spend time with your brother?"

"Yes, I have. To answer the question you truly want to ask, I have a date tonight."

"Good for you, getting back out there. I won't keep you. Please let me know how it goes."

"I will. Love you, Mom." I won't, but it'll end this call.

"Love you, too, Eva."

After the call with my mom, I work hard, and by three, I feel confident in the boards and the accompanying memorandum with deeper details. My phone chimes as I pad to the kitchen for water.

Jo: Can you talk?

Rather than respond, I call her.

"Hey, girl. Everything okay?"

"No, not at all."

"Please share with me," I implore.

"I overheard a bunch of the executives, including Shirley, talking while I was outside for lunch. They were discussing massive layoffs by the end of the month."

"Oh no! That's terrible. Thank you for the warning. I'll worry about it tomorrow. I have bigger things to handle first."

"Your date is tonight, isn't it? I'm sorry. I shouldn't have called today."

"Don't worry, lovely. I'm excited for tonight and won't let the rumors mess it up."

"Good for you. What are you wearing?"

"I'm torn between the emerald dress he's already seen and the blue one with the slit."

"Go with the blue. Show off those legs of yours. I'm crazy happy for you, E."

"Thanks, Jo. Let me know if you hear anything else."

"Will do. Have a great time tonight. You deserve a good man."

"Love you, girl."

"I expect details, exceptionally dirty and sexy ones, later in the weekend."

"I'll consider it. Bye."

I resolve not to worry about work until tomorrow. I take my time in the shower and make sure everything is buffed and shaved. Inwardly, I laugh. It doesn't matter in the slightest bit. I may not have had sex with Lachlan yet, but he's seen every inch of me.

I dry my hair while waiting for my skin to absorb the massive amounts of lotion I used. To quell some of my nerves, which surprise me, I grab a few crackers and cheese before applying my makeup. I slither into my dress, loop my fingers into my shoes, and descend the stairs.

At quarter past six, the doorbell rings. I don't check the peephole this time.

"Hey. Come in," I greet him again. This morning he was wearing his uniform. Now, though, he looks hot as hell, clad in charcoal dress pants and a crisp white shirt rolled to expose his muscled forearms. It wasn't until him that I realized arm porn is attractive. Then again, my exes weren't even close to as fit as Lachlan.

"Hi," he replies, handing me a beautiful bouquet of flowers. Interestingly, it includes many of my favorites, though I'm sure I never shared what they are. The grouping includes red roses, cremon, pink ranunculus, eggplant Calla lilies, limonium, and hypericum.

"Thank you. These are gorgeous." I attempt to put them in water in the kitchen, but he draws me into his arms.

His kiss is mind-bending. I've never felt so much from kissing alone. Each swipe of his tongue makes me more pliant in his arms. I drop the flowers and start to work the buttons of his shirt and increase the intensity of our kisses. When his shirt is open but still tucked into his pants, he pulls back.

"You can't kiss me like that before our date."

"If I recall, you kissed me first." I shake my head. "It doesn't matter. Why not?"

"Sultry kisses are for when we have time to be naked. We won't make our reservation. You look hot as fuck, you smell amazing, and I want to see the lacy lingerie you're hiding beneath this sexy dress after dinner."

"You're assuming I have lacy lingerie beneath this dress."

His jaw ticks before he manages, "Do you?"

I raise an eyebrow but don't answer his question. "We can go out another time."

"No. You deserve a perfect first date, and tonight you're getting one."

I tap my index finger on my lips.

"What are you thinking?"

"Can you change our reservation? You can find out the answer to your question before dinner."

"I can, but you may have to come with me to pick up Lilah."

"Okay. I sense a hint of dislike in your voice."

"I may not be able to properly kiss you good night."

"Hmmm. I'll survive."

Without further hesitation, he pulls his phone from his pocket and calls Morgan's, pushing our reservation back an hour. "Thank you," he manages before ending the call.

While he's talking, I unbuckle his belt, untuck his shirt, and set my mouth on his chest.

"Eva." My name comes out strangled.

I add space between us and meet his gaze.

"Are you bare beneath this dress?"

"Do you want me to answer you, or are you going to take it off?"

He threads his fingers with mine and leads me upstairs. In the middle of the room, he raises my arms overhead and commands me to keep them there. Squatting, he skims his fingers from my ankles up my calves. When he reaches the hem of my dress, he gathers it as he continues to climb. "You're stunning," he murmurs after tossing my dress to the floor. "Why no panties?"

"You know why."

"Remind me," he urges.

"Panties are pointless when you're close enough to touch me. Time to lose the rest of your clothes, Lachlan."

"Yes, ma'am."

I laugh softly and am immediately silenced when he stands before me naked as the day he was born with his eager length reaching skyward. *Yes!* Without another thought, I take a step forward and stroke him with both hands. Wrapping an arm around my waist, he guides me to the edge of the bed. His hands caress my sides and curl around to knead my breasts. The sensations he causes with his hands are beyond comprehension. Each sensual touch sends spikes of increased need through me, as if how much I need him could grow more.

Lachlan lowers his head and takes one taut nipple into his mouth while his fingers descend southward. When he plunges two fingers into my core, I slow my strokes. His thumb circles my swollen clit, and a needy sound falls from my lips. The beginning of an explosive orgasm builds in my low belly.

"Condoms?"

"Plural?"

"Hopefully," he replies.

I exhale slowly. "In the drawer." I point to the bedside table.

"I like how you were prepared for tonight."

"Didn't want to miss another chance to feel you deep inside me."

He pauses at my words.

I slow my strokes. "Lachlan. Did I say something wrong?"

He grabs the strip before replying, "No. You continue to surprise me each day."

"You do too."

He sears my mouth with his. I could survive on his kisses alone, but I don't want to. He pulls my lower lip between his teeth. The sting of his teeth is amazing.

"You like it, too, huh?"

"Guess so."

Hoisting me to the middle of the bed, he then climbs over me. I widen my thighs in invitation.

"You're perfect, Eva."

"Maybe for you. Despite my outward urgency and statement earlier, it's been—"

"Same for me. We'll go slow."

He tears a packet from the strip and rolls it on. Nudging my thighs wider, he settles between them and rests on his forearms. Our eyes are locked on each other as he pushes forward inch by glorious, torturous inch. My fingernails score his shoulder blades as I adjust to him.

"You good?" he whispers while closing in to kiss me.

"I need a minute before you move."

He lowers his lips to mine and kisses me as if he's never been in this moment before, which I know isn't true. He adds a sliver of space between us, and I drop my head. Sealing his mouth over mine, he withdraws slowly, then buries himself to the hilt again in slow increments. Each time he thrusts forward, he masterfully heightens my release to glorious levels.

I surrender to the demanding pressure and career over the edge into unmatched bliss. "Lachlan," I scream his name as my inner walls pulse around him.

His chest muscles tighten and strain before he empties into me with deep, hard thrusts. Lachlan lowers his forehead to my shoulder while we catch our breath.

A few minutes later, he pads to the en suite bathroom to dispose of the condom. I follow and clean up as well. When we return to the bed, he gathers me close and rolls us onto our sides. His eyes meet mine. They look different than before. The emotions he's been keeping under lock and key are obvious and transparent. I'm sure mine are as well.

Narrowing the gap, I set my lips to his and kiss him deeply. Otherwise, I might spill the thoughts in my head, including how neither of my other partners connected with me like Lachlan inside the bedroom. Clearly, I've been missing out.

"Care to share what you're thinking?"

I wrinkle my nose. "I will if you will."

"While I admit it's been too long for me, that was incredible and far exceeds every experience before it," he shares.

"I would go further than incredible and say exceptional." I crane my neck. "We should clean up and get moving."

"Promise to save the rest of the thoughts for another time?" he asks.

"Hell yes!"

With a tender kiss, he pushes to standing and helps me up from the bed. He turns on the water for the shower and motions for me to step inside.

"Can you keep your hands to yourself while we rinse off, or should I wait until you're done?"

"No promises, but you aren't waiting. Get in there," he demands.

I twist my hair up in a clip and join him in the steamy enclosure. Lachlan follows immediately. Aside from some kissing and touching, we manage to clean up and get out of the shower moderately quickly.

"This towel is warm," he states.

"I know. It's amazing, right?"

"Yes. It needs to be added to my bathroom as soon as possible."

I laugh and locate my dress on the floor. It doesn't take me long to slip back into it or for Lachlan to put on his clothes either. Once we're ready, we put the flowers in water and leave for our first official date.

With a sweet kiss to my forehead, he links our hands and leads me to the passenger door of his SUV.

CHAPTER SIXTEEN

LACHLAN

It dawns on me as I walk to the driver's side of my truck that this could be my last first date ever. While the order isn't normal by most standards, she's… I can't even put into words how well suited she is for me and Lilah.

Since my daughter was born, I never put my needs ahead of hers. Perhaps it was the wrong choice. Perhaps it was the right one because I hadn't met Eva yet. The nudges from Lia and the guys made me open up to the possibility of finding someone willing to take a chance on a single dad with a unique set of circumstances with his child's mother.

Eva squeezes my hand, dragging me back to the present. "You okay?"

"Better than okay." I pull into Morgan's lot and escort her inside.

"Good evening. Welcome to Morgan's, Mr. Hagen, Miss Washington. Your table is right this way."

Eva tightens her grip on my arm. "What are you up to?"

I smile. "Your best first date ever," I whisper for only her to hear.

The hostess escorts us to a small private dining room in the rear of the restaurant overlooking the harbor.

Once she leaves, Eva says, "You should've told me you went to all this trouble."

"It wasn't trouble. Plus, pushing our reservation was completely worth it in my opinion. Don't you agree?" I pull out her chair.

She replies once I'm sitting beside her, "Absolutely worth it."

Our server approaches with a bottle of wine and two glasses after we've had a few minutes to review the menu. I preselected wine and dessert—the wine because I know they needed to order it and the dessert because I love it and it takes an hour to prepare. The good news is Morgan's is closer to the daycare center.

"Good evening. Did you choose your appetizer?"

We place our entire order, and he leaves.

"Can I ask you a few questions?"

"Of course," I reply.

"How much do you like country music?"

I raise an eyebrow. "How?"

"Nearly every station in your SUV is preset to country," she states.

I drop my head. "Do you hate it? It's either love or hate. Truly there's no in-between." I'll give up country music for her.

"I'm not sure about that. I like some country music but not all."

"Meaning?"

"Popular musicians I like include Morgan Wallen, Lainey Wilson, and Chris Stapleton. Older musicians like Garth Brooks, Reba McEntire, and Kenny Chesney are fine too."

"I can work with that."

She laughs softly. "Tell me about your family."

I exhale sharply.

"You don't have to if it's a tough subject."

"You should know about them. It's kind of wrapped up in Lilah. My parents, Arthur and Bridget, have been married for forty-five years. I have twin brothers named Cormac and Duncan, who are eight years older than me."

"The picture in your office is of you and your brothers?"

"Yes."

Our server delivers our salads and refills our water.

She sets her hand over mine. "You don't have to tell me."

"I want to. When I learned about Clare's pregnancy, my family urged me to marry her."

"You refused?"

"As horrible as it sounds, I wasn't in love with Clare and didn't foresee a long-term relationship with her. My parents' marriage was one forged out of mutual understanding of two immigrant families. My mother wanted a guy who remained in Ireland. Don't get me wrong, I believe they love each other now, but they didn't in the beginning. Their marriage is about shared bonds, moving to America, and children, not passion. I didn't want to start a marriage out as barely friends and hope for the best knowing full well divorce isn't an option. I want all of it— shared bonds, children, mutual interests, and most of all, passion."

"They disowned you?"

"For lack of a better way to put it, yes. When I learned of Clare's diagnosis, I instantly put Lilah above everyone else, myself included. I only cared about her well-being. Sharing that I was moving away for Lilah didn't go over well. Despite my best efforts, my parents don't respond to my emails or calls." Eva is the first woman who asked, and I was willing to share every aspect of our story. That fact alone tells me she's special.

"I'm sorry. What about your brothers?"

"We talk occasionally, but I haven't seen them since I moved here. Both successfully chased their professional sports dreams. They're busy."

"Family is family. Grant and I have been in different states for over five years, but we always made time for each other. I'm sorry you didn't experience the same in the recent past."

"I am too. Lilah is amazing and perfect. I keep reminding myself, moving was the right choice, and they're missing out, not the other way around."

We dig into our entrées, which effectively ends chatting about my family. Honestly, it's been me and Lilah against the world since we moved here. Well... until Lilah spilled her cookies at Eva's feet. Since that moment, she has been on my mind. Little did I know she would move here less than a month after meeting at the party.

"Are you working in two weeks?"

I pause and run through the schedule in my mind. "No, I don't think so."

She takes a deep breath. "I realize it may be difficult, but will you come with me to a work event?"

"Of course. Why wouldn't I?"

"It's in Boston."

"Oh."

"I can ask Maggie to watch Lilah. That way she has company, and you won't worry."

"Yes. I want to attend with you."

"Thank you."

"Is this event fancy? Will you need to wear a smoking-hot dress without panties?"

Her skin turns a light shade of pink. "It's fancy-ish. I don't know about my lingerie yet. I'm meeting with Kelly to look for a dress next week."

"When you choose the color, let me know. I'll make sure my suit matches perfectly."

"Okay."

Our server approaches. "Sir, would you like your dessert here or to go?"

I glance at my watch and note that we have about thirty minutes before we must leave to get Lilah. "Here, please."

"Very well," he replies and scurries away.

"I didn't hear you order dessert," Eva notes.

"It needs to be preordered because it takes an hour to create."

"Oh. Wow! I'm intrigued."

"It's decadent and delicious."

She turns her gaze toward the harbor.

I thread my fingers into hers, causing her to look at me. "I love seeing you jealous of a nonexistent woman. I meant no dates when I said it."

"I don't know what you're talking about," she huffs.

"Your secret is safe with me. I had the dessert at Smithson's engagement party."

She wrinkles her nose at me. I lean over and kiss her tenderly. "Thank you."

Our server sets the dessert between us.

"That looks too pretty to eat," she states.

"Never." I scoop out a bite of the chocolate soufflé with coffee ice cream and offer it to Eva.

She moans when the decadent flavors hit her tongue. It sounds quite similar to ones I drew from her earlier this evening.

I bring my mouth near the shell of her ear. "You may not moan like that outside of the bedroom."

Her eyes flash with a thought, but I don't press her on it. "I'll try my best. This is by far the most amazing thing I've ever put in my mouth."

"Eva." This woman will keep me on my toes every day for the rest of my life if I let her in completely.

She laughs. "Dessert. Most amazing dessert I've ever put in my mouth."

I groan and request our bill. Offering Eva my arm, I escort her to the truck and drive to the center.

"Do you want to stay here or come inside?"

"Come inside, if you don't mind. I assume she knows we're going on a date tonight."

"Not at all. Yeah, she does." I enter the code and follow Eva inside.

"Mr. Hagen. Lilah had a good night. She's watching a movie in the school-age room. I'll get her for you."

"Thanks, Casey."

Soon thereafter, Lilah appears with her backpack on and ready to go home. "Hi, Daddy. Miss Eva, you look very pretty." She takes one of our hands in each of hers.

"Thank you, Lilah."

"How was your dinner?"

I lift my eyes to meet Lachlan's. "Very nice. Did you have a good time?"

"Yes. I like having fun here instead of learnin' all the time." We walk to the SUV, and Lilah hops into her seat with a little assistance from her father.

Lachlan opens my door and waits for me to settle into the passenger seat. Once he starts the truck, he takes my hand in his and drives toward the cottage. Lilah begins off the ride chatty, asking questions about our dinner, but after five minutes, the questions slow and then stop altogether.

"She fell asleep."

"Does she do that often?"

"It's way past her bedtime. The night we walked on the beach, she was snoozing when I arrived." Lachlan pulls as close to the cottage as he can.

After opening my door, he offers me his arm and leads me to the porch. "I had an amazing evening with you."

"Me too," she replies. Then, shaking her head, she adds, "With you."

"I understood." I lean in and kiss her softly. "Will you be at soccer in the morning?"

"Possibly. I need to go over the perfume project again before I send it to Shirley for review."

"Other than soccer, we'll be home all weekend."

"I'll let you know as soon as I finish the review. Good night, Lachlan."

"Sweet dreams, Eva."

She sets her lips on my cheek. "They won't be sweet. My dreams will be a replay of earlier tonight."

"Can't say mine will be any different. I'll call you after she's in bed." I can't seem to force myself to walk away from her despite my sleeping daughter in the car. I don't overthink it; I draw her into my arms, use the pillar of the front porch to obscure us, and kiss her deeply. "I want to strip you out of this dress again and have my way with you."

"I wouldn't object. However…."

"I know. I'll call you when I get home." With a quick kiss, I retreat to my truck.

I guess the guys were right. I needed to go on a date to find a woman willing to take on me and my little family. One actual dinner alone and I can see spending a long time with Eva walking beside us. Eva joining us for dinner and waking up with her on weekends. No, weekends would never be enough. Every day. I want to wake with her every single day. It would require dropping each wall I have around myself and Lilah and allowing her to see all of me. I'm terrified we'll be too much when you throw Clare into the mix.

CHAPTER SEVENTEEN

EVA

Despite a glorious evening out, I'm up quite early in the hopes of making it to soccer to watch the kiddos. I mean all three, but it's mostly for Lilah. Who am I kidding? I want to see both of them. Last night was by far the best first date I've ever had. The incredible sex beforehand was eye-opening. Delicious soreness exists in places it never has before, and I need more, so much more.

I have two solid hours to review the boards before sending them to Shirley.

With the boards and memo set up on the desk and around the room, I check and verify that the images match the notes and the storyboards are correctly labeled. Each board has my name above the company name, as requested by the perfumery. It's out of the ordinary, but I followed the instructions as requested. With painstaking precision, I take photos of the artwork and upload them to the office server along with a message to Shirley. I'm concerned more than ever about work with the information Jodie shared. How much trouble is the company in?

I rush through the shower. Last week I learned you can order ahead at the Perk. I do this morning, pick it up, and hustle to meet Lachlan and Lilah at the field. Unfortunately, when I arrive, Lilah has already joined her team.

"Morning, gorgeous," Lachlan whispers. "Lilah is going to be so excited you're here."

"Morning." I hand him coffee and a croissant. "Are you?"

He laughs softly, leans closer, and says, "More than you could ever know. I can share more later if you want. Did you finish your work?"

"Yeah, I sent it to her."

"How do you feel about the campaign?"

"Really good. My contact loved the preliminaries. I was shocked when they sped up the timeline, though."

"I'm sure it's perfect. Your brother is approaching from the right."

I drop my head in acknowledgment of his words and take a sip of my latte. Grant was never around to screen my boyfriends. I'm truly not sure how this will shake out. "Morning, Grant."

My brother hugs me loosely. "Morning," he grumbles in response. Then he greets Lachlan. "Hagen."

They exchange nods and watch the game. During the second half of the session, the kids scrimmage. Like last week, Lilah scores a goal and rushes to the sideline to make sure her dad was paying attention.

"Dadd—Miss Eva, you're here? Did you see my goal?" Lilah asks as she runs to her huddle.

"I am, and I did. Great job!"

Lilah raises her hand to me for a high five, and I comply.

The moment she's gone, Grant's gaze sears into Lachlan. *Great!*

"Have you two been seeing each other since the holiday party?" Grant asks.

"No," I reply. "I appreciate your desire to protect me, but Lachlan is a good man. A fact you are fully aware of. Plus, I'm older than you. I can take care of myself and make my own choices."

Grant looks from me to Lachlan and back again. "I'm sure you can, but after Cody...." My brother's response is quieter. "He did a number on you."

"Lachlan knows about Cody, every single detail," I inform my brother.

"I see." Grant crosses his arms over his chest and turns his attention to the field.

Grant is conscious of the fact that I don't let people in easily. By sharing my history with Lachlan, I let him in completely. I drop my hand and thread my fingers with Lachlan's. He squeezes lightly in support as Lilah scores another goal. When their scrimmages are over, Lilah and Caleb run over to us.

"Can you watch him for a minute while I get Corrinne?" Grant requests.

"Sure," I reply.

"Auntie, did you see my goals?" Caleb asks.

"I did. Great job!"

"Did you score when you played?" he wonders.

"Some." I was the leading scorer during high school, but stats weren't the point of the game for me.

"You played soccer, Miss Eva?" Lilah asks.

"Yeah, I did."

"It's awesome!" Lilah exclaims. "Daddy, can we get a goal for the backyard so I can practice?"

"Yes, we can."

"Yay!" Lilah turns her attention to me as Grant approaches with Corrinne. "Are you coming to our picnic today?"

"There's a picnic?" I ask her.

Lilah smiles. "Not yet." She tilts her head toward Lachlan.

Containing a laugh is difficult, but I manage it.

"How about we go home and clean up, then make more plans for the rest of the day?"

Lilah's shoulders drop. "'Kay. Will you come to our house, Miss Eva?"

"Definitely."

Grant lifts Corrinne. "Eva, can I have a word?"

I shake my head but follow him off to the side. "Grant, I'll be fine."

"I know. I wanted to apologize for questioning you. Of all people, I understand choosing yourself. Hagen is a good guy and an amazing dad. He's tightlipped about her mother and the circumstances. Has he shared the situation with you? No one knows the full story about her mother. Are you up for being her mom right away?"

"Yes, or I wouldn't have gone on a date with him. I appreciate your concern, truly I do. We have had honest conversations about our pasts, including Cody, Lilah's mother, and potential issues going forward."

"Okay. I can't bear to see you like you were after Cody again."

I hug him. "Lachlan won't hurt me in the same way Cody did."

Caleb runs over from where he was with Lachlan and Lilah, effectively ending our chat. "Let's go home!" my nephew announces.

"Hagen, a word?" my brother asks.

I drop my head. "Lilah, why don't you lead me to Daddy's truck?"

Lachlan sets his keys in my hand and squeezes before we walk away. Hopefully, Grant will apologize for being a jerk.

"Miss Eva, will you play soccer with me?"

"I would love to."

"Yay!"

I unlock his truck and buckle her into her seat. We chat a bit more, and Lachlan joins us.

"All set, sweet pea?"

"Yup."

"Awesome!" Lachlan replies.

"All set with Grant?"

"He apologized for being an ass. We're good. He did warn me about meeting your dad, though."

I huff. "Unfortunately, he's probably right. Dad will be tough. Mom will be easy, though."

"Why?"

"She will see I'm happy with you and Lilah."

"Good. We're with you as well." Without a second thought, Lachlan kisses me lightly. "Meet you at the house?"

"Sure." I steal another quick kiss and walk to my car. Lachlan's gaze is trained on me until I close my car door. We spend the afternoon at a picnic in their backyard until having s'mores on the patio before Lilah turns in.

Sunday is rainy, so we spend the day watching fairy movies, playing games, and coloring. After a long, sensuous kiss with Lachlan, I make my way back to the cottage, wishing I could sleep snuggled in his arms again. It was heavenly.

After an amazing weekend, I'm on a high when I wake up Monday morning. Soon it comes crashing down on me. Just after eight, the doorbell sounds. I whip it open, expecting to find Lachlan on the other side of the door. Unfortunately, it's not him.

"Joseph. Good morning." Thankfully, I'm appropriately dressed today.

"I'm sorry for stopping by unannounced, but I didn't want any evidence of the content of our conversation."

Not good. "Come in. Would you like a cup of coffee?"

"Sure."

I pour him a cup and refresh my own.

"I'm here as Maggie's friend, not in any official capacity." He takes a sip of his coffee.

"Understood."

"There isn't an easy way for me to say this. There have been rumors that your firm is going to be sold at the end of the month, resulting in staff reduction upward of 80 percent."

"Interesting. My best friend mentioned layoffs but not a closure late last week." Worry renews in my mind. Could I lose my job?

"Understandable. I'll be completely honest with you. Your design is impeccable and will be chosen."

Glee shoots through me. *Ohmigod!*

"However," he continues, "the team won't award it to your company with knowledge of the potential imminent sale. Do you have a noncompete agreement?"

"I don't think so. There was a clause in my old contract, but I don't recall one in my new one."

"Good. I strongly suggest verifying your understanding of your employment contract."

I can read between the lines. I need to check if the contract can be awarded to me individually and get it done ASAP. "How much time do I have?"

"End of the week at the latest."

"Thank you for checking on my accommodations. Everything is wonderful. I'll be sure to complete your suggestion as soon as possible."

"Glad to hear it. Good luck, Eva."

I escort him out, pull my phone from my pocket, and call Lachlan.

"Hi, sweetheart. Is everything okay?"

"No." I share my early, unscheduled morning visitor and request Alannah's office number.

"Good luck."

"Thanks. I'll call you later." I hang up with him and dial her office.

"Good morning, Craven Law. Alannah speaking."

"Hi, Alannah. It's Eva Washington."

"What can I do for you?"

I vaguely explain the situation and make an appointment later this morning. I recheck my office email and redial Lachlan.

"Are you free for lunch?"

"Sure. I can come to the cottage."

I laugh. "As much as I want to spend my lunch in bed with you, it isn't what I'm asking for today."

"Damn!" he laughs. "Yes. Where do you want to meet?"

"You tell me. Are there any good sandwich shops around here?"

"Yes. Vocatura's is the best. I'll grab lunch and meet you at the Short Sands gazebo. That work?"

"Perfect!"

"What kind of sandwich do you prefer?"

"Whatever their specialty is with salt and vinegar chips."

"Good luck, sweetheart. I'll see you in a little while."

"Thanks." I exhale slowly and hope for the best.

With a copy of my new employment contract and the team agreement in my tote, I head toward Alannah's office.

Nervousness gets the best of me as I drive. What if I lose this job? Then what? I just found Lachlan and Lilah. My thoughts are still spiraling out of control as I take a seat in her waiting room.

"Eva, come on in."

"Alannah. Thank you for seeing me on short notice."

"You're welcome. Did you bring your contract and the agreement with the team?"

I nod, hand them over to her, and wait patiently while she reviews it. Not a lot of time has passed, but it feels like ages.

"There is a noncompete clause in here."

"Oh." I slump in the chair.

"Don't get discouraged yet. Please share the details of your promotion and transfer to the Boston office."

I explain the parameters, including how the Boston office became a satellite office and the headquarters moved to DC. Alannah is furiously jotting down notes.

"I need to research a few things. If my recollection is correct, you would be able to accept the project individually and open your own firm here in Maine. I want to verify first before going any further."

I'm cautiously optimistic. "Okay. Thank you."

"When do you need to make the changes?"

"Jo… my contact suggested end of the week. I would prefer midweek, if possible. Please let me know what you need for a retainer fee as well."

"No problem. My assistant will prepare a letter for you and email it to you."

"I appreciate your assistance, Alannah."

"You're welcome. On a personal note, do you need us to bring anything to our meeting?"

"No. We've got dinner covered, but I appreciate the offer."

"I'll get back to you as soon as I can with a definitive answer."

I sigh inwardly and exit her office. Parking at the far side of the beach lot, I pluck off my shoes and wander across the sand to the gazebo. There are a handful of people on the beach enjoying spring break. According to my brother, the beach will be full from the end of May until late August. When I reach the opposite side of the beach, I catch Lachlan and Roxie approaching from the far side. He commands her to sit and sets down the bag. Instantly, his arms surround me, and he kisses me slow and deep.

"How did it go?" he asks after releasing me.

"Not sure yet. There is a noncompete clause in my new contract. Alannah is looking into whether it's enforceable."

"Okay. What are your options?" he asks, setting a sandwich, chips, and a raspberry iced tea in front of me.

After unwrapping my lunch and taking a huge bite, I reply, "This is amazing!"

"Yeah," he replies and works on his food.

"My options… I can leave things as they are and potentially not have a job in a few weeks. If I'm supremely lucky and the firm's attorney isn't too bright, I can earn the big client for myself."

"You did all the work, right?"

"Yeah, but I'm sure Shirley won't agree. She's still my boss and approved my submission to the team."

"Fair, but the concept and ideas were yours. Would you open a firm if you earn this contract?"

"It's an option. The budget and commission for the soccer team is sizable. It could sustain me for a while. Plus, I have Noelle and Caroline as clients as well. My clients, not ones assigned to me through the office."

"Was you owning your own company a potential plan for you before your impromptu meeting with Joseph?"

"It was always in the back of my mind but never something I actively pursued because I like my job. Until recently, it has been a great firm to work for." I can see the wheels turning in his brain. "How is it going with Roxie's training?"

When I say her name, she sets her head on my thigh. I pet her while I finish my lunch.

"Good. We worked on detection this morning. Late this afternoon, we're going to the Littleton house for a visit. Chase asked to meet her."

"That's sweet."

"Yeah. I'm glad her first case turned out positively."

"Agreed."

The ringtone sounds on his phone. He glances at it quickly. "I need to go. Dinner tonight?"

"Sure."

"Take this." He presses a key into my hand. "I'll meet you there after work." With a quick kiss, he runs off with Roxie matching his stride.

I clean up the debris from lunch and cross the beach to my car. As I walk, my phone rings. I glance at the screen. The number is from the office.

"Hello,"

"Hi, Eva."

Cody. The sound of his voice pisses me off instantly. "I have nothing to say to you."

"Please hear me out."

"No."

"Can you give me a minute to explain?" he pleads.

"No. Don't call me again." I hang up and climb into my car. After a quick stop at the cottage for my laptop, I head to Lachlan's and work on his deck for the afternoon. When I refresh my water, I get a text.

Lachlan: I should be there around six.

Me: Okay.

While my cooking skills aren't as sophisticated as Lachlan's, we won't starve. Earlier today, I noticed chicken defrosting in the fridge.

After a quick search, I found the items for fajitas. Fifteen minutes before they're set to arrive, I start making dinner.

Exactly when he said they would, Lachlan, Lilah, and Roxie come through the door connecting to the garage. I set the peppers, onions, and toppings on the table.

"Hi, Miss Eva," Lilah states, hugging me as soon as she arrives.

"Hi. How was school?"

"Good. I was with Isla all day. She's my bestie. Do you have one?"

"I do. Her name is Jodie."

She empties her bag and disappears to her room. She returns with her lunch box.

Lachlan kisses my cheek. "Li, please wash your hands." Then he feeds Roxie.

She complies and takes a seat. Without much discussion, the fajitas disappear in record time. We clean the kitchen while Lilah plays in her room for a little while before bed. Lachlan changes while I read with Lilah. He joins us in her room halfway through the second book. Wordlessly, he sits beside me. He may not have said any words, but his thumb rubbing circles on the small of my back certainly has my attention. Then again, anytime he touches me, every part of me pays attention from my head to my heart. I'm comfortable here.

We exit her room. He leads me by the hand directly to his bedroom. After a searing kiss, he says, "I didn't give you a key expecting you to make dinner for us."

"I wanted to. Why did you?"

"I like knowing you'll be here when we get home. Truthfully, I want you to stay each night."

I tilt my head up and kiss him sweetly. "I don't want to leave either, but it's crazy soon for me to stay."

He scrubs his hand down his face and presses his lips to my temple. "I agree with you in my head, but I know without a doubt that you care about us as much as we care about you."

"I do. We'll figure it out as we go. Okay?"

"Okay. Any word from Alannah?"

I shake my head. "No, not yet."

We take a seat on the couch in the master sitting room.

"Why are your hands shaking?" It's quite unlike him.

"I want to ask you something. I'm nervous because it's uncharted territory for me. Although almost everything with you is."

A host of options runs through my mind. I simply wait for him to continue.

"Would you allow me to add you to the list of people who can dismiss Lilah from daycare?"

"Of course. Why were you worried to ask?"

"Like I said, uncharted territory. I've never relied on anyone when it comes to Lilah. I'm grateful you're willing to do things with her, but I don't expect them."

"I understand, but I'm not Clare. I'm here for both of you."

Without another word, his lips are on mine, and our clothes pile on the floor faster than ever before.

CHAPTER EIGHTEEN

LACHLAN

As I'm leaving the center the next morning, I stop into the office.

"Morning, Mr. Hagen," Noelle greets me with a smile.

"Morning. I need to add a person to Lilah's dismissal list."

She smiles and rises from the chair. Pulling a folder from the file cabinet, she hands the card and a pen to me. While the information will be added into the computer, they require a signature to change certain aspects of a child's profile. Permitted people for dismissal is one of them.

I add Eva and sign before handing the card back to her. "Thank you. Also, I appreciate your guidance about Lilah needing more time to socialize with kids her own age instead of only me."

"I'm glad my suggestion was helpful. Lilah is a sweet girl."

"Yeah, she is. Have a nice day."

"You too."

Feeling a bit lighter, I climb into my SUV and drive toward the precinct. My demeanor shifts about a mile away from the center.

"Yeah, Cap," I answer my phone.

"There's a bomb threat and hostage situation at the regional courthouse. They've requested Roxie's assistance."

"I'm on my way. Who is the on-scene commander?"

"Luca Cappelli."

"Roger." I press the accelerator harder and hurry to the scene. Once I arrive, I suit up Roxie, and we locate the command center.

"Hagen, good to see you. Sorry about the circumstances," Luca greets me when I step inside.

"No problem. How can we help?"

"The suspect indicated he placed a bomb in the building and is holding the prosecuting attorney for his brother's case hostage unless his brother is released. Evacuation of the remaining people in the building is underway. Right now, we're examining our options. Roxie may need to search the building for the device if there is one unless I talk him down first."

"Understood. We're ready to assist, if necessary."

I exit the command center and wait with the other state police on scene. We walk toward a grassy area and await further instruction.

About an hour later, Luca sticks his head out of the command center. "Hagen."

"Yeah," I reply and join him inside.

"The suspect has surrendered. He gave me the location of the device and indicated it was a dud. Bomb Squad is checking it out."

"Understood." Thirty minutes later, Roxie and I are heading back to York. My phone rings at the halfway point.

"Hello."

"Lachlan, it's Alannah."

Anger and trepidation bubble to the surface. "What does Clare want?"

"Is that the only reason I would call you?"

"Lately… yes. I get it. You have your husband to commiserate with now."

Alannah laughs softly. "True, and you have Eva."

The mere mention of her name warms me. "Fair point."

"Her guardian understands why you don't want Clare to visit and is willing to work toward some kind of supervised visitation. However, she would like something to see how she's doing."

"Still not okay with in-person visitation at all. Such as?"

"I'm thinking a few photos and perhaps copies of her schoolwork," Alannah suggests.

I drag my hand down my face. "I'm fine with her drawings and stuff, but photos, I don't know. What is your opinion?"

"Legally, you don't have to offer her anything, and I'll share the same with her attorney and guardian. As your friend, I would give her older photos, which show nothing about where you live now. Also, Lilah's artwork tells her absolutely nothing about Lilah. Only that she's in school and thriving."

"Fine. Give me a few days and I'll send them to you."

"Hopefully, it will be enough."

I consider asking about Eva but quickly realize Alannah can't share with me. "Thanks, Alannah."

I hang up and call Eva.

"Hey. How was your morning?" she asks.

"Hi, sweetheart. Pretty good. Yours?"

"Great! I made significant progress on Noelle and Caroline's data points and a preliminary plan for their new brand and social media presence."

"Good for you."

"Thanks. I need to go. Alannah is calling me."

"See you for dinner." When I arrive at the precinct, I let Roxie run in the fenced area before eating lunch inside. It's warm out today but breezy and overcast.

We spend the rest of the afternoon out and about in the community. We make a stop at the playground, the beach, and the retirement home near the daycare.

When Lilah and I arrive at the house, Eva hasn't yet.

"Is Miss Eva coming over for dinner?"

"As far as I know, yes."

"Okay." Lilah disappears into her room.

I consider texting her because I'm worried. Why? Not sure. Pushing my concern away, I change and start dinner. She breezes through the front door as I close the oven. I meet her in the living room and greet her with a kiss just shy of inappropriate.

"What happened this afternoon? Your smile is wide and bright." I add some space between us but keep her close.

"I talked to Alannah, found a slinky but professional dress, and discussed watching Lilah with Maggie."

"Let's start with the easy question first. What color is your dress, and what does it look like?"

She grins at me. "It's navy, and I'm not sharing the style. You're going to have to wait."

"Fine. What did Maggie say?"

"Maggie agreed to watch Lilah and keep her for a sleepover as long as it was okay with you. The event doesn't end until ten, and it's in the city. She assumes the kiddos will be sleeping. Disturbing her doesn't make sense."

I'm shocked by the lack of trepidation flowing through me at the prospect of leaving my daughter overnight. "She has a point."

"She does. We need to let her know about the sleepover part."

"I'll consider it. What did Alannah say?"

Eva's face glows more. "Basically, the noncompete clause doesn't apply anymore."

"How so?" The timer for the oven sounds. I take her hand and guide her to one of the stools at the island.

"Generally, a noncompete clause is meant for me not to leave and go to a competitor or become a competitor in the marketplace myself. My company consolidated their holdings and moved the headquarters to DC. If I open my own firm here in Maine, there's no way they could say I'm taking business from them."

"Aren't you if you get the soccer team contract?" I set the pan on the stovetop and plate the lasagna.

She glares at me. "Arguably, I am taking the soccer team contract. With the knowledge that the team wants my design and the concern that my firm may fold, I stopped by the Cavallaro's earlier today and spoke with Joseph."

"What's his take?"

"I shared that Alannah also reviewed the contract between my company and the team as part of her due diligence. She noted their attorney was savvy and gave them the ability to select the designer individually, not the company. Joseph was already aware of the clause in the agreement with my firm."

"They must have been burned before," I state before calling for Lilah.

"Probably. Assuming nothing changes between now and the party, I will be awarded the contract personally."

"Congrats, sweetheart!"

"Thanks."

"Then what happens businesswise?" I ask her.

"If the company folds, I'll open my own with the team and daycare to start."

"Good for you." I move between her thighs and set my hands on her shoulders.

"Thank you."

I pull her closer. "For?"

"Supporting me however this plays out. You only want what's best for me both personally and professionally. I appreciate it."

"I do, and you're welcome."

Lilah joins us in the kitchen. "Hi, Miss Eva."

"How was school? Did you play with Isla today?"

Lilah frowns. "Isla wasn't in school today."

"Oh."

"But I had fun anyway."

"Glad to hear it."

After dinner, Lilah and Eva sit on the deck while I tire Roxie out throwing a ball for her. My girls chat and color beneath a blanket on the porch. The laughter echoing in my direction is amazing to hear. I can't imagine our days without Eva here.

They finish coloring, and Lilah heads inside for her shower. While she's gone, my phone rings.

"Good evening, Cap."

"Hagen. Sorry to bother you, but I wanted to reach out regarding the call this morning. Luca was briefed regarding some of the press coverage. Images of you and Roxie will be printed in tomorrow's paper. Whether they add your name to the caption is yet to be determined."

"I appreciate the heads-up. See you in the morning." I didn't actually do anything today, and yet my photo will be in the newspaper.

"Night."

I end the call and step outside again to sort through my feelings on this information. The photos could tip Clare off as to our whereabouts, and it stresses me out.

CHAPTER NINETEEN

EVA

The last week passed quickly. Our dinner with Callan and Alannah was canceled because the guys were held over at a call. Instead, Lilah and I played on the beach for a little bit with Charley and James. Alannah emailed me the list of students, and Lachlan is going to the high school with Craven next week to wrangle some volunteers.

I have checked and rechecked my purse more times than I care to admit. Nervous energy courses through me. I'm not sure if it's the work event or the prospect of being alone with Lachlan overnight. Don't get me wrong, Lilah is amazing, but tiptoeing around in their home is difficult. I feel like a teenager sneaking around in her parents' house, but the warden is a sweet, four-year-old girl.

Lachlan is due to arrive soon. Cocktail hour begins at six. Before I can recheck my purse again, the doorbell chimes.

An excited Lilah greets me with Lachlan a few steps behind. He looks beyond delicious wearing a suit minus the jacket.

"Hi, Miss Eva. You look like my dress-up Barbie right now."

It takes resolve to engage with Lilah when I want to step around her, kiss Lachlan deeply, and shout "Mine" for the world to hear. "Thank you, Lilah. Are you excited to hang out with Caleb and Corrinne?"

"My first sleepover is going to be epic!" she exclaims.

"Well, let's get going." I loop my fingers through the straps of my heels and lock the door. When I turn my back to check the lock, Lachlan slides his arm around my waist and draws me against him.

His heated breath tickles my exposed shoulder. "You are hot as hell in this dress. You're lucky we need to leave right now and this event is important. Otherwise, you would be naked in less than two minutes."

Heat pools between my thighs from his words. Forgoing panties was a smart decision. "I promise you can have your way with me later."

He kisses behind my ear and murmurs, "I can't wait to have no time limits tonight."

I exhale slowly. "Me too."

He steps back and offers me his arm. I slide mine around his, and we walk to the passenger door. Lilah successfully buckled herself in the back seat. After opening my door, he checks her and drives to my brother's house.

It appears the kids have been looking forward to this. Caleb and Corrinne are waiting at the door for Lilah to arrive. They hug and run into the playroom without a second thought. Lachlan hovers beside me, watching his daughter disappear from sight.

"Wow! Kelly made your dress? You look gorgeous, Eva!" Maggie states when I step inside their home.

"Your sister has skills."

"Go ahead, Hagen," Maggie urges him, noticing his discomfort.

As if she read his mind, he follows the path the kids took into the playroom.

"Tonight is going to be tough for him."

"Lilah will be fine. I promise," Maggie assures me.

"I know you're right, but he needs to figure it out for himself."

Maggie nods and hugs me. "He's a great guy. I'm happy for both of you. I hope your relationship works out."

Honestly, there isn't a chance of it not working out, but I won't share with Maggie yet. I should divulge my feelings to Lachlan first.

"Ready, Eva?" he asks upon his return.

"Yes. Please say hi to my brother for me," I request.

"I will. Have a great evening," Maggie offers as we step back outside.

After securing my door, Lachlan starts his SUV and pulls onto the road. If I've learned anything about him since we met, he needs time to sort his thoughts.

I press the modern country preset channel on his radio. I give him nearly half of the trip before I ask, "Want to talk or stew?"

He looks at me quickly and then returns his gaze to the highway. "Surprisingly, I'm good. You have made it possible for me to consider how my life could be with a partner. Noelle urging me to let go of Lilah a little played a role too."

"But?"

"No but. I trust a starkly limited number of people with my daughter. In fact, the list is only four deep, not including myself. Maggie is one of them. Lilah will have a great time while I get to spend an adult evening with you without worry. I have no concerns about touching you, kissing you, the clock, or how long until I need to be her dad again. Tonight, I'm your date. Nothing more or less as far as any other guests will know." He lifts our twined hands to his mouth and kisses the back of mine.

When we arrive at the posh hotel for the event, I'm a bit surprised. If Jo is correct, and the company is in trouble, it's an unnecessary expense. Unless... the team is likely footing the bill for this event. After checking my makeup in the mirror, I reapply my lipstick while waiting for Lachlan to open my door. Before turning, I slip my flip-flops off my feet. With my shoe in hand, I twist and slide my foot into it.

Before I realize what he's doing, Lachlan crouches before me, buckles the strap of my shoe, and presses a kiss to my ankle. *Sweet mercy!* Wordlessly, he reaches into the truck and grabs my other shoe from the footboard. He repeats his movements on the other leg.

Containing a sigh is impossible.

"You have a foot thing?" he asks, his big, calloused hand still wrapped around my ankle. At first, the roughness of his hands didn't make sense. Then when I saw the remodeling work he does at his house, like the fireplace and the beams in the living room, it became clear.

"No. Not used to being taken care of."

He rises to his feet and offers me his hand. With only a sliver of space between our bodies, he drops a sweet kiss to my lips, then says, "Get used to it. It isn't going to change as long as you're mine."

I manage a slight nod.

"Time to accept the contract, sweetheart." His gorgeous smile makes my knees wobble.

With my purse in hand, we make our way into the ballroom for the dinner and presentation. As soon as we have our table cards, Lachlan is thrust into meeting a ton of people. We speak with Joseph Cavallaro and his immediate supervisor, Kate Hightower. Then I greet Shirley.

"Hello, Shirley. Nice to see you. I would like to intro—"

"You brought a date?" Shirley's tone is sharp and incredulous, as if she wasn't offered a plus-one.

"My invitation included one, so yes."

"I see." The wheels in her head are turning. I consider going down the rabbit hole but don't.

"As I was saying, Lachlan, this is my boss, Shirley."

He extends his hand to her. "Eva speaks highly of you. Pleased to meet you." His greeting is smooth and polished.

"You as well. I'll circle back with you after the presentation," she states and walks away.

Lachlan leans in and whispers, "She's a gem."

I turn my head and stifle a laugh as best I can. A server approaches, and I take a plate and fill it with a few appetizers to share with Lachlan.

"Ohmigod! You're here!"

Jo. I spin around and hug her immediately. "I miss you so much! Hi, Keisha." I introduce them to Lachlan.

"You left out that he's smoking hot, E."

I shake my head and direct my words to Lachlan. "Jo is my coworker, and Keisha is her lovely wife. Their five-year anniversary is in a few weeks." Jo looks amazing. Her wrap dress highlights her hourglass shape, and the emerald hue complements her shiny ebony hair. Keisha is equally stunning and statuesque with a column dress accentuating her supermodel body.

"Pleasure to meet you both." He pops an appetizer in his mouth.

Jo looks between me and Lachlan more than once before he takes the hint.

After swallowing he asks, "What would you like to drink?"

"A white wine, please."

"Ladies, anything for you?" he asks Jo and Keisha.

"I'll come with you," Keisha offers. "My wife needs to catch up with her bestie."

Lachlan kisses my cheek and offers Keisha his arm.

Before they're out of earshot, Jo says, "Gurl! He's... there are so many words and not enough time to use them all."

A huge grin grows on my face. "Yeah, he is and then some."

"He can't tear his eyes away from you. Your dress is something else. I'm crazy happy for you," she gushes.

I glance toward the bar and meet his gaze. Then I return my attention to Jo. "Thanks. I am too. Grant's sister-in-law is an amazing designer. How are things at the office?"

"Strained. Everyone is on edge with the rumors."

"Makes sense. Anything more than layoffs?" I ask. I don't plan on sharing the information from Joseph even with her.

"No, that's all."

"Miss Washington?" A young brunette with a headset approaches me.

"Yes."

"I'm Dani. I need to go over a few points with you for the presentation."

"Of course," I reply.

With a side hug, Jo steps away. Dani offers me a synopsis of the presentation and when the project winner will be announced. I thank her, and she hurries away, presumably to the next candidate. I don't need to do anything except walk up and shake a hand or two if I win. A few other people from my department stop by and offer good luck on the project.

I turn to look for Lachlan again and find he's listening to Keisha and Jo at the bar.

"Eva." My name in Cody's stone-cold voice makes me preemptively angry. No, angry isn't the right description. Disgust grows in my chest.

I face the man who made me question everything I was looking for and if everlasting, loyal love was possible. I may not be there yet with Lachlan, but it's certainly feasible.

"You look stunning," Cody admits, setting his hand on my forearm and leaning in to likely kiss my cheek.

"Don't touch me." I yank my arm away, wrap it around my midsection, and take a step back. "What are you doing here? You don't even work in the same department."

"I came to support my girl. I messed up huge. I miss you so much," he states while narrowing the space between us a tad.

"I'm not your girl." A sense of calm and protection surrounds me before Lachlan touches me. I feel him approach.

Lachlan's hand curls around my lower back and grips my hip possessively. He drops a searing kiss on my lips. "Sorry it took so long to get back here, gorgeous. The bartender needed to grab a new bottle of wine, and your friends are hilarious."

"No problem."

"Who are you?" Cody asks.

Lachlan extends his hand to Cody. "I'm sorry. We haven't been properly introduced. I'm Lachlan, her boyfriend." The difference between them is stark, especially standing face-to-face. Lachlan towers over Cody and makes him look like a boy without trying.

Reluctantly, Cody shakes his hand. "Boyfriend? You started dating?"

A knot of fury tightens in my belly. "Excuse me. It's been a year. You cheated on me and got engaged. You have no right to question what or who I do."

With my possessive words, Lachlan's fingers dig deeper into my hip. It's official, I've fallen for Lachlan and his sweet daughter. Now, I need to tell him.

Inexplicably, Cody continues talking. "You don't understand. My engagement to Chelsea was fake."

I raise my hand to shut him up and consider his words. "Did you sleep with Chelsea while we were dating?"

"It isn't that simple," he replies.

"Yes, it is. Were you unfaithful to me?"

Cody's head drops, and he mutters, "Yes."

At his response, Lachlan shifts and draws me closer.

"Then I have nothing to say to you."

"You don't understand. I was trying to save your job," he presses on.

I frown. "I would love to know how sleeping with Chelsea saves my job."

Fortunately or unfortunately, I'm not sure which yet, the president of the team steps onto the stage. Before turning away, I add, "Cody, do not contact me. Also, don't call from the office hoping I'll pick up again either. I don't have anything to say to you, nor do I choose to hear excuses you believe will justify your despicable behavior."

I face Lachlan and kiss him lightly. "We're at table four."

Cody is dumbstruck and hasn't budged an inch. Shirley casts a stern look in his direction. He shuffles to her table and takes a seat beside her. *Interesting.*

Lachlan pulls out my chair and waits for me to sit. Once he's beside me, he whispers, "I'm crazy proud of you for putting him in his place."

I turn so my mouth is near his ear and only he can hear me. "It felt good to claim me, didn't it?"

"I won't lie. It was phenomenal. We haven't really talked about a label."

I lean back a bit and meet his gaze. "No, we haven't. Do we need one? Boyfriend seems juvenile. We're more than that."

"Agreed."

"We're together. A label isn't necessary, is it."

"Not at all."

The presentation starts, effectively ending our conversation. From the information Dani provided, my project announcement is near the end of the program. I listen and applaud when necessary. Paying attention grows increasingly difficult while I attempt to ignore the streaks of heat zipping up my leg from Lachlan's fingers drawing circles on my thigh.

Nearly an hour later, my project is up for announcement. Despite Joseph's assurance that I've already earned the contract, I'm nervous.

Lachlan takes my hand in his and says, "You've got this."

I nod tightly and direct my attention to Joseph at the podium. "After a painstaking process, we have finally selected our new logo and branding scheme. All the credit goes to Eva Washington."

Lachlan turns my face to his and kisses me. "Go, sweetheart."

As I make my way to the stage, I catch a confused look on Shirley's face. Before I reach the stairs, she storms toward me.

"What have you done? This is my account!" she screams.

I don't have the opportunity to respond before Lachlan is standing between us and security is storming in our direction.

"Are you okay?" he asks.

"Yes. She didn't touch me."

Joseph settles the crowd and continues with awarding the next project while Lachlan guides me to the table and immediately out of the ballroom.

When we reach the lobby, we encounter Shirley again. Security merely escorted her from the room but nothing else.

"What did you do?" she fumes.

Lachlan has his hand linked with mine and his body turned to shield me from her.

Squaring my shoulders, I answer, "I crushed this project, and the team awarded it to me, not the company. Their decision has nothing to do with me personally."

Venom drips from her words. "I will get to the bottom of this mess. You can't take our client. You have a noncompete clause."

Instead of sharing what I've learned about the clause, I simply reply, "I did nothing wrong. Have a nice evening."

I turn on my heel and walk straight out the door into the chilly evening. I inhale a few times. I'm not sure how I thought earning this huge project on my own would feel, but terror concerning Shirley's wrath isn't it.

Sliding my hair over to one side, Lachlan sets his lips to the exposed skin while he holds me from behind. "You did everything right. It will work out."

"I hope you're right."

"Do you want to go back inside or go home?"

Before I can answer, Joseph steps through the front doors and greets us again. "I had no idea she would react unprofessionally. I'm sorry for putting you in that position."

"Frankly, I knew it wouldn't go over well. However, her accosting me is outside of the possibilities I considered."

"Kate will reach out to you next week to discuss next steps."

"Thank you. I'm looking forward to fostering a solid working relationship for the team. I'll speak with my attorney before then," I share.

"Congratulations, Eva."

"Thank you." He leaves.

Lachlan turns me in his arms and kisses me sweetly. "Ready to go home and celebrate properly?"

I raise an eyebrow at him. "How does one properly celebrate earning a lucrative contract and likely starting her own business?"

Lachlan glances around us before lowering his voice. "Naked, steamy, a little dirty, and all night long."

"Let's go home."

Maybe someday it will be true. At least for tonight… it is.

CHAPTER TWENTY

LACHLAN

Without further hesitation, I escort Eva to my SUV. Like when we arrived, I crouch before her and assist with her shoes. Honestly, I will take any opportunity to touch her. You would think the drama of tonight would be over.

"Hey, I need to talk to you," Cody shouts in our direction.

I'm kicking myself for not paying better attention to our surroundings. My vigilance decreased considering she's confronted or been confronted by both her ex and her boss already this evening.

I rise to my full height, shielding her. "Eva was quite clear. She has nothing more to say to you."

My words anger Cody more. "I'm not talking to you."

"It's okay." She slips on her flip-flops and stands with the door and me between her and Cody.

"What did you do, Eva? I thought you were smarter than that."

"Excuse me? I didn't do anything except my job."

"You cast stones at me for cheating on you, but you must've done something for the team to award the contract to you personally," Cody states.

"Don't lump me in with you. I crushed the design, nothing more."

"What about him?" Cody points at me. "I'm sure he's connected to the team somehow. I mean… look at him. He's clearly an athlete. You aren't that good at designing marketing campaigns."

I feel anger roll off Eva from his words. The notion that she would only get the account on her own if she had an inside contact is preposterous.

She glances at me and asks, "Would you like to tell him, or should I?"

"Go ahead, gorgeous."

Eva stands tall and proud, looking directly at Cody. "He's a police officer with no connection to the team whatsoever."

When Eva discloses my profession, Cody clams up. However, Eva isn't finished giving him a piece of her mind.

"Oh, you thought I chose a brainless man who spends all his time in the gym. Did you know me at all? Then again, I briefly dated you, which was a mistake of epic proportions. I'm going to reiterate my words from before. Do not call me, email me, write me, or send a carrier pigeon with a message. I never want to see or hear from you again."

"Eva, don't be like this."

"Like what? Strong. Independent. Resilient. Not your doormat anymore." My gorgeous woman turns to me and says, "Take me home."

She's everything. Not only is she the things she mentioned to Cody but so much more. I kiss her and close her into the car. As I round the hood, Cody retreats a few steps, adding space between me and him. "I suggest you walk away, Cody. She won't change her mind. Something you would know if you cared about her at all."

I settle into the driver's seat and pull out of the spot. Cody hasn't moved, and I don't care one bit. I thread my fingers into hers and rest them on her thigh. Most of the ride is silent as far as words. Truly, there isn't anything to say. She was clear and honest with Cody. Hopefully, he'll listen this time. I pull straight into my garage and close the door behind us.

"I'm grabbing a water. Want one?" she offers.

"No, I'm fine. I'm going to let Roxie out, and I'll be right in."

"Okay," she replies, traipsing into the kitchen.

I release Roxie from her kennel, and she immediately lopes into the kitchen and rubs against Eva, who bends down and bestows love on my partner in crime. When Roxie is satisfied Eva feels better, she heels near the French doors. I follow her outside and stand on the deck while she runs around. When Roxie finishes checking out the boundaries of the yard, she trots up the steps and sits by the door. After letting her in, I arm the security system and tug at my tie as I walk to my bedroom.

The moment I cross the threshold, I see Eva wiggling out of her dress. Containing my reaction is impossible. "Holy fuck!"

She turns in the direction of my voice and doesn't cover herself. It's hot as hell. "What? It isn't as if you haven't seen me naked before."

I grin. "You went to a work event bare beneath your dress?"

"Yes."

"You're my dream woman, and I need to feel you vibrate with pleasure beneath me right now."

"Awww. saying sweet and dirty things in one sentence." She walks in the opposite direction.

I expeditiously remove the rest of my suit and pile it on the floor. "Get over here, woman, so I can worship you properly."

We close the gap between us and tumble onto my bed. Sealing my lips over hers, our kiss explodes. An undercurrent of desire pulses through me, yet I force myself to slow down. Beginning at the top of her foot, I kiss and lick my way up her long, lean legs. Each touch of my mouth on her skin causes goose bumps to skitter over her body.

"Lachlan."

This beautiful woman has burrowed her way deeper than anyone else, and I yearn to let her unravel me completely. "Yes, baby."

"Get up here, please."

"I love it when you beg, but we have all night," I reply, lifting my gaze to meet hers.

"I need to feel you inside me now. Later you can work on your tactile map of my body."

Without a second thought, I scramble up and meet her lips before answering, "Yes, ma'am."

Her glorious laugh surrounds me as I protect us both. The sweet sound stops the moment I bury myself deep inside her.

Keeping her out of my mind, heart, and soul is a futile endeavor. Each thrust brands us together. She screams my name, and her inner walls clench around me. Together we free-fall over the cliff into pure ecstasy.

When our panting decreases to steady breathing, she asks, "Will we keep getting better...?" Her question trails off.

"I certainly hope so. Ready for me to study the lines, dips, and curves of your body for my tactile map?"

"Completely."

Hovering over her beneath the sheet, I shimmy southward and press a kiss to the top of her foot. A sweet moan echoes toward me. With painstaking precision, I follow the contours of Eva's frame. Each nip forces shivers to cascade along her flawless skin. She arches off the bed, silently begging for me to settle between her thighs.

"Lachlan."

"Yes, gorgeous."

"I want you to explode inside me again."

I hurry a little but don't heed her request instantly. I slide a layer of latex over my length and penetrate her as deeply as possible. We find our rhythm easily this time and surrender to the thunderous pleasure we create. Once we clean up, I wrap her in my arms, and we fall quickly to sleep.

Near eight the next morning, I wake, tug on a fresh pair of boxer briefs, and slip out of the bedroom. Once Roxie is fed, I brew coffee for the two of us. I stare at her a bit longer than I should before nudging her.

Like when she watched Lilah for me, she's sound asleep in my bed as if it's ours. I want it to be ours. I'm not questioning whether Eva can make us happy. She already does. My concern is when Clare drops the other shoe, can we survive it?

"Are you going to share?" Eva mumbles from the bed.

"Yes, but you need to put on some clothes first."

Without a second thought, she sits up, the sheet pooling at her waist. Her full, pert breasts on display tempt me to take her again. "Why would I do that?"

"We don't have enough time for me to worship you properly again before we need to leave."

"Nothing wrong with hard and fast."

"Really?"

"Absolutely."

"Drink up, sweetheart. Your statement has me planning to act ungentlemanly this morning."

She gulps half the cup and sets it on the night table. Uncovering herself fully, Eva turns and positions herself on all fours before me.

"You're as insatiable as I am."

"True. Get over here and make me come before we run out of alone time," she demands.

Without further hesitation, I sheathe myself and climb onto my bed behind her. I drag my length along her core before plunging into her to the hilt.

"Lachlan. Yes!"

I smirk and set a quick, steady pace with my hands gripping the swell of her hips. My release coils at the base of my spine. To push Eva to the edge faster, I slide one hand around her and rub circles with my fingers on her swollen nub. Before long, she's meeting me thrust for thrust, and heat barrels through me with Eva screaming with pleasure seconds later.

Given our short timeline, I kiss down her spine and withdraw from her. When I reach the bathroom, I turn to see her a few steps behind me. She starts the water and steps into the shower while I dispose of the condom and brush my teeth. When I join her, she's nearly done.

"Sorry, no time to shave my legs this morning," she shares.

I kiss her hard and deeply. "I don't care if your legs are as prickly as a porcupine. I'll still want to make you scream my name in the throes of passion."

"Good to know. Hustle up. This spacious shower gives me ideas. Sexy wishes we can't fulfill right now." She kisses me lightly and steps out of the tiled enclosure.

"Are you going to share your dirty thoughts involving my shower?" I ask while washing.

"Eventually." She winks at me, brushes her teeth, and leaves the bathroom wrapped only in a towel.

Despite my need to be alone with Eva, I miss my daughter. Finding a balance in the future will be a necessity. Then again, if Eva moves in....

A few months is soon considering Lilah. I push my desire to have her closer all the time away and dress to pick up my daughter.

"Ready to go?" Eva asks, tapping her foot on the hardwood floor.

"Are you nervous to pick her up?"

"No. Can I be honest with you?"

I frown at her. "Aren't you always?"

She scowls at me. "Yes. I missed her last night. Please don't misunderstand, I thoroughly enjoyed our… adults-only time, but—"

"I completely understand. I did too. Let's go. I'm sure she's driving Maggie nuts."

When we arrive, the kids are sitting at a small picnic table on the front porch, coloring.

"Daddy! Miss Eva!" She runs over and wraps one arm around each of us at once. "How was your work thing?"

Relief and a bit of pride slither into my heart. We are fine after taking a huge step. "Sweet pea."

"Morning, Lilah. It was eventful."

"Did you get the job?" Lilah asks.

"I did."

"Yay!" She raises her hand for a fist bump. "I knew you would get it!"

Eva complies. Maggie joins us on the front porch soon after we arrive.

"Morning. How did it go?"

"Miss Eva got the job!" Lilah informs her.

Maggie smiles. "Aren't you the cutest pint-sized cheerleader of them all?"

Eva shares the details of last night more fully and accepts Maggie's congratulatory wishes. "Ready to go home, Lilah?"

"Yes. I need to share my epic sleepover with Roxie and get some doggy kisses."

I laugh. "Can I tell you a secret?"

Lilah nods quickly.

"Roxie is in the truck."

"Really?"

"Yup. We need to go to Miss Eva's for a little while, so I brought her along."

"Perfect!"

Lilah returns to her seat and starts cleaning up her coloring space.

"Is Grant here?" Eva asks.

"No, he went for a run."

"Okay. Can I grab her stuff, Maggie?"

"Sure, it's on the island."

When Eva steps back outside with Lilah's bag, the kids are saying their goodbyes.

"Daddy, can we host the next sleepover?"

"Sure."

The kids say, "Yay!" at once.

After a short greeting with Roxie, we drive to the cottage once I assure Lilah that she'll have plenty of time to share the activities of her evening. When we arrive, I walk Roxie around the perimeter with Lilah while Eva heads inside.

"Honestly, how was it?" I ask her.

"Awesome. Did you have fun?"

"I did. Last night was a big deal for Eva."

"I can stay with Miss Maggie whenever you need to do adult stuff."

Confusion streaks through me. "What do you mean?"

"So you can spend time with Miss Eva alone."

"Oh, okay. Thanks, sweet pea. Let's go inside." We climb the back stairs, and Lilah knocks on the sliding door.

"Your house is pretty, Miss Eva. The beach is right outside!" my daughter shares when Eva opens the door.

"I know. I love that too."

I hear their conversation while I show Roxie the remaining exit. We spend the rest of the afternoon together coloring, baking a cake, and then cooking a huge dinner. I can't wait for days like today to be possible in our home. One we share with Eva as well.

CHAPTER TWENTY-ONE

EVA

First thing this morning, I prepare an extra cup of coffee and log into my work email. The first notification is from Shirley with a video conference request for eleven today.

With that information, I trudge upstairs and change into more appropriate clothes. Once properly dressed, I return to my office and text Lachlan, hoping to take my mind off the impending sense of dread filling my chest.

Me: Good morning.

Lachlan: Hi, beautiful. Did you sleep well?

Me: Not as well as I did with you.

Lachlan: We didn't sleep much.

Me: No, but with you is better than without.

Lachlan: You really like me, then?

No, I love you, but I'm too chicken to fully open myself up to you and Lilah. Deep down, I know not saying the words doesn't make it less true.

Me: Perhaps. I'll see you for dinner.

Lachlan: Looking forward to it.

With my mood significantly better, I note an email from my contact at the perfumery. After reading the contents, the fear in my gut dissipates. Her words are glowing and ecstatic about the boards I presented for the campaign. She wants to set up a meeting at my earliest convenience to discuss my outlined strategy for release. I suggest Thursday at eight in the morning. Morning would work better for me than evening. I would prefer to spend my evenings with Lachlan and Lilah.

The next on the list is from Kate Hightower, scheduling a meeting for Wednesday to discuss the finer details of the timeline to roll out the new branding to coincide with the beginning of next season. I accept the invitation and move on.

For the next few hours and two more cups of coffee, I watch the clock tick down to my call with Shirley. My internal pep talk is the only thing keeping me from running a few miles on the treadmill.

With a lump in my throat, I click the link.

"Eva. I appreciate your willingness to join this call."

"Good morning, Shirley," I reply, gritting my teeth.

She continues, "Your decision to hijack the team account has given management pause."

"I didn't hijack the account. I had nothing to do with the team awarding the contract to me alone. You saw and approved my submitted boards."

"Be that as it may, your employment at this firm will be terminated on Friday. Please draft a memo of your pending clients complete with due dates and draft boards, if any."

I'm applauding myself internally for not submitting Noelle and Caroline's client information. "I understand. My work for this company has been nothing but exemplary. It's a shame you feel that blaming me will give you the result you desire. You think because I'm in Maine, I haven't heard about the layoff rumors?"

"Excuse me?"

"More than one source has shared that the company is in trouble and layoffs are imminent."

"Why aren't you fighting for your job?" Shirley asks.

I smirk to myself. "If you feel you have grounds to fire me, by all means, give it a try. I'll explore all avenues available to me once I've been properly notified. Have a lovely day, Shirley."

I end the call. After hustling upstairs to shed my conference-call-appropriate clothes, I grab my laptop and a notebook. A rush of ambition fills me. If I'm fired, I will be prepared to forge my own path. Despite the ocean outside the cottage, there's only one place I want to be—Lachlan's. First, I make a stop at the Perk for a latte.

"Hey, Eva," Kelsey greets me when I step inside the coffee shop.

"Hi, Kelsey."

"What can I get for you?"

I give her my order and wait over to the side. I notice Lachlan approaching through the window, but he doesn't see me. He's with Craven and another officer I've never met before. After he crosses the threshold, he catches my gaze and walks straight to me. I'm not sure how he'll react to running into me unexpectedly.

Without a second thought, he draws me against him and kisses my lips. Well, he answered the question in my mind about his preference for sharing our relationship.

One of the guys says, "Get a room," but I'm not sure which, probably Craven.

Lachlan waves him off. "Hi, gorgeous. What are you doing here? Is everything okay?"

"Not really. Coffee, then I'm going to work on your deck."

"Your morning didn't go well?"

"No. Shirley fired me effective at the end of the week. I told her I would wait for actual and appropriate notice before I comply with her exit memo request."

"Good for you."

"Thanks."

He eliminates the space between us so his words are private. "It makes me happy knowing you'll be at the house when we arrive."

"Me too."

"Good."

Kelsey approaches the counter. "Hello, Hagen." She hands me my latte, which I lift in gratitude.

"Hi, Kelsey," Lachlan replies.

"What can I get for you?"

"A coffee and a bagel sandwich, please."

"No problem. I'll add it to Craven's order."

He laughs heartily. "Much appreciated." He turns back to me. "What's your plan?"

"I'm going to call Alannah and give her a heads-up. Then I'm going to make some notes about my files, specifically the team and the perfumery. I want to have proof the work was mine alone."

"Smart. We should be home about six. I planned on grilling burgers for dinner. I'll do it when I get there, okay?" He kisses me again.

Craven indicates they need to hurry to a call. Kelsey shoves his food in his direction, and then they're gone.

"Happens all the time for them," she states.

"Oh, I know. I have a few things on my mind. I'm going to head out as well. Have a nice day, Kelsey."

"You, too, Eva."

By the time Lachlan, Lilah, and Roxie arrive home, I've completed my desired tasks as well as a to-do list for when I'm officially fired. Writing it down helped me realize I can be my own boss and do it well. Perhaps I should be angry, but I'm not. Perhaps a little scared that I won't be able to bring in enough business to support myself initially is accurate. Then again, if I'm awarded the soccer campaign, that won't be the case.

"Hi, Miss Eva," Lilah greets me.

"How was your day?"

"Good. Yours?"

"So-so, but it's better now."

Lilah smiles. "It's pretty awesome when we're together, isn't it?"

"Yeah, it is."

She hugs me and bounds into her room to play before dinner. Once we finish eating and clean up, Lilah reads to Roxie before bed. She hugs us both before Lachlan tucks her in. For the first time, I purposely stay overnight, and it's perfect.

Like after I watched Lilah for Lachlan's call, the morning routine was smooth and easy. However, Lachlan deserves all the credit for instilling those things in Lilah early on. It's radio silent the next day. However, my midweek meeting with Kate Hightower is filled with insider information.

"Eva, thank you for taking my call," she states.

"Of course. How can I assist you?"

Kate goes on to share that the team has informed Shirley and Colton they will only work with me and the contract with the company allows them to choose me individually. Colton is Shirley's boss as well as Cody's father, and the contract was duly executed and signed by Colton. Kate demanded all content and boards be turned over to me individually immediately.

I thanked her and set up an in-person meeting at the team facility in a month to complete the rollout plan. I mark the calendar and check my messages. I have two emails, which aren't pressing, and a voicemail from Caroline indicating they need to reschedule our meeting because she and Noelle are ill.

As the week passes, the tides turn in my direction. It's clear from my calls and contact with clients that Shirley and Colton are attempting to salvage the company. The kicker is they need me to do it.

First thing on Thursday, the perfumery indicates they plan to work with me alone and no one else at the company. My contact, Maisie, informed me that Colton reached out to the perfumery and shared that I would be fired. When they learned this news, the international company demanded my contact information and assignment of the contract to me.

Once I learn about this development, I reach out to Alannah again and request she complete formation of my company as soon as possible. I also inquire if she knows of any available office space.

As soon as I end my call with Alannah, Colton calls me directly.

"Miss Washington, it's my understanding that Shirley verbally notified you of your termination earlier this week."

"That's correct."

"Sharing the information with you was premature on her part."

"I see. Well, I'm not willing to work for this company any longer. She accosted me at dinner and has been crass and rude since the team chose me to run this account. I did nothing wrong. The contract allowed the team to select me individually, as I'm sure you're now well aware. Also, my call with the perfumery first thing this morning yielded some additional support for my leaving. It appears you informed them I would be fired, and they chose me as well."

Colton stammers. "I... umm—"

"Save it. Shirley used me to get the account knowing the company was in dire straits. That's why Boston meetings were canceled. I was being canned either way. What you didn't count on was the team and the perfumery walking away from your company."

"Miss Washington—"

"No." I consider not asking but opt to anyway. "Did Cody truly start dating Chelsea behind my back at your request?"

"I don't know what you're talking about," Colton answers.

"It makes complete sense now." Not only was the company in trouble, but Cody learned I was going to be fired. "Was it your idea or his to cozy up to the company president's daughter?"

"Mine," he answers harshly.

Damn it! Cody wasn't lying to me. It was a setup from the beginning. Except... he was unfaithful to me. Infidelity is a deal-breaker for me. A fact he knew. More importantly, there's no comparison. Lachlan makes me feel whole and worthy of the love I've been seeking. Lachlan and Lilah are the ones for me.

"Sir, my resignation letter will be forwarded to you by close of business tomorrow."

"Please reconsider. We need you," my former boss begs.

"No. I will not save the company. It's been a pleasure working for you." I end the call and exhale. Any moment the reality of my words will come crashing down on me. I wait and nothing. I wait a little longer until exhilaration passes over me, not fear. I can be my own boss, control my schedule and the clients I take on. More importantly, I can continue to build a relationship with Lachlan and Lilah.

Elated, I download the files I need and draft my resignation letter. In addition, I copy and save the contents of my portfolio before logging off the company server. Without a doubt, the firm will lock me out as soon as Colton calls the IT department.

Near four, I throw some clothes into a bag and head to Lachlan's. My letter is scheduled for delivery by the end of the day. Before I go inside, I send a text to Jo.

Me: We need to talk. Call me ASAP.

My phone rings as I'm disarming the security system at Lachlan's. I slip off my shoes and answer.

"Ooohhh, girl! You are the talk around here. What happened?"

I smile and share every detail with her.

"I'm ecstatic for you. You took control. Now you have a new love, your own business, and a stunning location to meet your ocean needs."

"Me too. What about you? Did you lose your job?"

"Not sure yet," she answers.

"Well, I need an assistant, even one who lives in New York City."

"Are you serious?" The glee in her voice is obvious.

"Absolutely. Think about if you're willing to work for me and let me know."

"I'll talk to Keisha tonight. You're the best ever, E."

"Bye, Jo." I end the call and hoist my bag onto the island. When I grab a bottle of water, I notice a card addressed to me.

Eva,

I missed having you nestled against me last night while I slept. See you when I get home.

Lachlan

My heart beats faster, and I hold the card against my chest nearly swooning. I need to share my feelings with him. I'm terrified of scaring him away. Does it matter if we don't say the words out loud? He shows me every day, just like I do.

Resigned that I won't find the answer today, I curl up with my notebook on the deck. I review my new business list and enjoy the waning sunshine until my little family comes home.

"Miss Eva, we're here," Lilah calls from the threshold.

I gather my stuff and join them in the kitchen. "Hi, sweetie. How was school?"

"Good." She empties her bag and disappears down the hall.

"Hi, sweetheart. How was your day?"

"Eventful. Yours?"

"Our call today went well," he replies.

"Good."

"Are you going to share the details with me?" His voice is shakier than normal.

"Of course. I figured you would want to change like normal first."

He exhales, takes my hand, and leads me into the bedroom. "Is it that or you want to watch?"

"A little of both." I tell him about my day and leaving my job officially.

"Your boss admitted to using his son to save the company?"

"Yeah, he did."

He frowns at my response but adds, "I'm proud of you for going into business for yourself!"

"Thanks. I called Alannah about finishing the business formation and potential office space."

He cants his head in question. "You need office space?"

"Considering it as an option. I asked Jo to be my assistant, but I don't expect her to move here. The room at the cottage is small for a full-scale operation."

"Okay. What else would you need?"

"The office itself is fine. When I have a large project like the soccer team, I need space for the boards somewhere other than the desk."

"Makes sense. Dinner?"

"Sure. Will you share about your call?"

He frowns again. "I don't want to scare you."

"Now I need you to tell me."

"Roxie was tasked with checking a stash house this morning, and it went well."

"Why would that scare me? You and Roxie enter after the others clear the building, right?"

He drops his head. "Sometimes, I purposely ignore the fact that Washington is your brother and you have a clue about police procedure. Yes, that's true."

"You're fine. Roxie is fine, and the raid was successful. A win, no?"

He hauls me into his arms and kisses me until there's a knock on his door. A door which isn't fully closed. Lachlan reluctantly releases me and answers.

"Come in, Lilah."

She pushes the door open only enough to slip through.

"I'm starrrrving!"

"Do you know what day it is, sweet pea?"

"Thursday." Realization crosses her face. "It's pizza night!" She turns on her heel and rushes out the door.

It doesn't take long before we hear her open her stool and start to pull out the necessary items. With another kiss, we join her and make homemade pizzas for dinner.

After reading to Lilah, we curl up on the couch and promptly fall asleep.

CHAPTER TWENTY-TWO

LACHLAN

Since Roxie joined YPD, her cases have been successful, which is a double-edged sword. I'm grateful it's going well with my new partner but still concerned about Clare. I will always worry about her finding us.

My phone rings as I park in the lot at the precinct. A sliver of fear slices through me when I see Alannah's name first thing in the morning.

"Morning, Lachlan. Sorry to call this early, but I have great news."

"No problem," I reply with some of my fears dissipating.

"I received a voicemail from Clare's attorney and guardian late last night. She's happy with the photos and artwork you provided."

"What's the catch?"

Alannah laughs softly. "There isn't one, exactly. She would like you to send more of the same going forward."

Not terrible. "How frequently are we talking?"

"Quarterly."

"Okay. I can work with that. I'm almost afraid to ask, but what about her visitation request?"

"Counsel didn't mention it in her voicemail."

"I understand. She either changed her mind, or her attorney talked her out of it for now?"

"Probably the latter," Alannah replies.

"I appreciate your help and the call. Have a great day."

"You, too, Lachlan. Oh, before I forget. Callan has the final list of volunteers for you. He added Caden last night."

"Sweet. How is he doing?"

"Great. His first season of college basketball went well. Callan and I were able to catch most of his home games and a few away ones."

"Glad he's finding his way. How are you feeling? Craven may have slipped up sharing information about your growing family."

"Other than forgoing heels, I'm pretty good. Thank you for asking, but please don't share with anyone else."

"I won't. Bye, Alannah."

With relief still pumping through me, I hustle inside for roll call. Once it ends, I retreat to the training area with Roxie. We work on a few things each morning unless we're on a call. While I throw a ball for a few minutes, I dial Eva.

"Morning, Lachlan."

"Hi, gorgeous. How are you holding up?"

"I'm good. Excited at the prospect of being completely in charge."

"Never going to happen," I admit.

I imagine her pursing her lips. The sultry move makes me thicken every single time. "I'm only talking about my work. The rest is negotiable."

"I accept."

She laughs. "I thought you might. You're easy."

"Only for you, sweetheart."

"Everything okay there?"

"Yeah. I talked to Alannah, and she gave me a good report about Clare," I share with Eva.

"You must be relieved."

"Cautiously, but yes, I am."

"Is Lilah going out tonight?"

Now I laugh. "Yes, she is. What do you have in mind?"

"Not what you're thinking. Well, maybe…. We need to finalize the volunteer assignments and verify that the route and security are properly set. The other item is to request the necessary supplies for the water stations from the park department."

"As long as I can make you scream my name at least once this evening, I'll happily do whatever else needs to be done."

"I can work with those parameters. See you later."

I finish my training with Roxie and take her out into the community by joining Craven and Gugliotti at the high school during lunch. Before I know it, the day ends, and I'm picking up Lilah from the center.

"Come on, Daddy. We need to get home to see Miss Eva before I come back to play with my friends."

My heart expands in my chest. In this moment, I resolve to ask Eva to move in with us. First, though, I need to finish her surprise. I give myself the completion deadline of the race and hurry to the house.

Lilah is unbuckled and waiting to be released once I reach her door. "Miss Eva. Miss Eva, where are you?" she calls as soon as she's inside.

Eva doesn't answer.

"Daddy, her car is outside."

"We'll find her. Don't worry." Regardless of my words, a thread of worry trickles into my mind.

"Miss Eva," Lilah calls again.

The longer it takes to locate her, the more concerned I become. We check the entire house to no avail.

"Daddy, she's outside," Lilah informs me and slides open the door before running to the far end of the yard, where it looks like Eva was weeding along the fence.

"Hi, Lilah," Eva greets her after pulling out her earbuds.

Relief cascades through me.

My daughter hugs her close and spills the events of her day. Once she's done, she asks, "What about you?"

"Today was mixed for me."

"Why?"

"Well, my job is ending, which is a little bit sad."

"'Kay. That's the bad, right?"

"Yes. The good is I'm starting my own business on Monday."

"You are the boss?" Lilah asks.

"I will be."

"Yay!"

One little word and a huge smile expands on Eva's face. She's the perfect example for Lilah, and I'm grateful my daughter spilled cookies at her feet.

"Are you and Daddy going out while I play with my friends?"

She shakes her head. "No, we need to work on race stuff."

"I'll have enough fun for both of you," Lilah states.

I catch Eva's gaze. From the rosy color to her cheeks and the way she shifted her thighs, I know the dirty thoughts in my mind when my daughter said "fun" are the same ones in hers.

"Sounds perfect. Why don't you put your bag and stuff away? I'll be right in," Eva suggests.

"On it!" Lilah runs toward the house but slows to a walk at the base of the deck.

I offer Eva my hand, and she takes it. With a glance toward Lilah, I sweep Eva into my arms and kiss her slowly and deeply. When I'm ready for air, I pull back slightly. "Are you good?"

"Yeah. I was honest with her. I'll be full-on excited when I get the official go-ahead from Alannah."

"What dirty thoughts floated through your mind?"

I don't need to explain further. We're tethered together, and I love it.

She shakes her head. "Only you have ever noticed my physical reactions. Don't worry, I'll share my ideas with you as soon as we get back from taking Lilah."

"Not even a little teaser?" I ask.

"No, no teaser."

I frown, then kiss the tip of her nose. She gathers the tools while I drag the tarp covered in weeds to the rear of the yard and dump them into the woods along the boundary.

When we return from dropping Lilah off, we decide to tackle the tasks for the race before twisting up my sheets. I know it's the right choice, since I prefer not having time limits when I explore her sweet-smelling skin.

She pulls out the checklist, and we start at the top. We make it to the middle before we need to place calls and send a few emails. While she's talking, she paces the length of the island in her bare feet and skintight leggings. I love how comfortable she is here. Not true. I love her. Sharing those feelings is another story. If I say it out loud, it will be real. I'll open myself and my daughter to devastating heartbreak.

Aren't you both already there?

"This is all set. What's left on the list for tonight?"

I push my thoughts away and glance at it again. "Only ordering the medals. We have it set to go. It needs to be paid for, which means talking to Cap. I'll take care of it on Monday."

"Perfect." She saunters over to the table and closes her laptop. Turning to face me, she lifts the hem of her shirt as she approaches. When her taut abdomen and the underside of her breasts are visible, the work tone echoes around us.

Without a second thought, she drops the hem of her shirt and follows me into the bedroom.

"Can you pick up Lilah?"

"Of course."

"If necessary, can you bring her to soccer?"

She sets her hands over mine. "What are you worried about?"

"I'm not. For maybe the second time ever, I want to ignore my duty and stay with my family." My gut tightens when I realize my word choice.

Her eyes widen, but she doesn't press me on it. Now isn't the right time to have a discussion about our feelings.

"We'll be here when you get back." She tilts her chin up and skims her lips across mine. "Get ready. I'll be in the living room."

I drop my head. *Damn it!* I finish dressing while my mind spins with things we need to say and discuss. Then I join her in the living room. "Eva, I…."

"I know. I… too."

"How?"

"You show me every single day with breakfast deliveries, sweet notes for me to find, allowing me to get to know both of you, by standing beside me when I went toe-to-toe with Cody, and by asking what I need. We'll get to a point where we share in words. Actions are enough right now."

"You see how I feel about you?"

"Yes. We can talk about this more when you get home, Lachlan. Be safe."

I kiss her deeply. "Thank you."

"You're welcome."

"Roxie, come."

With Roxie beside me, I hurry to the garage door. After a sharp look back, I slide Roxie's gear on and rush to the scene. Through my truck, I call Cap.

"What is the situation?"

"We have a car chase between Carol and Andrew Nichols. Carol is the custodial parent. It appears there was a confrontation at their usual custody transfer spot. The business owner called in the scuffle before Carol took off in her car with their daughter. The business owner claims the father was acting erratically. He allegedly shoved Carol and was shouting at her loudly, but the business owner couldn't hear the words or what the issue was. Andrew, the noncustodial parent, gave chase. Vehicles crashed on Route 91 near the Highland Farm Preserve. Carol is seriously injured. Their seven-year-old daughter, Penny, left the vehicle. It appears she willingly followed her father into the preserve."

"Okay. Did the first on scene start their search from the main entrance?"

"Yes."

"Do we have an article, or is Roxie walking a grid?"

"A grid."

"Understood. We'll enter from the east and move toward the road."

"Roger. Keep me informed," Cap orders.

I pull to a stop along the eastern edge of the property. I grab an extra flashlight for myself and attach one to Roxie's vest near her shoulder. More light will be helpful.

Once we're ready, I command my partner to track. An article would be helpful, but we don't have one this time. "Roxie, *such*."

We walk the length of the preserve in a straight line to the south edge, then turn north and continue. We make four turns before Cap asks for a progress update.

"Hagen, status?"

"Four turns, nothing yet."

"Roger."

We continue searching for thirty more minutes before Roxie alerts. Pausing, I pan the flashlight in a circle around me but find nothing. Roxie barks and points her nose toward the sky. When the beam of light hits Andrew, he jumps down from the tree, taking me to the ground with him. A searing pain streaks up my left arm. I attempt to fight him off, but he's strong. Freakishly strong.

"Roxie, *fass*."

At my attack command, Roxie latches on to his arm and pulls on him long enough to distract my assailant. I scramble to my feet and order Roxie to stop. "*Halt*." Immediately, she releases Andrew and heels. "*So ist brav*, Roxie. *So ist brav*."

"You're under arrest for assaulting a police officer and whatever else the state deems appropriate." I cuff him and state his Miranda rights.

"She can't do this to me," he wails. "Penny is my daughter. It's my night with her."

A shudder pulses through me. This could be me. I don't mean running Clare off the road but a difficult custody situation.

I tighten my grip on his bicep. "Quiet." I press the call button on my radio. "Hagen to command.

"Go, Hagen."

"I have apprehended the noncustodial father. No sign of Penny."

"Roger. Need backup?"

"Yes, to pick up the search from this spot. Both Mr. Nichols and I will need medical attention."

"Roger. Garcia and Montgomery are heading your way."

"Why would she do this to me?" Andrew mutters.

"Sir, I suggest you be quiet."

"Do you have kids?"

I shake my head and refuse to answer him. Not happening. My personal life is exactly that—personal.

Montgomery and Garcia arrive with haste.

"You good, Hagen?" Montgomery asks.

"My arm is pulsing, so that can't be good. I'm sure Penn can fix me up." I instruct them about the grid we were walking. "Head south two people wide, and when you reach the edge of the property, turn back."

Garcia answers, "Roger. Go get checked out. Your arm looks gross."

I laugh because there's nothing else for me to do. It helps me ignore the throbbing pain in my forearm and the fact that my sleeve is crimson. "Thanks, Garcia."

"Anytime. Levity is my coping mechanism."

I nod tightly. "Roxie, *hier*." She falls in step with me. "Mr. Nichols, let's go." Slowly but surely, we make our way to the command post.

The moment we arrive, Smithson takes Mr. Nichols to a cruiser. Before I can say a word to Cap, Penn ushers me to his rig.

"Got yourself good, huh?"

I shake my head. "Idiot jumped out of a tree on top of me. I don't know what sliced open my arm."

Penn pats the gurney in the rig, urging me to sit after climbing in.

"Roxie, *blieb*." I follow him.

He cuts away my sleeve and examines my arm. His facial expression tells me the cut is deep.

"I need to go to the hospital, don't I?"

"Yeah. I can't close this here. I'll clean it up and let Carly know you're on your way. Anyone you want me to call for you?"

I raise an eyebrow at him. "What are you talking about?"

"You know the rumor mill is sophisticated and highly detailed around here. Can't keep a relationship a secret for long."

"I'll call her myself. She will freak if it's someone else."

"Fair. How does Washington feel about you dating his sister?"

"We're good," I reply. "I need to speak with Cap before we leave."

"Don't take too long."

"Yes, Penn." My response is sarcastic. The burly guy laughs as I step outside again.

As I approach Cap, I hear over the radio, "We found Penny near one of the fairy castles at the south end of the path." I believe Garcia is speaking. "She's cold and has minor lacerations on her arms and legs. Could be from the accident, though."

"Roger. Vaughn and Auberon are heading your way," Cap replies. "You should be riding toward the hospital by now." His stare is pinned on me.

"I wanted an update about Penny before I left. I'm going." I raise my hand in feigned surrender.

"Give me your keys. I'll bring your vehicle to the hospital for you," Cap offers.

I dig into my pocket and give him my keys.

"Have you called Eva yet?"

I open my mouth to speak but fail.

"No, it isn't a secret," Cap answers my unasked question.

"I will. Right now."

"Get going," he orders.

I nod and scroll to her name in my phone. "Roxie, *hier.*" Roxie jumps into the ambulance before Penn closes the door as I press Send.

CHAPTER TWENTY-THREE

EVA

Picking up Lilah was smooth, once the staff verified I was on the official list. She was sound asleep, and I successfully maneuvered her into her bed without waking her. Near midnight, my phone startles me awake.

"Hey, sweetheart," Lachlan greets me.

Panic rushes through my body, recalling when Grant was injured during an incident. "Are you okay?"

"I will be, but I would prefer not to have Lilah at York Memorial. I can explain it to her later. However, I know you won't be willing to stay away."

My heart is pounding in my chest. I'm talking to him. Clearly his injury, whatever it may be, isn't that serious.

"Eva. Baby, breathe." His words filter into my thoughts.

I inhale slowly and exhale even slower.

"Good girl. Lia is on her way there to watch Lilah."

"Uh-huh."

"I promise you, I'm going to be fine. I...."

"I'll be there soon. I...."

I throw back the covers on his bed, then tug on my leggings, a tank, and his Chicago Bears hoodie. I freshen up in the bathroom and pull on my shoes in the foyer as Lia approaches the front door.

"Evening, I'm Lia. Pleasure to meet you in person, Eva. Your brother talks about you all the time."

"Thank you for coming."

"Of course. I've got Lilah."

I don't hesitate any longer. I run to my car and speed away. The seven-mile drive feels like an eternity. Hurrying inside, I blindly turn the corner and plow into a tall, fit guy.

Said guy grabs my upper arms to steady me. "Whoa, Eva."

"Grant." Relief washes over me.

"You have real feelings for him, don't you?" Only my brother would be able to follow up with this question. He has been able to see through me since childhood.

"Yes. Please take me to him."

Without further hesitation, he leads me past reception and into the emergency department. With a light knock, Grant pushes open the door. Lachlan is sitting on the bed with his feet hanging over the side. Roxie is next to him with her head on his muscular thighs.

"Thanks, Washington," Lachlan states.

Grant drops his head and closes the door behind him. I'm frozen a mere step inside the room, staring at Lachlan.

"Come here, sweetheart."

I force my feet to move, stopping between his legs. I set one hand on his chest and the other cups his face. He grips my hip, drawing me in more.

I claim his lips in a searing kiss, partially because I can but mostly to verify he's truly fine. I kiss him until the fear in my chest dissipates to palpable levels.

"It's a nasty cut. A long, deep one requiring stitches. Not a big deal."

"I appreciate what you're saying, but I needed to see for myself," I answer and kiss him more.

We're lost in each other and don't hear the nurse knocking on the door.

"Well, hello," a bubbly voice sounds from my left. "Hagen, I see you have been keeping secrets. Nice to see you again, Eva."

"Hi, Carly."

Lachlan frowns. "How do you two know each other?"

"I met her when I had drinks at the inn with Maggie." I purposely leave out our walk on the beach and dirty promises. Promises which he has fulfilled without reservation and quite well. No reason for me to share those details with Carly.

"Dr. Templeton is on her way to close your wound," Carly shares. "Need anything else?"

Lachlan bruises my hip with his fingertips before replying, "I'm good."

An hour and fifteen stitches later, Carly reappears with his discharge papers. "You're set to go. Cap and a few others are waiting in the lounge. Do you want to stop there or have them come here?"

"We'll see them on the way out. Thank you, Carly."

"Anytime. I'm glad to see you changed your mind about having a fling, Eva."

A huge smile widens on my face. "Me too."

Carly closes the door.

"What is she talking about?" Lachlan asks instantly.

"When we met, I may have said dating was off the table. A fact you already knew."

"I changed your mind, though."

"Yes, you did. Let's get you home," I say.

He commands Roxie down from the bed, threads his fingers with mine, and we walk to the lounge. Captain Ramirez, my brother, and Smithson remain.

"Penny will be fine. Her mother has a long road ahead of her, but the doctors are optimistic," Cap offers.

"Thanks for the update and the support."

Smithson bro hugs him and extends his hand to me.

I wrinkle my brow in confusion.

"Can I have your car keys, Eva?"

I drop them into his open palm.

"I rode to the scene with Cap since we're neighbors. He'll follow you to Hagen's and give me a lift home."

"Much appreciated."

"It's what we do," Smithson replies.

I open the rear door for Roxie, and she jumps in. Once Lachlan is settled in the passenger seat, her head is flat on the console. The guys line up behind me, and we caravan to his house.

Luckily, Grant seems comfortable with Lachlan and I and hasn't said another word about our relationship or the fact that I'm spending the rest of this morning there with him.

We wave goodbye and step into the house. Lia is sound asleep on the couch. Lachlan nudges her, and she wakes.

"You gonna make it?" she quips.

He smirks at her like an older brother would. "Yeah."

"Good."

"Thanks for coming over. It means a lot."

"We're family. You know that," Lia replies. After a quick hug, she closes the front door behind her.

"Can you take her gear off? My arm is throbbing."

"With a bit of guidance, sure," I reply. Successfully, I remove Roxie's gear and stow it in the garage. "I'm fine. Go check on Lilah to wash the concern off your face."

He drops his head and complies. Ten minutes later, he shuffles into the bedroom, fussing with his uniform.

I set my hand on his chest, and he pauses. The look in his eye is hard to gauge. I can't tell if he's angry or happy he has me here in this moment. "Will you let me help? It isn't as if I haven't seen each hard, sculpted inch of you before."

His signature panty-melting smile appears on his face, and then he nods in approval. I start with his vest but don't make it very far. He laughs and guides me step by step. A few minutes later, he's down to his boxer briefs and socks. Despite the circumstances, it's arousing being told what to do. I push away my thoughts, or at least I try.

"The answer to whatever you're thinking is yes."

I exhale sharply and meet his intense gaze. The type of gaze that would lead a girl to think a man would never leave and would support her every single day for the rest of her life. "You have no idea what I'm thinking."

"No, but I would bet if I slip my hand between your thighs, you're wet and ready for me."

A shiver cascades over me from head to toe. "True, but now isn't the time for it to happen or for me to share with you."

"I accept your words as true. However, I still want you to share your thoughts."

I guide him to the edge of the bed. He takes a seat, and I tug off his socks. His uninjured arm curves around me and draws me between his legs. I bend forward and kiss him, then whisper my thoughts.

"Interesting. Did you know you might like that before?"

"No, only happened with you." No man before him made me feel safe enough to be honest behind closed doors about my sexual desires.

"Well, we shall explore your realization another time."

"Promise?"

"Promise."

I kiss his forehead and add space between us. "Need anything else before you go to sleep?"

"You."

"I'll be right back. I'm going to set the alarm and grab water for you." By the time I return to the bedroom after completing those things and checking on Lilah myself. Lachlan is sound asleep. I strip off my clothes, set an alarm, and slide into the bed beside him until morning. Well, for a few hours, anyway, since it's already morning.

Just past seven, I hear a tiny knock on the door and footsteps hurrying away. Without disturbing Lachlan, I slip out of bed and tug on more clothes. As I pass the front door, I disarm the security system.

Lilah is in the kitchen poised to pull out her stool. "Hi, Miss Eva. Is Daddy at work again?"

"He came back a little while ago. What would you like for breakfast?" I consider whether I should share about his injury but decide it isn't my place.

"We should take care of Roxie first," Lilah reminds me.

"Of course. Why don't you let her out, and I'll get her food?"

"Roxie, come," Lilah states.

Without hesitation, Roxie walks beside her to the French doors. Lilah opens the slider door and waits. After a few fast laps around the yard, Roxie returns. Lilah admits her back into the house, and Roxie scurries to her bowl.

"What would you like before soccer?"

"Pancakes with smiley faces."

"Okay." I pull the pancakes from the freezer while she gathers the face-making items like strawberries, whipped cream, bananas, and blueberries for eyes.

I don't need to look up to feel him approaching us while we decorate.

"Good morning, ladies."

Lilah laughs. "I'm not a lady, Daddy." Then her face falls. "What happened to your arm?"

"Come here, sweet pea." Lilah complies, and Lachlan shares how he was injured at work.

"Your arm will be fine, right?"

"Absolutely. Just a cut. It already feels better."

I can tell from the tight set of his jaw that isn't the truth.

"Good. Is the girl going to be okay too?"

Oh. My. Heart. She understands the core of his job is helping people. It's heartwarming.

"Yeah, she will be."

"Good." Lilah kisses his cheek and hurries back beside me. "Wow! Miss Eva, your smiley face rocks!"

"Thanks." I set her plate on the table while she takes a seat. "Why don't you eat and then get dressed for soccer?"

"'Kay."

When I round the island to make coffee, Lachlan traps me against the counter.

"I could get used to you being here each morning," he whispers and presses a discreet kiss to the curve of my neck.

"Me too. Is it the right time, though?"

He lifts a shoulder. "You're the first and only woman I've allowed to be near my daughter. How the hell would I know?"

I laugh softly. "As amazing as being surrounded by you feels, we need to leave soon, or she'll be late."

"I'll fumble around making coffee while you shower and get dressed."

I nod and attempt to move, but he isn't ready to allow me the privilege. After another sweet kiss behind my ear, he backs away.

When I finish dressing, Lachlan is nearly done as well. We arrive at the pitch with five minutes to spare. Aside from a few shocked looks that Lachlan is present, the session runs smoothly.

The last few weeks have been a whirlwind. Aside from dinner with them each night, I've been going home to the cottage. We've slipped up a few times, but usually, I sleep alone.

Before I left after dinner, I prepared Lilah for her event today.

"I'll meet you at the center at three, and then I'll bring you home."

She nods and looks up at Lachlan. I understand her fear. She's afraid I won't show, and she'll be alone while her friends' moms are present.

"Would you like a pinkie promise?" I offer.

Lilah's eyes widen. "What's a pinkie promise?"

I grin at her. "First, you hook your pinkie like this." I bend my pinkie and turn my hand toward her. She mirrors me. "Then, we hook our fingers together and say, 'Pinkie promise.'" With our fingers linked, we say in unison, "Pinkie promise."

Lilah releases my finger and throws her arms around my neck. "Good night, Miss Eva. I'll see you tomorrow."

I get up early the next morning and run six miles on the beach. Booting my laptop when I return, I have a meeting request from Jo. *Weird.* Weirder, it's for ten minutes from now.

With coffee in hand, I settle into my chair.

"Morning, lovely."

"Morning."

"What has you extra glowy this morning? Did you have a sleepover?" Jo accuses with her eyelashes fluttering as if to say "about time."

I laugh. "No, no sleepover last night. I already went for a run. What's up?"

"Is your offer still available?" my bestie and former office mate asks.

"Hell yes!"

"I'm crazy excited. How do we make this happen?"

With a huge grin on my face, I answer her questions and give her a few items to take care of for technology purposes. If she doesn't have a computer or printer or whatever, we need to order it as soon as possible.

"Do you have anything pressing right now, or can we chat about personal stuff?

"I have a few things to do before tea with Lilah, but we can catch up a bit." I spill all the recent details from the end of the dinner to the calls with our old boss and Lachlan facing off with Cody. Not exactly true, but his presence made me stand my ground more firmly.

"Good for you. It seems Chelsea dumped him as soon as his father and Shirley realized they weren't safe from the impending implosion of the company."

"Honestly, I'm fine. I don't wish them ill will, but I don't want to talk or think about them anymore."

"I'm proud of you, E."

"Thanks, Jo. I need to get this done before tea. Love you."

We end the call, and I spend the next few hours reviewing paperwork from Alannah about forming my business and administrative items. After a light lunch and a shower, I don a spring sundress and strappy sandals.

After a calming breath, I input the code at the center. Nervous butterflies flutter in my belly, and not the kind I get from Lachlan.

"Good afternoon. Which student are you here for?" Casey, if I recall correctly, asks.

"Lilah Hagen," I reply.

"Right this way." Casey leads me through the center and out a rear door.

I've never seen anything so cute in my life. There are numerous round tables set up with tablecloths, floral centerpieces, and colorful cups and plates. My nervousness increases when I see Maggie. *What is she doing here?*

"Eva?" She circles the table and hugs me.

"Hi, Maggie."

"Lilah invited you?" she asks.

"Yeah."

"How sweet. I love catering this event. When Noelle and Caroline offered me the job, I was thrilled to handle this unique get-together. Have a great time."

Before I can settle myself completely, Lilah bounds through the door with a flower in her hand and a small gift bag. "Miss Eva, you're here!" I crouch to allow her to hug me at her level. She presses a kiss to my cheek, and her smile widens. "You look pretty."

"Thank you, Lilah. So do you. I love your sparkly shoes."

She points her toe for me to admire them a little more closely. Then she takes my hand and leads me to one of the tables. Wiggling into the chair beside me, she waits for Noelle to begin the program.

"I'll be back after a song," Lilah shares and pushes off the chair.

"Okay." I nod and shift my attention to the grassy area to my right.

A woman in scrubs hurries through the doors and takes one of the empty seats at my table. "You look familiar," she states. "You came to the emergency room with Lilah."

"Yes. Janet, right?"

"Good memory. Nice to see you again."

"You as well."

The kids sing a sweet song about love and their mothers to the same tune as "You Are My Sunshine." After a boisterous round of applause, the kids rejoin their guests for pastries and tea—iced tea served in teacups.

"What did you think of the song, Miss Eva?"

"It was perfect, sweetie."

Her smile doubles in size, though I'm not sure it's possible. She digs into the brownie on her plate.

As I glance around the group, I notice the array of guests. It's clear some are grandmothers, aunts, and even older sisters in addition to the mothers present. I'm grateful Lilah felt comfortable to ask me to attend. I would've been bummed if she invited Alannah like previous years.

Lilah sets her hand on mine, and I look at her. Her eyes are filled with tears, but none have fallen. It's as if she willed them to stay put.

"Are you okay, Lilah?"

"I'm great! Thank you for coming."

"Pinkie promise, remember?"

She nods furiously, then stands to hug me again. "Can we go home now?"

"If you're ready to leave, we can."

She bolts out of her chair, rushes to Casey, and animatedly explains she's leaving. With the task complete, Lilah walks back to me and escorts me to get her things. With her purple unicorn backpack and nap items from her cubby secured, we head outside only to have Noelle follow us out with Lilah's car seat.

"Eva, thank you for joining us today. Lachlan left this for you this morning."

Well done, Eva! Parenting 101. Kids need a car seat. "The event was wonderful. Thank you for reminding me."

Noelle nods. "While we set this up, Caro and I reviewed your proposal and are looking forward to implementing your suggestions. Perhaps we can meet in a week or two to finalize the order?"

My nerves are frayed, hoping this seat is secure. "Of course. I'm glad you love my plan. Would you mind checking this?" I motion to the back seat.

"Not at all." Noelle tugs on the seat itself as well as the latches securing it into my car. "It's perfect. Hop in, Lilah."

"Thanks, Mrs. Morgan." Lilah climbs in and buckles her belt.

I verify it's locked in place, close the rear door, and thank Noelle again.

When we arrive at the house, Lachlan isn't home yet. Without a second thought, Lilah empties her backpack, stows her lunch box, and drops the naptime items in the basket in the laundry room.

"Can I help you cook again?" Lilah asks me while I peruse the fridge for dinner options.

"Sure. Any idea what's on the menu?"

"Grilled chicken, 'roni salad, and special s'mores when it gets dark enough," she answers.

"Let's get started, then," I offer.

Step by step, we work to make the macaroni salad with the prepared pasta in the fridge. By the time he arrives home, we're nearly finished grilling the chicken.

"How are my ladies this evening?" he asks, finding us on the patio.

"Great!"

Lilah dishes the entirety of our afternoon with minute details, including Janet talking to me. We finish dinner and enjoy the warm evening by eating outside. A few hours later, after a s'mores festival including peppermint patties instead of chocolate bars, Lilah curls up in her bed before the last soccer session of the season tomorrow morning.

CHAPTER TWENTY-FOUR

LACHLAN

Each night Eva leaves makes me wish I could work faster on her office. Yes, it's in my home, but I want it to be hers—the office and, more importantly, the home. There isn't much left, but my injury is not helping matters. While it isn't major, I don't want to prolong my recovery by doing too much. With a helper for two or three days of solid work, I can finish it. I resolve to ask for assistance from an unlikely source today. After feeding Roxie, I prepare a coffee and shuffle to Lilah's room to wake her.

Giggles meet me before I cross the threshold. "Roxie is silly. Her tongue is rough."

I smile at my daughter and partner. "Time to get up for soccer."

A frown materializes on her face where a smile typically appears when I mention soccer. "It's the last one, though." She pouts.

"I know, but I'm fairly certain your goal will arrive in the next few days so you can practice through the summer."

"Okay. Thank you, Daddy."

I leave her room only for her to call me back.

"Daddy?"

Hovering at the threshold again, I reply, "Yeah, Li."

"I love Miss Eva. Is it okay for me to tell her?"

Instantly, my chest tightens, and the hairs on the back of my neck stand up. "Of course you should tell her." *Pot. Kettle.* "What brought this on?"

"She takes care of me, lets me help with cooking, and she came to my tea. I had a mom for the first time. Miss Alannah is smart, pretty, and nice, but she doesn't live here."

"Miss Eva doesn't live with us." *Yet.*

"She doesn't sleep here, but she's always with us."

Mostly accurate. "True. You can share whatever feelings you have with Miss Eva when you're ready."

"Can I call her Mom?"

My heart clenches. I'm at the top of the roller-coaster hill and need to make a choice before the car plummets to the bottom. "You'll have to ask her that question, sweet pea."

"'Kay. Is she coming to soccer?"

"As far as I know, she is."

Lilah throws the covers off and rushes unnecessarily around her room to get ready. "Perfect. Eggs for breakfast, please?"

"Your wish is my command, sweet pea."

Her giggles follow me down the hall. My phone chimes with a notification as I pull out the pans to cook.

Eva: Morning.

Me: Morning, sweetheart. Wish you were here to share eggs with us.

Eva: Me too. See you soon.

Lilah and I devour the eggs and toast before packing up for soccer. This session is the last one and includes snacks, as well as an awards ceremony. Ideally, I'll be able to request assistance from my accomplice beforehand and, more importantly, before Eva arrives.

I park a few spaces away from Washington. He's alone with the kids this morning. "Need a hand?"

"Thanks," he replies as I reach for Corrinne.

She leaps into my arms willingly. "Hi, sweetie. You givin' your dad a tough time this morning?"

She shakes her head and points to Caleb. "Him." At least I think that's what I heard her say.

I stifle a laugh and usher Lilah to the pitch. "Let's go play some soccer."

The kids cheer, and we walk toward the field.

After we leave the kids with the coaches, Washington states, "Thanks, Hagen."

"No problem."

"How's the arm?"

"Healing but a hindrance just the same," I offer.

"What do you mean?"

I scan the field in search of Eva. "I completed the living room and started remodeling the office for your sister."

Washington turns to face my profile. "You're building Eva an office at your house?"

"Yes, and with my injury, I need help to finish it before she rents office space."

"I'm stuck with you, aren't I?" His question was serious but with an amused undertone.

"Yes, if she'll have me." *If I can work up the courage to say those three little words.* I see Eva approaching.

Washington nods. "I may give you crap, but you're a good guy. If Eva chooses you, I'm fine with it. When do you want help with—"

"Morning, Lachlan," my gorgeous woman states. She slides her fingers into mine and kisses my cheek. "Hi, Grant."

"Hey," Washington mumbles.

We stand side by side and watch the kids play. After the awards are handed out, they have cupcakes and cookies in the early hours of the morning.

The kids hug before climbing into their car seats.

"Hagen, I'll call you to work out the details," Washington states.

"Sounds good. Thanks."

"What details?" Eva asks.

Think quick. "Maggie wants to assist with the last-minute stuff for the race, if necessary." *A small white lie.*

"Oh. We don't need help, do we? We only need to verify the volunteer schedule and pick up the signage. Plus, we have almost a month to pull it off."

"I think so. I'll let her down easy. We make a great team, and she kind of forced us to work together."

Eva laughs. "She did that, didn't she?"

"I'm not mad about it. Are you?"

"Not even a little. It gave us an excuse to spend time together."

"I didn't need one."

"Perhaps the word is *cover*. We used the planning as cover to keep prying eyes and ears out of our business," she suggests.

"Fair. I didn't need either one. I wanted to spend time with you since our stroll on the beach."

"You mean when you shared each dirty thought in detail with me?"

"Admit it, you liked it."

"Your candor took me by surprise initially, but I love it now."

With a wink, I kiss her and usher her toward her car. "I'll see you at home."

We hang out around the house for the rest of the day. After Lilah reads stories to Roxie, who has become her favorite listener, Eva leaves for the evening.

"I'll call you when I wake up," I offer, leaning against the front door.

"Okay. Dinner after work?"

"Of course." I haul her against me and kiss her to the brink of dragging her into my bedroom and never letting her leave. *Patience. Finish the office.* "Good night, beautiful. Please text me when you get to the cottage."

"I will. Night, Lachlan."

I watch until her car disappears onto the street. Fishing my phone from my pocket, I text Washington.

Me: Thanks for offering to help. I'm off Tuesday and Thursday.

Washington: I'm available Wednesday and Thursday.

Me: I'll see if I can switch with someone.

Washington: Sounds good. We can finalize tomorrow at the precinct.

I spend the next thirty minutes looking for someone to swap shifts with me. Craven does without a second thought. I consider working on the office a little, but it isn't the right move. Attempting to finish the built-ins alone is stupidity of the highest order. I let Roxie outside and wait for her to return.

Eva: I'm here.

Me: Sweet dreams.

Eva: You too.

I smile, lock up, and finish off my latest book before turning in for the night.

At the crack of dawn, I roll out of my lonely bed and run a few miles on the treadmill before my shift. Today is a difficult day for my house. This year, I've taken the coward's way out. I'm working. I can lie to myself and say it's to allow the other dads to properly celebrate the special women in their lives, but it would be a straight-up lie. Until this year, Lilah didn't seem to care or notice when Mother's Day happened despite Alannah attending the tea with her.

I was surprised she didn't blurt her feelings yesterday when Eva was with us. The poem with her handprint she created at school is sitting on the island, itching to be bestowed upon its rightful owner. Who? It should be Clare, but nothing about our life rises to the level of traditional. Frankly, Eva has done everything for both of us. It's part of the reason I want her here… for Lilah. For us. No, I need her here for me. She makes my heart pound when she smiles. Her presence alone calms me to my core. I'm better with her beside me. Yet I can't own it and say the words. *Why?*

The answer is simple. Terror. I'm terrified to believe I deserve the happiness we both seek. Eva and I desire the same things: a home, a family, and a dog or two. More than that, we want a love to grow old with. Every fiber of me is screaming "she's the one," and yet saying those words seems impossible… for both of us.

I scrub my hand down my face, catching a glimpse of the gift on the island. Peeking in on Lilah, I grab breakfast and wait for Lia to arrive.

"Morning, Lia."

"Morning. Still sleeping?"

Roxie walks casually toward her, and Lia reaches down to pet her head.

"Yeah. I'll be back later. Eva may arrive before me."

Lia nods. "We've known each other since your first day in York Beach. Do you realize that when you mention her name, you relax instantly? Does she know how you feel?"

"Is it obvious to everyone?"

In comparison to Eva, Lia is tiny. She tilts her chin up to look at me fully. "Only people who know you well, which includes me. You're noticeably happier, and so is Lilah. The mere fact that you allow Lilah to be with Eva one-on-one should be enough for you to let yourself fully own your feelings. Take it from someone Cupid smacked with an arrow when she least expected it. Not saying the words doesn't make it any less true. The three words only make it official."

I drop my head. "Thanks, Lia."

"It's my pleasure to push everyone I know toward coupledom. It's pretty amazing."

"I'll keep it in mind, future Mrs. Blake."

"Say hi to Finnegan for me."

I laugh and reply, "Will do." I move to the garage door, and Roxie hurries to my side without being called. "*So ist brav*, Roxie."

With Lia's words in addition to my own thoughts, I drive to work. She's absolutely right. I love Eva in the deepest recesses of my soul, and she deserves to hear the words. Thankfully, I'm on desk duty today, and it's blissfully uneventful.

On the way to my truck, I get a text from Eva.

Eva: Any ideas for dinner?

Her question is innocuous, but also something a woman, my better half, Lilah's mother would ask of me each night. I want her to be that person. Even more than before, I need to finish the office, ironically, with her brother's help. Rather than reply, I call her.

"Hi, beautiful. How was your day?"

"Fine. Yours?"

"Desk duty was boring. I'm leaving now. Want me to pick up something?"

"Sure. I can place an order at the inn. Does that work?"

"Yes. I'll be there soon." I end the call and exhale heavily. Blurting my feelings over the phone isn't the right decision. I'll show and share when I ask her to move in.

Eva: Food will be ready in twenty-five minutes.

Me: On it.

Resolved, I drive to the restaurant and wait for our order. After taking off Roxie's gear with our dinner in hand, I cross the threshold but don't see my ladies. Roxie guides me to them by following their sweet voices.

"Hi, Daddy. Miss Eva came over early."

I set the food on the outdoor dining table. "Hi. I'll be right back. Roxie needs to eat too."

Lilah pops up from her chair and rushes past me. Her words, "I'll do it," trail behind her.

Without another thought, I slide my arm around Eva and draw her flush against me. Before I can manage to say hello, she fists my shirt and kisses me hard. Each time we kiss is like the first time but better. What I mean is, the sensations are the same but grow each time. To avoid getting carried away, I draw her lower lip between my teeth and pull back slightly. "Hey, beautiful. I'm happy you're here."

"Me too."

Lilah's voice carries through the French doors. "Sit. Good girl, Roxie." After a few minutes, presumably for Roxie to eat, Lilah says, "Let's go outside." Soon, they appear at the door.

"Ready to eat, Lilah?" I ask my daughter.

"Did you get me 'roni and cheese, Daddy?"

I shrug. "Miss Eva ordered dinner."

"Oh." She turns to Eva expectantly.

"Macaroni and cheese is your favorite, huh?"

Lilah nods enthusiastically.

"Interesting. I like it with lobster."

"Yuck! Is mine plain?"

Eva giggles. "Yes, yours doesn't have lobster."

"Yay!" Eva places the dish in front of my daughter, and she digs in.

I take a seat beside Eva across from Lilah. Without prompting, Eva ordered my favorite dish from the menu as well. We eat mostly in silence.

When Lilah finishes, she slides off her chair and stands beside me. If she intends to whisper, she fails miserably. "Can I get the gift now?"

"Sure."

Eva frowns, and Lilah rushes away from the table. With a flourish she returns with the gift bag from the island.

"Miss Eva, I made this for you." Lilah shoves it toward Eva.

Eva's gaze meets mine, and I drop my head slightly. With precision, she removes the paper. Emotion wells up within her. It's clear at least to me by the way she inhales deeply and holds it before releasing the breath slowly.

"Will you read it to me?" she asks.

"Sure." Lilah takes the paper and stands before Eva as if she's giving a presentation. "I'm growing like a flower with all your love and care. All your hugs and kisses and good times that we share. I'm growing like a flower. We know that this is true, so I made this picture to say I love you."

"It's beautiful. I love you, too, Lilah."

"Really?"

"Yes."

A bashful smile grows on her face. "Can I ask one more thing?"

Eva's eyes meet mine again. I nod to share I know what her plan is. Ideally, I convey the same to her.

"Of course. Ask away."

"Will you be my mom?" She anxiously awaits an answer.

"It would be my honor."

As if the world will continue infinitely, Lilah throws her arms around Eva and kisses her cheek.

After releasing Eva, Lilah asks exuberantly, "Daddy, did you hear?"

"Yeah, I heard."

"I'm so happy," she exclaims and carries her dish to the trash with Roxie padding behind her.

Eva focuses on my face and asks, "How long have you known she was waiting to share?"

"A week or so. It needed to come from her this time, no heads-up."

"I appreciate it."

We clear the table and hang out until Lilah turns in for the night.

CHAPTER TWENTY-FIVE

EVA

With a coffee from the Perk, I hustle to the center for my meeting with Noelle and Caroline. I'm running late this morning because last night Lachlan and I got carried away. More accurately, we were lost in each other and have been since Lilah's gift and request over the weekend.

I park at the center and silence my phone. Before I can, I find a message from Lachlan.

Lachlan: Morning, beautiful. Have a great day!

Me: Morning. Thank you. You too. I'll see you for dinner.

With a sigh, I exit my car and ring the bell. If I use Lilah's code, it will make it appear as if I'm picking her up.

"Good morning, Miss Washington. Noelle and Caroline are expecting you."

I laugh. "Two Mrs. Morgans is a tough one, isn't it?"

Casey asks, "How does that go?"

"I think it's Mesdames, shortened to Mmes. Though I'm not sure how to say it properly."

"Sweet. I'm going to use that."

"Of course." I thank her once she shows me to the conference room.

"Morning, Eva. I'm excited to get started on this," Caroline states when I enter the room. It never ceases to amaze me how put together she looks. Aside from her shiny raven hair and striking blue eyes, she exudes confidence in any room. Plus, I don't think she worries if a student dirties her clothes either.

"Hi. I am too."

Noelle breezes in after we greet each other. "Morning, Caro, Eva."

We reply in kind and get started. I share the chart I created for them and explain as we review it.

"Here are places where you can improve your website traffic. I created a draft website for you to review. The link is in your emails. Let me know what you think, and I can make changes before it goes live."

"This is fantastic! Better than I imagined," Caroline offers.

"Thank you, Mrs. Morgan."

"We can absolutely move to a first-name basis," Noelle adds.

"Perfect. For the specialized plan aspect, Caroline, I have an action item for you."

"No problem. How can I help?"

"Either we need to go through how you start one, or you can write up a synopsis."

"What do you mean, go through?"

"A role-play, if you will, as if I were coming to you for my child."

"Lilah doesn't need a plan," Noelle offers.

A wide smile blooms on my face. "No, she doesn't."

"Do you see that, Noelle?"

"Yes, I see the giddiness on her face. I take it things are going well?" Noelle asks.

"Walked right into that one, didn't I?" I mutter.

"Yeah, you did," Caroline replies.

The three of us laugh softly. I nod and answer, "Yes, they are."

"Happy to hear it," Caroline states.

For the next hour, we finish going over my plan, and they intend to review the draft website over the next few days. As I leave the conference room, I see Lilah playing outside.

She rushes to the door and throws it open. "Hi, Mom. Are you here to pick me up?"

"Not yet. It's still morning, sweetie. I had a meeting with Miss Noelle and Miss Caroline."

"Oh, okay. Love you."

"Love you too."

When I turn back into the room, I note my conversation had an audience. I smile and exit the center. Before leaving the lot, I check my messages.

Jo: The proposal for our new client is ready on the server.

Jo: I love, love, love my new job. Comfy clothes, unlimited coffee.

Me: I'll review it soon. I love, love, love my business and you for taking the leap with me.

Jo: xoxo

I scroll through my inbox and find nothing urgent, then head to my next appointment. I have three options for office space. The realtor has two options to show me today. The third is subletting from Alannah. Finishing my now-cold coffee, I loop my arm though my purse and climb to the first possibility.

"No, I don't care. Get it done," I hear Susie, my realtor, on a call at the door of the first potential space. "Come in, Eva."

"Everything okay?"

She waves me off. "Yeah. Initially, my son decided to take a gap year. In the last few days, he's changed his mind. Now we're rushing to complete applications in the hopes he can attend college in the fall."

"Good luck to him," I offer.

"Thank you. This space has two offices and a medium-sized conference room. It's 750 square feet, and the rent is $825 per month. There's ample parking and double security doors in the lobby. Feel free to look around."

I wander away from her and check out the space. It's nice and clean, but I don't want to commit to more space than I need. True, I can pay the rent with the profits from the contract with the team, but an office this large seems unnecessary right now.

"What do you think?" Susie asks.

"It's nice but too much."

She nods but tries to convince me anyway. "This location is prime and won't last forever."

"That's the thing. Generally, my work is virtual or on-site at my client's business. In fact, I came from an on-site appointment."

"I understand. Perhaps the next office, which is much smaller, will be more to your liking."

"I can meet you there."

"Fifteen minutes?" Susie suggests.

"Sure."

I'm conflicted about renting an office so soon. Either way, I suck it up and walk through the second space with Susie. It's half the size of the first option, but again, why would I pay for it right now?

"I appreciate your efforts, Susie. I'm going to take a few days to think about it."

"Of course. Please give me a call either way," she requests.

"I will. Have a nice day."

To shake off my uneasy feeling, I decide to walk on the beach despite the early tourists crowding the space. I pluck off my shoes and deposit them on the passenger floorboard. After stowing my small purse in the glove box, I lock the doors and wander to the sand. The breeze is light, and the salty air is soothing. Once my angst passes, I opt to work on Lachlan's back porch. The pergola offers the perfect amount of shade.

When I pull into the driveway, I notice a familiar car. *What is my brother doing here in the middle of the day?* Worried, I rush inside and find them leaning against the kitchen island. Lachlan is hot as hell in low-slung athletic shorts and a YPD shirt with a hat on backward. It's sinful to look as good as he does right now, especially with my brother beside him. I can't do anything about the desire rushing through me. Roxie greets me as well.

I pat her head and ask, "What's going on? What are you doing here, Grant?"

My brother gulps the rest of his water. "Good luck." His words were directed at Lachlan. "We'll talk later, E. Love you." Grant offers me a side hug and steps through the front door.

"Lachlan, is everything okay?"

Before he answers, he draws me into his arms and kisses me boneless. His kiss is everything, but this one is different. Our tongues tangle, and our hands move over each other until he pulls back, pressing a tender kiss to my forehead. "Yes. Everything will be perfect. I made a decision. Truthfully, it was a while ago, but Lilah is braver than I am. To some our relationship is fast, but I don't care. I also know this goes against your request for slow-and-steady progress. I'm rambling." He reaches for my hand and leads me toward his office. "With the living room complete, I started work on the office. From the beginning of my planning and my first pin, I was building it for you."

"Me?"

He drags his free hand down his face while we stare at a closed door. Without saying another word, Lachlan pushes it open. There's no way this is the same room. The office was barren, dark, and drab. The only reason it looked like one was the desk in the middle of the spacious room. Now, it's beautiful. The walls are dove gray. The bay window is surrounded by cream-colored built-in shelving and cabinetry. He included a window seat with plush pillows in coordinating shades of purple and a fluffy blanket. The desk is massive, and the sitting area looks cozy.

"You did this for me?"

"Yes. I recall you mentioning the office at the cottage is too small for your new business. Honestly, you shared about the size when you weren't the owner. Something about needing space to spread out. I believe you stated you would need to use the dining area for larger projects." He lifts my hand to his lips and kisses the back. Then he walks over to the shelves along the wall, turns a lock of sorts, and pulls along the edge. A wooden easel-like stand the length of the bookcase comes forward. I wouldn't know it was there without him showing me. It blends into the cabinetry seamlessly.

"Lachlan."

"Will this work for the presentation boards?" His question is soft and laced with concern. Concern for what, I'm not sure.

A single tear rolls down my cheek. "Yes, it's perfect."

"Eva, I…."

I love you, Lachlan.

"Don't rent office space. Use this one. Make this your home." He scrunches his face as if he isn't conveying his feelings well. On the contrary, he's speaking loud and clear without those pesky words. "I want you to be here with us always."

"How soon are you willing to share your home with me?" I wonder aloud.

His mouth slants over mine, and he kisses me hard and with a possessiveness I've grown to expect from him. Secretly, I love it. Pulling away, he threads our fingers, rushes to his bedroom, and brings me straight into his huge walk-in closet.

"Where are your clothes?"

He winks and makes my heart melt more. "I moved them into the back or 'his' portion of the closet so you can have the 'hers' part."

The look on my face must convey my lack of understanding. We take a few steps and turn the corner. This area is a mirror image of the front half.

"Wow! I never came in here other than to steal your Bears hoodie."

"You mean *your* Bears hoodie."

First a custom office and now offering a prized sweatshirt. Perhaps saying those three important words aren't as terrifying as I've made them out to be. Stifling my giggle is impossible. "Think we can move my stuff while Lilah is at parents' night out after I take her for a girls' afternoon?"

"Two nights? You're going to make me wait two more nights?" He pouts.

"Don't whine. I need time to pack. The good news is I don't have a lot. The only things at the cottage are my clothes, a few personal items, and office equipment."

He scoops me up from the floor and turns us in a circle. "I can survive until then to have complete access to you. I can't wait to whisper my dirty thoughts in your ear from the moment you wake up until you slip into dreamland tightly cocooned against me."

"Yes, to all of it. Yes." I take a quick glance at the clock. "Do we have enough time before picking up Lilah?"

"There's always time to make you scream my name."

Expeditiously, our clothes pile up on the floor. Somehow, I manage to take off mine faster than Lachlan. When he looks up, I'm naked, standing at the side of his bed. Our bed… almost.

He eats up the space between us, hauls me into his arms, and shifts us horizontally onto the bed. Feverishly, we chase our release as one.

With a few minutes to spare, we pick up Lilah together at the center and have dinner on the beach.

CHAPTER TWENTY-SIX

LACHLAN

Unfortunately, duty calls on Friday morning when I would rather spend the day moving Eva into my house. I set up a delivery of flowers and breakfast to the cottage for Eva in the parking lot. Apparently, I'm taking too long in my SUV. Roxie is pushing her nose against my hand repeatedly.

"What's wrong, girl?" I ask, then check my mirrors.

Without a response, I finish checking my messages and hop out. When I do, Roxie is dutifully waiting for me to let her out as well. I buckle her vest and lead her inside.

"Morning, Hagen," Craven calls, coming toward me.

"Hey."

"Cap was looking for you. Something about a meeting with Captain Snow."

I frown. I'm not scheduled to meet with her. "Thanks." I stow my bag, and we knock on the frame of Cap's door.

"Come in, Hagen."

Roxie heels beside me before I can command her. "*So ist brav.*" I turn my attention to Cap. "Morning. Did I miss something?"

Cap shakes his head. "No. Captain Snow set up a meeting for 11:00 a.m. to chat with me about expanding the K-9 program here under our supervision. Would you be willing to sit in?"

"Absolutely."

"Great," Cap replies.

To pass the time between now and the meeting, I take Roxie outside to the training area. We work on her tracking by walking a grid. Thirty minutes later, my phone rings. When I see who the caller is… *This can't be good.*

Fear courses through me. "Morning, Alannah. What's wrong?"

"Morning. You're right, my call isn't for a great reason."

I steel myself for whatever she may share next. "Clare is missing from her halfway house. She slipped out after bed check two nights ago and hasn't returned."

Instantly, I compute the distance and time it would take to get here by car—about eighteen hours with a few stops. If she got on a plane, she would be here already. I've done the math almost weekly since Alannah shared about the halfway house.

"Lachlan. Lachlan." Alannah's voice pierces my thoughts.

"Yeah. I'm here."

"Don't spiral. We don't know where she is, that's all."

"Are you kidding me?" How could Alannah not understand the stress not knowing causes? "For the last four years, I knew exactly where she was. I knew she couldn't show up here. I knew Lilah was as safe as I could provide for her. I need to call Noelle. Thanks, Alannah."

"I'll keep you informed when I get more information."

I end the call without so much as a goodbye and immediately dial the center.

"Good morning, Rooms to Learn and Grow. This is Casey. How may I direct your call?"

"Hello, Casey. I need to speak with Mrs. Morgan. It's urgent."

"Who may I ask is calling?"

"Lachlan Hagen."

"Which Mrs. Morgan?" Casey inquires.

"Either is fine."

"Please hold, Mr. Hagen."

While I wait, I walk to the picnic table and take a seat. Less than a minute later, I'm back on my feet pacing the length of the wooden furniture. For the first time in my life everything is going well. Lilah is thriving, and my relationship with Eva is moving forward

"Good morning, Mr. Hagen. This is Noelle. How can I help you?"

"Morning, Mrs. Morgan. There has been an issue with Lilah's mother. I need to make immediate changes to those allowed to dismiss my daughter."

"Understood. What would you like to amend?"

"As of this moment and until further notice, only I'm allowed to pick up my daughter from the center."

"Understood. What is your phone password?" Adding people to the dismissal card requires a signature. Normally, so does revoking privileges. They have a backup password for instances like this.

"Lake View Wildcats."

"Very well. We'll see you at the end of your shift. Is there anything we can do in the meantime for Lilah?"

"No, thank you." I scrub my hand down my face. To calm myself, Roxie and I continue walking a practice grid pattern in the training yard until my meeting with Captain Snow.

After giving Roxie some water, we enter the precinct and take seats in the small conference room. A few moments later, Snow joins us.

"Hagen, nice to see you again. May I?"

"You as well. Of course."

She reaches down to pet Roxie. "Hi, girl. How is it going with her?"

"Great. Her basic training is on point."

Before she can take a seat, Roxie and I are sent out on a call for a bomb threat at the high school. I meet up with Craven, who is already on the scene.

"What's the situation?"

He turns in my direction. "Principal Kisel received the threat via email fifteen minutes ago. She alerted me, and I called it in. The students have been evacuated and will be transported home once the buses arrive. Davis, who was with me in the building today, is handling the backup sweep of the building for stragglers."

"Understood. Let me know when Roxie can begin her interior search. I'm going to scan the perimeter now."

"I will," Craven replies. "Hey, you good?"

I huff. "No. There's some stuff going down with Lilah's mother. I'll be fine. Thanks for asking."

"Roxie, *voran*." We start at the front entrance and work to the east around the perimeter of the high school. When we reach the rear of the building, I update Craven. "Hagen to command."

"Go for command," Craven replies.

"Eastern and rear of the perimeter are clear."

"Roger."

We continue around the remainder of the complex and rejoin Craven at the main entrance. "Exterior is clear."

"Roger. You may proceed inside."

We start our search in the gym, including the locker rooms and weight room. Luckily, we come up empty. I continue to the main office and then travel from west to east in the building. "Hagen to command."

"Go for command."

"Basement and main level are clear. Proceeding to second floor," I inform Craven.

"Roger."

Slightly more than an hour later, I exit the building. "Roxie, *so ist brav*. Craven, all clear."

Upon hearing my words, Smithson and Van Doren enter the building, headed directly to the main office.

"Thanks," Craven responds.

"Welcome."

He glances at his watch. "You don't have to stay. The only people who remain are the detectives."

"Appreciate it."

"Of course."

"Roxie, *hier*." We leave the scene. I praise Roxie some more and load her into my truck. Before pulling away, I check my phone. I have two missed calls and a few texts. The preview on the top slices my heart open.

Eva: What is going on? Are you okay? Did I miss something?

I swipe open the rest of the notifications and note they're from Alannah and the daycare. With expedience, I hurry to my daughter. I enter the building quickly and find Lilah curled into a ball in Noelle's lap. Intermittent sobs echo around the room.

"What's wrong, sweet pea?"

"Miss Eva didn't…. We were supposed to shop for you today. She didn't come."

Fuck! I forgot. Not only that, but I also didn't give either of my girls a heads-up. "Lilah, please look at me."

My daughter unburies her face from the crook of Noelle's arm.

Before I can explain, Lilah adds, "Did she leave us?"

My heart shatters into tiny little pieces for her. "Eva not showing up is completely my fault. Please don't be upset with her. Be angry with me. I'll explain on the way home."

"No." The definitive word leaves Lilah's mouth.

"Want to try again?" I urge her.

"No, you're going to fix Mommy," Lilah demands.

Noelle looks directly at me, presumably to see how I'll respond to my daughter's second statement.

"Yes. I will. We need to find her first. Grab your stuff, please."

Lilah scoots off Noelle's lap and walks into her classroom.

"Good luck," she offers.

"Thanks. I'm going to need it. She most likely won't be back tonight."

"Understood."

Lilah yanks on my hand. "Let's go, Daddy. You need to say sorry."

Noelle smirks, and I hang my head. *If only "sorry" is all it's going to take.*

After buckling Lilah, I tear out of the parking lot and consider my options. Eva could be anywhere. If I had to narrow it down, I would say the beach, Maggie's, or the lighthouse. In the interest of time, I drive to the Nubble, since it's the closest to the daycare. *Please don't let it be Maggie and Grant's,* I inwardly beg. I don't want to admit I messed up. Nor do I care to admit to her brother that I haven't mustered the courage to tell her how I feel in words. Actions, sure, but not words.

I speed up the winding road to the Nubble Lighthouse. Given the time of day, it's not overly busy. I scan the lot for her car and come up empty.

"Her car isn't here, Daddy," Lilah shares after investigating.

"I see that."

"Where to next?"

Arguably, Grant and Maggie's is before the cottage. "We're going to drive by Maggie's to see if she's there."

"Why?"

I reverse from the spot and head down the hill. "Remember that Eva is Caleb and Corrinne's aunt?"

Lilah bobs her head in understanding.

"Well, that makes Grant Eva's brother."

"Got it. Hurry, Daddy."

I pull onto their street and creep toward the house. I don't even pull into their driveway, since she isn't here. I turn onto the road and hustle toward the shore. Throwing my SUV in Park at the far end of Short Sands Beach, I walk around the hood and open Lilah's door.

"Can you put on your sweater, please?"

She reaches into her purple unicorn bag and tugs it on quickly. Hopping to the ground, she waits for me to let Roxie out. With Roxie on one side and Lilah on the other, we hurry to the far side of the beach, searching for Eva. Reaching the end, we turn back toward the arcade side and walk in the direction of the cottage. We are at the beginning of tourist season, but Friday evenings generally have limited people on the beach.

Within twenty minutes of our arrival, we traverse the entire beach to no avail. I consider returning to my truck, then see movement on the upper balcony of the cottage. It must be her.

"Lilah, I see her. Let's go!"

I reach down and scoop my daughter up. Pain shoots up my arm, but I ignore it and take off running down the shore on the backside of the cottages with Roxie trotting beside me.

CHAPTER TWENTY-SEVEN

EVA

"What the hell is going on?" I ask Casey when I arrive to pick up Lilah for Father's Day shopping.

Given my agitated state, Caroline joins the conversation. "What is the issue?"

"Casey has informed me that I'm no longer on the dismissal list for Lilah. Can you confirm for me?"

Caroline steps into the office and taps on the keyboard. "Casey is correct. It appears the change was made this morning."

"I see. Is Lilah here and okay?" Anxiety and dread flood my body. He would've called, right?

Caroline excuses her employee from the conversation. "I shouldn't share that she's even here. Lilah is fine."

"I appreciate the information. I'm going to leave now in the hopes she doesn't see me. I have no doubt she'll be upset and think I blew off our shopping date."

"We'll keep a close eye on her," Caroline assures me.

"Thanks." With a heavy heart, I slip out of the center unnoticed by Lilah. Once settled into the driver's seat of my car, I text Lachlan, hoping for an instant reply.

Me: What is going on? Are you okay? Did I miss something?

When it doesn't come, I pull out of the driveway. Aimlessly, I drive and find myself at the Nubble Lighthouse. Here is as good a place as any to sit with my thoughts. I grab a blanket from my trunk and set it on the rocks. In my mind, I go over the last few days. Everything is—was—no, is amazing. I stayed up too late last night packing the rest of my clothes. I press my fist to my chest, hoping to quell the ache building there. I let him in. I let them in. All the way in. *Hell, this hurts.*

I allow the soothing sound of the salty waves below to wash over me, wishing it'll help. It doesn't. A while later, I swipe the blanket from the ground and retreat to my car. Briefly, I consider stopping at Grant's but don't want to spill my issues yet. I also don't need a lecture about going too fast or choosing wrong.

I trudge to my car and drive to the cottage when truthfully the only place I want to be is at Lachlan's. They are home to me, and the rapid timeframe in which falling for them happened is shocking, but....

I push away my wallowing thoughts for the moment and key myself into the cottage. The sight of my packed clothing opens the dam I had successfully put in place to keep my tears at bay.

Swiping over the ball of my cheek, I lock the front door and climb to the master balcony. I burrow into the corner of the couch and listen to the usually calming sounds of the ocean below and drift off to sleep. I shift and blink awake to the sound of my name.

"Eva!"

"Mommy!"

Bark!

I look over the edge of the balcony to the shore below. My little family is standing with their eyes pointed upward.

"Can we come up?" Lachlan asks.

"No." Crossing my arms over my chest, I shake my head.

Lachlan grips the back of his neck. "I need to explain. I royally screwed up."

I sigh heavily. *Isn't communication what you wanted this morning? You can't ask for it and not give it in return.* "I'll be right down."

Lilah cheers. "Hi, Mommy," she greets me and throws her arms around me when I open the door. A flood of relief tempers the anger in my chest a bit.

"Hi, sweetie."

Lachlan steps over the threshold with Roxie at his side. His gaze is pinned on me while I speak to Lilah.

"I'm only mad at Daddy for no shopping," she informs me.

"I see. What do you say to coloring a fairy or two while we talk?"

She fist pumps and shouts, "Yes!" While I procure the coloring book and crayons stashed in my bags, she sits at the round dining table.

"All set for now?" I ask after setting her up to color.

"I'm good."

A beat of silence passes between Lachlan and me before he says, "Roxie, stay."

I tilt my head in question but don't voice it. He's concerned for her safety. To add a little more privacy, I lead him outside to the back porch. We'll have a direct line of sight, plus Roxie's head is on Lilah's leg.

Lachlan reaches his hand toward me, but I don't uncross my arms to take it. "I'm so sorry. Alannah called this morning and shared that Clare is missing. She has been gone long enough that if she chose to, she could be near here. My first call was to the center to change her dismissal procedures."

Oh, Lachlan. "Does she know where you live?"

He shakes his head. "Not that I'm aware of, but with the press Roxie is getting, it's possible she narrowed it down to this area."

The dull ache in my chest lessens slightly. "You should've called."

"I know."

"You let me down. You forced me to let her down." I point at my sweet daughter inside, who is immersed in a world of pixie fairies.

"I know. I'm sorry. I truly forgot you were taking her shopping this afternoon. I assured Lilah it was my fault, not yours."

"It's the truth."

"It wasn't about you. It was about the extra protection Roxie offers."

"Explain more," I demand. His words soften my anger a bit.

"Normally, I leave Roxie in the truck when I pick up Lilah. However, now with Clare unaccounted for, I would take her inside with me for pickup. It gives me another set of eyes and ears in case something goes awry. It was never about you. I trust you completely."

"You have a crappy way of showing it," I retort.

He eliminates more of the space between our bodies and reaches his hand out again. This time, I allow him to take mine. "It won't ever happen again. I promise."

I glance inside and see Lilah happily coloring. "The fact that you would give us up for Lilah is admirable and heartbreaking at the same time. However, I won't allow it to happen. I do not consent to breaking up. You made a stupid decision or at least failed to keep me informed. If we're going to be partners, you need to talk to me about everything, especially Lilah's safety, or we won't work."

"We won't? Why would you volunteer to be part of the wreckage that is my life?"

"Did you quote a Nate Smith song?"

He shrugs. "How do you know it's from a Nate Smith song?"

"Perhaps your taste in music is rubbing off on me. Either way, I refuse to give you up, either of you. For the first time, I'm happy in all aspects of my life—notwithstanding this afternoon. Did you invite me to move in and build me the perfect office to turn around and kick me out?"

"No."

"Do you want to continue building a life with us?"

"Yes."

With my heart in my throat and a tightness in my belly, I ask, "Do you love me?"

"Yes. I love you, Eva. It has taken me too long to say the words. Somehow, and without me realizing it, you bored deep into my heart and soul. I never plan to let you leave."

"Good. I don't plan to. I love you both more than I thought possible. You told me daily with your actions. I appreciate hearing how you feel as well. We can figure this out."

"What happens if she shows up here?"

"We handle it like the news of her leaving her housing. No, it'll be better than we handled today because we're a team."

"What if I need to move?" Lachlan murmurs.

"Where?" The silence stretching between us is deafening, and he shifts his weight. "Never mind, it doesn't matter. I choose you, both of you. If it means I need to relocate to Florida, I will. The beauty of being my own boss is working anywhere I choose. However, it would be a mistake to uproot Lilah simply because her mother may know where she lives. It isn't fair or reasonable. Besides, are you willing to give up Roxie?"

"Are you serious?"

"Yes."

He tugs on my hand and draws me against him. The familiar warmth of him unravels the rest of my anger. I understand his position, and I'm confident he won't shut me out again.

"Shielding her has been solely my job for the last four years. Knowing Clare was in an institution under lock and key was my saving grace. Adding in the press for Roxie, my worry levels increased significantly."

"Why didn't you tell me you were concerned about the coverage?" I ask with my cheek against his sculpted chest.

"You were handling so much with your job. I didn't want to add more."

"Lach—"

"I will never fail to share information again."

I lift my head and look into his eyes. "I'm going to hold you to your promise."

"Can I kiss you now?"

"Yes, please."

Lachlan lowers his lips to mine and kisses me like it's the first time. Initially, he's tentative, but once he realizes I meant what I said, our lip-lock turns heated and passionate, bordering on inappropriate, considering Lilah can see us. Adding a sliver of space, I ask, "Does she want to go back to the center?"

He lifts his wrist and checks the time. "It's too late. What do you say to pizza on the way home?"

"Yes, sounds perfect."

With my hand in his, he leads me into the cottage for probably the last time.

"Did you 'pologize and fix Mommy?"

I laugh heartily, burying my face in Lachlan's arm.

"Yeah, I think we're good. What do you say to pizza and moving Mommy's stuff into our house?"

A wide smile grows on Lilah's face. "You're going to live with us?"

"I am. Okay with you?"

"Yes, yes, yes!" Lilah hops off her chair and throws her arms around my legs.

An unfamiliar wave of happiness washes over me. These feelings are absolutely welcome. We make a few trips to our cars and stow my belongings. After securing dinner, I follow Lachlan home. We eat and then haul my personal belongings inside.

"Can I read longer tonight?" Lilah asks.

"Sure," Lachlan replies. "Take Roxie. We'll be right in."

"Roxie, come," Lilah commands.

Dutifully, Roxie lopes after her into her room.

Once story time ends, we move boxes to their appropriate rooms and turn in ourselves.

CHAPTER TWENTY-EIGHT

LACHLAN

It has been two weeks since Alannah's initial call regarding Clare. Alannah checks in with Clare's attorney and guardian about twice a week. So far, nothing new. She hasn't returned, nor has she shown up for work. While I have added Eva back onto the dismissal list, we agreed I'll handle drop-off and pickup at the center with Roxie until the situation with Clare is resolved.

"Morning, Hagen," Garcia greets me before roll call starts. She's a great addition to our department.

"Morning."

The chatter ceases when Cap steps into the room. "I'll keep this brief. Your assignments are posted on the board. Any questions?"

With no one raising their hand, Cap states, "All are dismissed except Officer Hagen."

The rest of the department filters out of the room after finding their assignments on the board. My phone vibrates in my pocket, but I don't check it.

"Morning, Cap."

"Morning. Please follow me."

Roxie walks beside me to his office.

"Take a seat," he states. "As you're aware, the K-9 program was recently reinstated with Roxie. Additionally, though you were called away, I was able to speak with Captain Snow about the preliminary aspects of expanding the program here in York."

I acknowledge his statement.

He continues while setting three thick books and then three binders on the desk. "In order for the program to be successful, we need a leader to head it up. Despite my love for training and how much I miss it, I can't add it to my plate. I want that person to be you. To do so, you need to pass the sergeant exam. The next time it'll be given is in November."

"Seriously?" Nothing could make my life better right now. I have a beautiful daughter and a gorgeous woman to share my life with and now my dream job.

"Yes. We want to add at least one, if not two more canines to our department over the next five years. You'll be tasked with vetting an officer to take on a canine partner and getting him or her through their training. Then collaborate with Snow to procure another dog."

A nervous feeling courses through me. The only time I've felt this way recently is at home with Lilah and Eva. For the first time, I could be happy at home and at work. "Thank you. Do you have a suggestion for the next officer?"

Cap smiles. "I do, but I'm wondering if you would come to the same conclusion. Who would you suggest?"

"Garcia."

"Glad we agree. Study and let me know if you have any questions. Washington was the last one to take the exam, for your information. The binders are Snow's program she uses with her department. Read it and study it, then amend it to work for our department."

"Thanks, Cap. I won't let you down."

"I know. Keep me up to date about Garcia when you talk to her."

"Will do."

"On another note, how is the 5K planning wrapping up?"

"Excellent. Eva and I still need a few vendors to confirm drop-off locations and times. Otherwise, everything is set."

"Glad to hear it. Kelsey and I will be there. I foresee at least my wife walking with the kids."

"I registered, but I'll be working, not running."

"Glad to hear the planning went well."

"Eva and I were thrust into it when everyone else bailed."

He raises an eyebrow but says nothing. Curious, but I don't call him on it, especially after the amazing job he just offered me. "I'm set."

I rise from my seat. "Thanks for the opportunity, Cap."

"You're welcome."

We shake hands before I exit his office and pluck my phone from my pocket to call Eva. Instead, I find a voicemail from Alannah.

"Lachlan, call me when you get a minute. I received an update about Clare."

My stomach bottoms out, and I set my hand on the wall to ground myself. It's impossible for me to tell from the sound of her voice if the update is good or bad. The scenarios in my head zigzag from benign to catastrophic in the blink of an eye. I lead Roxie outside and take a seat on the picnic table in the yard. I release Roxie, then return Alannah's call.

"Good morning, Craven Law. Alannah speaking."

"Hi, Alannah."

She sighs. "Hi, Hagen. Are you ready to hear the news??

I scrub my hand down my face. "Don't truly have a choice, do I?" I huff. "Sorry, I got amazing news from Cap this morning, which is why I didn't call sooner. What is the update?"

"Police outside Auburn, Massachusetts, found an abandoned rental car with Ohio plates by the side of Route 20 about ten days ago. They traced the rental back to a Charlotte Jones."

My stomach knots tighter the more Alannah shares. Each one of Clare's alters had a first name beginning with the letter C and her true last name—Jones. "Did they determine if Charlotte is Clare?"

Alannah answers, "They ordered the car towed. The rental company was contacted, and they sought to get the car back. The Auburn police department fingerprinted and cataloged the contents of the car before turning it over. In a duffel in the back seat, they found a letter with your name on it and York, Maine. Nothing else to indicate your address. The fingerprints are a match to Clare Jones of Chicago, Illinois."

"She was on her way here." A statement not a question. Despite the way I handled it, my instinct to increase security around Lilah was on point.

"Likely."

"I'm almost afraid to ask... have they located Clare yet?"

Alannah exhales slowly. "No, they have not."

"Okay. Who contacted you?" I wonder. My vigilance needs to remain in place until her whereabouts are known.

"Her attorney reached out late last night."

"Thank you for calling, Alannah."

"You're welcome."

I stand and work off some of my anger by throwing a ball for Roxie. Fifteen minutes later, I reenter the building and share the information I learned with Cap.

"None of that sounds promising for Clare."

"No, it doesn't."

"Please keep me informed."

"I will. I'm going home to talk to Eva. I'll be back after lunch."

"Understood."

I hop into my SUV with Roxie and drive home for lunch. Abnormal, yes, but this news warrants an in-person conversation.

The moment I cross the threshold, I see my gorgeous woman dancing in the kitchen. She has no clue I'm here yet, and her dance moves exemplify the same. I watch her for a few solid minutes before releasing Roxie, then slowly follow her.

When Eva feels Roxie against her leg, she casts a look of worry in my direction. "Hi, is everything okay?"

Before answering, I pull her against me and kiss her urgently. "Sort of. Not really. I'm not sure." I share the update Alannah gave me with her while I make a sandwich.

"I'm not sure if that's good or bad news," Eva states while we sit at the island.

"Me either." I take a few bites of my sandwich.

"She doesn't have our address."

"I love that."

"What?" she asks with a wrinkle in her nose.

"Our address."

She offers me one of her genuine smiles. "Me too."

"I have more news," I admit, nearly polishing off half of my sandwich.

"What kind?"

"Amazing. Cap asked me to sit for the sergeant exam in November."

"Congrats! I'm proud of you!"

I grin as wide as possible. "There's more. The reason for taking this exam is to allow me to run a K-9 unit at YPD. He wants to add up to two more canines in the next five years."

"Ohmigod!" She peppers my cheek with kisses. "You must be ecstatic!"

"I am. When I chose YPD, it was for a position below my skill set, but it was for Lilah. Cap petitioning to add Roxie and even more is beyond what I could've hoped for."

"I'm happy for you."

"How is your day going?" I ask.

"Aside from your amazing career update, I have secured a second soccer club to revamp their logo. One of the teams in Florida reached out to Kate Hightower to inquire about the new design, and she recommended me. I retained Alannah to negotiate the contract for me."

"Career progress all around today. I hate to rush out, but I need to get back to the precinct. We should celebrate soon."

"Sounds perfect. Go, I'll clean this up."

After a quick kiss, Roxie and I hustle out the front door. Cap sharing the expansion with me and Eva's news are the only good bits of today. On my way back to the precinct, I answer a call from Alannah.

"Twice in one day. This can't be good."

"Ehh. Not sure. Clare's attorney reached out again. There has been no update regarding her whereabouts. However, Mr. and Mrs. Jones would like to speak with you regarding the situation. They believe you will have a better idea where Clare would go."

"I don't and do not wish to speak with them. I may not have wanted to be with Clare long term, but I was willing to co-parent with her if it were an option. They ignored and overlooked her symptoms for years and disowned her when her medical care got too hard. Now they want my help? No, I have none to offer."

"Okay. I'll tell her attorney."

"Sorry about my tone. My day has been up and down so far. Also, thank you for helping Eva with her contract."

I hear the smile in Alannah's voice. "No problem. Happy to help a fellow boss babe at the beginning of running her own business. I heard your redecorated office was spectacular."

"Huh, good to know. Sorry you won't have company just yet." I smile inwardly, knowing my better half is bragging about me.

"No worries. I was only trying to help, and I have the space. Have a good afternoon, Lachlan."

"I'll try."

I return to the precinct and finish my shift. There were no calls requiring our assistance. I was able to visit one of the elementary schools during their science fair. I have been wrestling with what, if anything, I should tell Lilah. I decide not to share anything with her yet. Is it the correct call? I'm not sure.

It takes a few days for the other shoe to drop, and then I have no choice but to share unfortunate details with my daughter.

"Hello, Alannah," I greet her as she approaches the front desk four days later. "I'll get Craven for you."

She shakes her head. "I'm here to see you."

I drop my head briefly, and Roxie nudges me with her nose. "Let me call Cap and get someone to cover the desk." I have no doubt the news isn't good.

I pick up the receiver and dial.

"This is Captain Ramirez."

"Cap, it's Hagen. Do you have someone to spare for the desk? Alannah is here with news about Lilah's mother."

"I'll send Davis. Give me five minutes."

"Roger."

Davis arrives quickly, and Alannah, Roxie, and I walk outside to the park across the street.

"Clare's attorney called. They located her remains at the morgue near Worcester, Massachusetts. She was identified as Jane Doe. Apparently, after your refusal of knowledge, her parents reported her missing. Unbeknownst to them, there was already a report filed by her guardian. With two separate reports for the same woman, the police dug deeper. Plus, Mr. and Mrs. Jones called all the hospitals and medical examiners, making waves about failing to notify them."

"How could the medical examiners notify them? She didn't have identification on her." I'm afraid to ask, but I do anyway. "What were the circumstances of her death?"

"Suspected overdose, possibly purposeful," Alannah shares.

Conflicting feelings filter in and out of my body and mind. The sense of grief for a woman I barely know but who is the biological mother of my daughter. The palatable relief knowing once she learns about her mother's death, Lilah will move on. "I'm not sure what to say."

"Nothing."

I grip the back of my neck. "What happens now? Did her guardian or family claim her? Will there be a service?"

Alannah sets her hand on my forearm. "I'll get you the answers to those questions."

"Thank you for sharing in person, Alannah."

"You're welcome. Please let me know if you need anything."

I drop my head. "I will." I escort Alannah to her car and then walk straight to Cap's office.

He waves me inside. "I take it the update wasn't pleasant," he surmises.

"No. Clare died. Aside from that information, the details aren't plentiful."

"Understood. Go home. If you need time off for services, put in a request," Cap states.

"I will." I'm not sure if I should add anything else. "Roxie, *hier*."

Like earlier this week, I head home at lunch and share the news with Eva while I change and lock my weapon in the safe.

"How terrible," she offers. "I'm sorry. How do you feel?"

"Mixed and angry."

"Please explain," she asks.

I finish changing and take a seat beside her on the bed. "Despite making strides by allowing Clare to see Lilah's artwork and sending old photos, I kept her as far away from my daughter as I could. I'm relieved but filled with shame, and surprisingly a bit of grief."

"Shame because you're relieved you don't have to worry about Clare anymore?"

"Yes."

"It's understandable, and no one would fault you for your feelings. You were protecting Lilah. Clare made her choice nearly five years ago. The relief isn't because she's gone. It's because all the pressure you were under to protect Lilah over and above what a normal father would carry was lifted. Grief is normal for any loss, regardless of how long you have known a person. You cared about Clare. To be honest, I felt similar when my mom had her stroke. I was terrified the woman I loved would be gone forever."

I press a kiss to her temple. "Do you have time for a walk with me before picking up Lilah?"

"Of course."

Less than thirty minutes later, we stroll the rail trail near the cottage with Roxie for two laps. For the most part, it's comfortably silent. It turns out to be exactly what I need to filter my thoughts and feelings about Clare and how it impacts my life… and my daughter's.

Afterward, we pick up Lilah from the center and return home.

"Will you sit with us for a minute, sweet pea?"

"Sure. What's wrong, Daddy?"

"Do you remember when you told the lady at the Perk you didn't have a mom?"

Lilah nods. "I meant I didn't have a mom who lived with me."

I exhale sharply. "Okay. Your mom's name was Clare. She was sick and couldn't take care of you."

"So you did by yourself," she supplies.

"Yes." I close my eyes and settle myself to share this news with my daughter. "Clare died a few days ago." The timeline is off, but I don't want to give too many details.

"Oh. Are you sad?"

"Yes."

"Why?"

"Clare gave me one of the best gifts ever."

Lilah frowns. "What?"

"Not what, who. Clare gave me you."

Silently, she ponders my response before asking, "Can I go play?"

"Sure."

She pushes off the couch and walks to her room with Roxie following her closely.

"How are you feeling about that?" Eva asks.

"Not sure. Lilah had no relationship with Clare. Her reaction is logical, I suppose."

"Lilah will be fine. We're here for her if or when she needs to talk more."

Tugging her close, I absorb the calm she offers… hoping she's right.

CHAPTER TWENTY-NINE

EVA

The last four weeks have passed in a blur. We celebrated Lachlan in a low-key way for Father's Day. Thankfully, Lilah seems to be handling the news of her mother's death well. The fact that Clare truly didn't have a role in her life is key to Lilah processing the situation.

"Time to go," I call from the kitchen.

Lilah turns the corner dressed but rubbing her eyes. "It's early, Mommy."

I laugh softly. "I know, sweet pea. Races are usually first thing in the morning. The good news is we'll be done around lunchtime."

She shrugs and locates her shoes. Once she's set, I search for Lachlan. He hasn't made a peep since he rolled out of bed.

"You okay?" I ask, finding him staring at his clothes in the closet. "We need to get going."

"Working on it."

I step between him and his perfectly hanging clothes, none of which will work for today's event. "What are you nervous about?"

His arms collapse around me, and he draws me close. "I'm nervous about meeting your parents."

"They will love you like I do. I mean, it won't be instant, as you're stealing their only daughter, but by the end of the day, it'll be fine. I promise."

He kisses the top of my head. "I'll be right out, beautiful."

Twenty minutes later, we walk to the registration area for the race. Thankfully, our volunteers are ready and willing despite the early hour.

"Morning, Hagen and Eva. Hi, Lilah," Craven greets us once we join him there. Caden and Alannah say hello as well.

"Thank you for coming and helping out," I offer.

"How was your first season of college ball and, you know, college, Caden?" Lachlan asks.

"The basketball went well. We finished second in our conference. I'm excited for the rest of my career. My classes are awesome. It helps that I knew I wanted to study cybersecurity before I enrolled."

"Sweet. Good for you." Lachlan verifies the assignments. "Caden and Alannah, you're on registration duty. Please collect the donations, if any. Give runners a packet. They'll get a completion medal and T-shirt at the end of the race."

"No problem," Alannah replies.

A throng of people rushes toward us.

"Wow, that's a lot of people," Lilah observes.

"Yeah. It is." I turn my attention to them and announce, "If you're a volunteer, please move to your left. If you are here to check in as a participant, please shift right."

The crowd parts, following my instructions, and we're thrust into a flurry of activity for the next two hours before the race is set to start.

Lachlan and I opted not to run despite registering to do so. The initial moment of truth happens when Grant approaches the registration table with his family and our parents.

"Morning, Grant." I hand him the packets for him and Maggie, plus cute numbers for the kids. With a second packet in hand, I circle the table and hug my parents. "Thank you for coming."

"We wouldn't miss this. Anytime I'll earn a medal for completing my morning walk, I'm in," my mother remarks. She has made great strides since her stroke, and my father has taken his health more seriously as well.

"I'm glad we could organize your award for you. Mom, Dad, please meet Lachlan and Lilah." My mom, a former third-grade teacher, is tall, thin, and always has a smile on her face. After selling the EggStop, my parents have been enjoying their retirement.

Lachlan extends his hand to my father, who shakes it. Attempting to shake my mother's hand is thwarted by Lilah's words.

"Mommy, you forgot Roxie."

A smile widens on my mother's face, and my father nods curtly. They didn't meet Cody until after we were engaged. Introducing Lachlan and Lilah now is a tacit signal they're sticking around.

"You're right, I did. Mom and Dad, please meet Roxie as well."

My father crouches to greet Lilah and pet Roxie while Lachlan is pulled in for a hug by my mother.

Smithson approaches from our left. "Eva, Captain Ramirez is looking for you. Something about an issue with the barricades near mile two. Nice to see you again, Mr. and Mrs. Washington."

"You as well, Zack," my mother replies.

"Where can I find him?" I ask.

"I'll take care of it, sweetheart," Lachlan offers.

"Okay."

"Pleasure, Mr. and Mrs. Washington. Hopefully, we can chat more after the race," Lachlan states. "Li, please stay with Eva and Roxie." Even though there's no concern about Clare any longer, Lachlan continues to be overprotective of Lilah. Over time, I'm sure it will decrease to normal dad levels as opposed to overprotective alpha dad.

"Okay, Daddy."

Lachlan kisses my cheek and leaves to locate Captain Ramirez and fix the issue.

"Why don't we move to the start area?" I suggest. I loop Roxie's leash around my wrist, and Lilah takes my hand. My mother falls in beside me with my father behind us talking to Grant. If I had to surmise, he's checking Grant's opinion of Lachlan.

"You failed to mention he's a cop like your brother," she accuses.

"Did I?"

My mother dips her chin and glares at me. "You did. You also failed to mention he's quite handsome as well as how serious you two are so soon."

"I didn't purposely omit it. To me, it doesn't feel fast. Like with Grant, his job is a calling. He helps people every single day. It's honorable." We are about halfway to the start line.

"It is. I'm surprised is all," she adds. "Lilah is the cutest."

I smile. "She's amazing."

"Where is her mother?"

I shouldn't be surprised by her concern. "I'm her mother."

"You know what I mean, Eva."

"It's a long story, which I'll willingly share with you at another time."

"Thank you. Aside from those points, you're happy here?"

I look down at Lilah and Roxie. "I am. More than I've ever been before, and it's because of them."

"I'm glad you found a man willing to stand beside you instead of in front of you."

"You never shared your disapproval of Cody before. Why?"

"I wasn't about to tell you he was wrong for you. You needed to figure it out on your own."

"Thanks, Mom." I give her a side hug and leave her at the start line with my father and Grant.

Lachlan jogs to my side to start the race together.

"Everything fixed?"

"Yup, all set. Let's do this!"

I raise the bullhorn and announce, "Good morning and welcome to the First YPD 5K and Toy Drive. We appreciate your support for this event. On your mark, get set, go!"

As I say go, Lachlan fires the pistol into the air. Lilah cheers, and the participants take off. The three of us plus Roxie hop onto a golf cart and drive to the finish line. A seasoned runner can finish this distance in twenty minutes or less.

"Mommy?"

"Yeah, sweet pea."

"This is super fun!"

"It is," I reply with a proud grin on my face.

"Can we do it again next summer?"

I glance at Lachlan, who has a huge smile plastered on his face. "If they host it again, absolutely."

"Yay!"

We park along the side of the finish line and wait for the first finisher. The first-place male is Donovan Davis with a time of 18:48. The first-place woman is Esme Garcia with a time of 19:56. Over the next hour, we award medals and T-shirts while directing the participants to the food trucks in the park.

It was sweet handing my parents their completion medals. I didn't mind the sweaty hugs one bit.

"We'll see you at Grant's for the barbeque, right?" my mother asks after securing her medal around her neck.

"Yes, we'll be there."

"Perfect. See you later. Bye, Lachlan and Lilah."

"Mommy's mom, you forgot Roxie," Lilah reminds her.

Without missing a beat, my mother crouches beside Lilah and pets Roxie. "Thank you, Lilah. I wouldn't want to miss your dog."

Lilah wrinkles her nose. "Daddy's special police dog."

"Oh, I see. Well, goodbye, Roxie."

By noon, we have returned the route and the park back into prerace condition. The trash bins will be emptied tomorrow morning by the refuse company.

"Ready, gorgeous?"

"Yes, but can we stop home before going to Grant's?"

"Of course. Is everything all right?"

"Yeah, I need to clean up a bit. I'll be quick as long as you stay out of the bedroom. It's hotter than I thought it would be today."

Lachlan laughs, then kisses me. "It's July, babe. Of course it is!" He leans in and whispers, "I don't plan on staying out of the bathroom while you shower."

A shot of desire zips through me, and I shake my head. From the beginning he has been straightforward with his sexy words. I'm still surprised I love it.

I only went over my self-imposed time limit by five minutes. I'm fully blaming Lachlan. He wasn't kidding. He leaned against the sink and watched me shower. I must admit, I'm shocked he didn't jump in with me.

"Why didn't you join me?" I ask as he turns onto Grant's street.

Lachlan whispers, "I want to continue making an excellent impression on your parents. Lateness is unacceptable, although please know I wanted to soap you up to feel your skin warm beneath my fingertips."

Holy hell! I squeeze my thighs together, hoping to quell the ache. I fail miserably.

"I'll make you scream my name, muffled behind my hand later tonight, multiple times to satisfy the throbbing between your legs," he whispers and presses a kiss to my cheek before hopping out of the car to open our doors.

Lilah scampers around the house in search of Caleb and Corrinne with Roxie close behind her.

"You follow. I'll go through?" I suggest.

"Sure," Lachlan replies. With a kiss, he disappears around the corner of the house after our daughter.

Even before Clare died, I thought of Lilah as mine. Now I could make it official, a notion I plan to discuss with Lachlan... eventually.

In the house, I find my brother and parents hovering around the island.

"Did you come alone?" Grant asks.

"No, they went around the side because Lilah heard the kids playing," I answer.

"Makes sense. How is your new business venture going?"

"Excellent," I reply with a huge smile on my face.

"Good for you, sweetie. Tell us more," my mother urges.

I share what went down with my old firm and the new soccer team contract in the works.

"We're proud of you, both of you. We truly didn't share our feelings well when you and your brother turned down taking over the restaurant. Now we realize the sale was the best option for us and for the two of you," my father states before hugging us.

"Thanks, Dad," we reply together.

Then Grant adds, "We should get outside and start cooking these ribs."

I wrinkle my brow. "No further questions about my relationship? Trust me, I'm not looking to discuss in detail, but I'm surprised," I admit to my parents.

A huge smile grows on my mother's face. "We don't need more information per se. We can see you're in love and happy. I would like to know how you met, but that's merely anecdotal."

"I see."

"Plus, Grant is his coworker and has mentioned Hagen more than once over the years. More importantly, he's seen you two together, and he approves."

Turning toward my brother, I accuse, "You told them about the office, didn't you?"

Grant shrugs. "If I did?"

I bump his hip. "Thanks, bro."

"Anytime. I talked to Hagen at soccer, and you're happy. I know how that feels, and when you find it, you hold on with both hands. I'm surprised you broke through his hard exterior shell. You managed to get him to open up to you and share his life. No one else has come close. You two will be fine," Grant adds.

After another round of hugs, we join the rest of the family outside and fire up the grill for an amazing dinner.

CHAPTER THIRTY

LACHLAN

"Pens down," the proctor states from the front of the room.

I lean back in my chair and mull the last three hours. The exam was tough, but I think my preparation over the past three months was enough. I'm confident I passed. I worked out a schedule to prepare for the exam, purposely taking extra desk shifts and burying my nose in the study guides nightly.

I walk to the front of the room and turn in the booklet. The moment I exit the building, the crisp air hits my lungs. I inhale slowly and exhale. With a smile, I settle into the driver's seat of my car and turn on my phone. I'm not surprised the only message is from Eva. Everyone else offered well-wishes before the exam, including Washington, Smithson, and Cap.

Eva: I'm proud of you, Sergeant Hagen. Love you.

Me: Thank you, gorgeous. Love you. I'll be home soon.

Before driving home, I make a stop at the Perk. I grab coffees and scones for us and place a special order to be ready in a few weeks. With my food in hand, I step through the door from the garage. Roxie rushes over to greet me, followed closely by Eva.

"You let Roxie get to me first?" I accuse and set down the pastries.

"She has twice as many legs."

I chuckle, lift her into my arms, and kiss her until we're both panting. "Do you have a spot in your schedule for me to ravage you from head to toe with my lips and hands?"

"Oh, how I love your dirty words. Hell yes! Being the boss allows me sexy time in the middle of my day."

"Happy to hear it. It won't change." I take a few steps toward the master bedroom. "Wrap your legs around my waist," I demand.

Eva complies without hesitation. I slide my hands along the sides of her body, raising her arms overhead and dragging her shirt up at the same time. Her hands settle on my shoulders as I toss her shirt to the hardwood floor. After I set her on her feet near the bed, she makes quick work of my Henley, then focuses on removing my belt. My lips travel from the bow of her mouth, along her jawline, and down the curve of her neck. Goose bumps erupt on her skin when my lips meet the hollow of her collarbone.

"Lachlan." My name sounds raspy and needy.

"Nope, not hurrying today, sweetheart." I continue my quest to mark her inch by inch. Once I reach her toes, I lick, nip, and suck my way up to her lips. The expression on her face his priceless. "What's wrong?"

"Nothing, except your time is up. I need you to fill me and make me scream."

"As you wish." I widen her thighs with mine and bury myself to the hilt in her.

"Ohmigod! Yes!"

"Already?"

Eva giggles softly. "No, but it won't take long. You were edging me on purpose."

"Me? I would never."

"Yes, you would."

I would. Together we pick up our pace and chase bliss together. Once we catch our breath, we clean up and dress.

With another kiss, I say, "Let's pick up our daughter and get started on pizza night."

After a round trip to the center, we return home with Lilah and prepare homemade pizzas on Friday instead of Thursday this week.

"What kind of pizza do you want, Li?" I ask my daughter.

"'Roni and cheese, please," she states.

"For you, my love?"

Eva wrinkles her nose and smiles at me. "I'm thinking pepperoni and sausage."

"Let's do this!"

Lilah laughs heartily at my enthusiasm while Eva grins at me. Nearly an hour later, we take slices of pizza to the table. Lilah fills us in on her day while polishing off her plate.

"Do we have stuff for brownie sundaes, Daddy?"

I shrug.

Eva saves me. "Let's go look, sweet pea."

They walk into the kitchen as if they are getting away with something, though I can see their every move. I hear giggles and whispers. They approach the dining room table again, hand in hand.

"Daddy, will you go out and get chocolate sauce and whipped cream while Mommy and me make the brownies?"

"Sure."

My ladies high-five, and I grab my keys, wallet, and phone. I kiss them both and add, "I'll be back soon."

It's rare for me to be completely alone. Normally, I would relish the silence. Today, not so much. When I park at the store, my phone vibrates with an incoming call.

"Good evening, Cap. Is everything okay?"

"Yes. I may have seen the results from the exam that was administered earlier today."

"I see."

"I am not supposed to share them until next week."

"Would you be willing to share if I didn't hear it from you?"

Cap laughs. "I would. Congratulations, Sergeant Hagen."

"Thank you."

"Mum's the word."

"What word? Have a nice evening."

"You as well."

I hustle through the store and collect the requested ingredients, then check out and return home. When I step inside, the smell of freshly baked brownies wafts toward me.

"Yay! Now we need to wait for them to cool a little," Lilah informs me.

"What should we do in the meantime?"

"Build a fort," my daughter suggests. "Then we can come back up, build our sundaes, and eat them in the fort."

"Deal," I reply. "You get started gathering the pillows and blankets, but Li—"

"Walk," she completes my sentence. "I like Miss Scarlett, but I don't want to see her at work again."

I stifle a laugh as Lilah walks away. After she disappears around the corner, I surround Eva in my arms.

"I have some news to share."

"Do you?"

"It's hush-hush until next week."

"You passed! Who? When?" Eva peppers me with kisses. "Never mind. I'm so proud of you. We should celebrate later."

I look left to verify Lilah is out of earshot. "Naked?"

"Absolutely."

I agree and kiss the elegant curve of her neck. It's one of my favorite spots on her body.

While we were talking, Lilah has made numerous trips into the basement with blankets and pillows.

In a breathless huff, she says, "I'm done. Can we build now? I need somewhere to take a nap."

We laugh and follow her downstairs.

"Can it be huge, Daddy?"

"Absolutely."

"Can we leave it up?"

"Yes."

"Yay!" Lilah cheers. For the next thirty minutes, she instructs, and Eva and I follow without question, securing and holding up the walls until they're perfect.

"Sundae time," Eva announces.

With bowls teeming with warm brownies, vanilla ice cream, chocolate syrup, sprinkles, and whipped cream, we return to our fort and laugh and talk until bedtime for Lilah. After cleaning our sundae bar dishes and ingredients, we turn in as well. More accurately, we twist up our sheets well into the wee hours of the morning.

CHAPTER THIRTY-ONE

EVA

A few weeks and a low-key Thanksgiving holiday have passed since his promotion.

"Lilah, are you ready?" I call out to her.

"I'm ready, Mommy. Are the cupcakes?"

"Definitely. Check them out," I urge her.

Lilah is celebrating her birthday a few days early at the center with cupcakes decorated with her favorite fairies' powers. There's a water-themed one for Silvermist, one with a flower garden for Rosetta, a chocolate cupcake decorated with animals for Fawn, and even a frosty one for Periwinkle.

"Miss Kelsey is awesome! I bet they will be yummy too!"

I smile at her. "I'm sure they will be. Let's get you to school."

With a huge grin on her face, Lilah skips to the garage and buckles herself into her seat. I set the cupcakes in the back of my new SUV and climb in after checking her buckle.

Noelle greets me at the door to assist. "Hello, Lilah. Aren't these pretty."

"Miss Kelsey made them," Lilah informs her.

"I see. Go ahead inside. I'll put these in the lunch area for safekeeping," Noelle offers.

"Thanks."

"Birthday celebrations are cherished around here."

"Glad to hear it. I'll see you later when I pick her up."

"Sounds great! I was going to email you, but since you're here, Caro and I are going to announce the new location at the beginning of the year. Does the timeframe give you enough notice for the necessary website changes?"

"Congratulations! Definitely. I'll pencil you in for a meeting before the holiday."

"Perfect! Have a great day," she offers.

"You too!"

I leave the center and return home to wrap up my workweek with a video conference with my junior account manager.

I can hear the tone as I rush into the office. I push the Accept button and flop into my chair. "Hey, Jo!"

"Hey. Slow drop-off today?"

"She's celebrating her birthday with her friends at school. Tomorrow we're having a small party for her, then a sleepover with a few friends, including my niece and nephew."

"Sweet!" Jo gives me a quick synopsis of the files she's handling and the upcoming deadlines.

"Great! The Florida team logo is in the works. I have a few draft concepts. They're on the shared drive. Please look and let me know which one you like best. I need to submit those before the holiday. The perfumery campaign will start running the first of the year."

"Wish Lilah a happy birthday from us. Talk again next week."

"Later, Jo."

I sigh and smile, closing my laptop. Although I'm sure the house is perfect and everything is ready for tomorrow, I go over the campaign again. The basement is prepared for a party centered around animals with a hint of Fawn. Woodland creatures adorn the walls, and we ordered cookies and cupcakes with the same theme.

Near three, the doorbell rings. I frown when I see Lachlan standing on our front porch.

"What are you doing?"

Clad in jeans and a puffer coat, holding a huge bouquet of flowers and a large box with a red bow, he replies, "I wanted to deliver these myself." Stepping inside, he hands me the flowers before kissing me deeply.

I smell them once he releases me. "What are you up to?" Giddiness overtakes me.

He points to himself. "Me? Nothing. Is there a rule that says I can't bring my better half flowers and a gift for no reason?"

I tilt my head, then accept the box. "No, there isn't. What's the occasion, though?"

"Birthday dinner out with Lilah."

I purse my lips. "We're having dinner for Lilah, yet I get beautiful flowers and a gift?"

He shrugs and replies, "Yes."

"Now I'm confident you're up to something."

"We will pick you up at five."

"You don't know this yet, but I'm not a fan of surprises."

"I'll keep your preference in mind… in the future. I'll be back in a few hours. Love you."

"Now I know you're up to something and conspiring with our daughter."

He feigns shock but says nothing.

"I'll be ready. Love you."

With a quick, nearly chaste kiss he's gone. Can't blame him. If he kissed me deeply again, we would be dancing toward our bed.

I hurry into the bedroom and tear open the familiar box. Inside, I find an emerald sheath dress with three-quarter bell sleeves. It's beautiful, and it'll fit because he asked Kelly to make it for me. Settling my nerves regarding the true meaning behind tonight's dinner, I dress and apply a little makeup.

At five on the dot, Lachlan, Lilah, and Roxie enter the house.

"Wow! Mommy, your dress matches mine," Lilah states.

My gaze pins to Lachlan. "Yes, it does, sweet pea."

"Did you know?" she asks.

"No, Daddy surprised both of us."

Glee is plastered on her face. "I love 'prises and gifts. I have a gi—"

"Not yet, Li," Lachlan warns her. He moves closer and kisses me lightly on the lips. "Lilah, please go get your dress coat so we can leave."

"Okay." She skips toward her room.

"Hi, again."

"Hi. You look gorgeous."

"Thank you. This dress fits perfectly. I gather there is more up your sleeve for tonight?"

"Maybe one or two things," he replies and kisses me again. Scooping my coat from the back of the couch, he gathers my hair in his hand and helps me into it.

An inappropriate shiver cascades through me. Well, inappropriate timing, not for the idea. "Thank you."

"I see you, sweetheart."

I turn to face him. "I have no idea what you're talking about."

"I will pull your hair again at a later time… when we're alone."

I swallow hard as Lilah joins us, wearing a black pea coat with a huge pink flower on the lapel. "Let's go. We have special dinner to have."

"As you wish, almost birthday girl," Lachlan replies.

Lilah giggles. "You're silly, Daddy."

"Roxie, crate." She lopes to her crate, and he locks it.

Lachan offers me his arm and Lilah his hand and escorts us to the car. Once we're both in our seats, he rounds the car and drives toward our destination.

I turn to look back at Lilah. "Do you know where we're going for dinner?"

She nods enthusiastically. "Can I share?"

"Only where we're going for dinner," he reminds her.

"We're going to eat dinner in a snow globe," Lilah informs me.

"Sounds awesome," I reply, threading my fingers with Lachlan's.

He lifts our hands and kisses the back of mine. Lilah left out the best detail about our dinner. Despite the fact that it's early December, the snow globe is on the grassy area near Short Sands Beach. String lights attached to a temporary pergola provide additional illumination.

"It's amazing!" I admit as we approach.

"This is super cool," Lilah exclaims.

"I thought you knew about this already," I wonder aloud.

"I know the plan, but I haven't seen it, Mommy." The underlying sass is strong in her response.

"What else is Daddy up to?"

Lachlan gives Lilah a stern "don't spill the beans" look, and she shrugs without offering any additional top-secret details.

Lilah steps inside first. It's cozy in the plastic bubble. An elegantly set round table with three chairs is in the center. There is a small hallway, if you will, where it looks like a staging area.

"Good evening. I'm Matteo, and I'll be serving you this evening. Your menu has been preplanned. I shall serve drinks and your appetizer immediately."

I lean over the white linen tablecloth and whisper, "Thank you."

Lachlan kisses my temple before replying, "You're welcome."

"How do you know Matteo?"

"He's Lia's cousin. He's a personal chef and caterer. He mostly works with athletes and celebrities."

Matteo slips back inside with our sodas and a plate of bruschetta.

"Yes, tomato bread!" Lilah states.

If I'm not mistaken, I hear Matteo chuckle as he returns to the serving area where he's plating our food. The three of us make quick work of the bruschetta embrata. Dutifully, Matteo tops off our drinks, removes our appetizer dishes, and slips away again.

"Daddy, this is so cool!"

Lachlan grins. "It is."

After a brief break, he returns with Lilah's dinner.

"Mac and cheese and nuggies! Thanks, Mr. Matteo."

"You're welcome, Miss Lilah."

He leaves and returns with our dishes. I'm not shocked when he serves me macaroni and cheese with lobster and sets a large filet with sides before Lachlan. For the most part, we devour our dinner in silence. It isn't because we don't have anything to say, but Matteo's food is phenomenal.

"Is everything to your liking?" he asks.

"Each morsel is amazing. Thank you," I offer.

"You're welcome."

Lilah's plate is licked clean, and she's sitting quietly, but her foot is bouncing up and down as if she can't contain the secret she's carrying any longer. "Daddy, is it time yet?"

"Almost. We need to finish our dinner."

Soon thereafter, Lachlan and I are done with our meals, and Matteo clears them away.

"Would you like your dessert course now or later?"

"Later, please. We're going for a walk," Lachlan replies.

Glee materializes on Lilah's cherub face. "Are you sure about outside? It's cold."

"Yes, the woman we love won't worry about a little cold air at the beach."

I smile and follow them outside. While I adjust the buttons on Lilah's coat and then mine, Lachlan grabs two white boxes and flashlights from Matteo and nods tightly. We take the concrete staircase down to the sand and turn right. It's a short distance from there to the rocky cliff framing the edge of the beach.

While we walk, Lachlan pours his heart out. "Five years ago, my life changed instantly. I became a father to a precocious princess who keeps me on my toes. I was determined to protect her with every fiber of my being from anything that may harm her, including my ineptitude at solo parenting. In doing so, I walled us off in our own private bubble. It was calm, quiet, and safe. Fast-forward to last year, when my sweet daughter falls at the feet of the woman of my dreams. You single-handedly broke through the hard gray wall around my little family brick by brick and made it brighter. We have two huge questions to ask you today."

Lilah is looking up at Lachlan with wide eyes and a huge smile on her face. "Can I go first?"

He lifts his shoulder as if thinking what the best plan is. "We should open them together."

"Okay," Lilah replies, seemingly unhappy with having to share this moment. "On three?"

He nods and turns the box to open in my direction. Lilah does the same.

"One, two, three." With a flourish, they open the two nondescript white boxes. Inside each box is a decorated sugar cookie. One has "Adopt me" and one has "Marry me" in elegant icing prepared by Kelsey.

I laugh softly. "I think those are backward."

Lilah shoves her box into my right hand and grabs the correct one.

"Go ahead, sweet pea," Lachlan urges our daughter.

"Miss Eva, will you be my mommy 'ficially?"

I crouch in front of Lilah, set the box on the sand, and take her hands in mind. "I would love to."

Lilah throws her arms around my neck and whispers, "I love you."

I swipe the tear rolling down my cheek. "I love you, Lilah."

Lachlan extends his hand to me when our daughter releases me. Once I'm standing, he lowers down to his knee before me. The ring box is closed in his hand. "Eva, will you make me the happiest man on the planet and walk beside me for the rest of my life?"

"Yes."

Lachlan rises from the ground and kisses me deeply. Pulling back, he murmurs, "I love you, Eva."

"I love you."

Our sweet daughter interrupts our moment a little early. "You forgot the pretty ring."

"You're right, sweet pea, I did." He loosens his hold on me and opens the box between us. "What do you think?"

I stare at the old mine Asscher cut, double-prong ring with my mouth agape. "You were nervous?"

"A little. If you hate it, we can pick something else."

"No. It's perfect." I never thought there was a man out there for me until I met Lilah. She brought her father into my life. I couldn't ask for more to start our family together than two lifetime proposals at once.

He slides the ring on my finger and kisses me again. Lilah is clapping and cheering beside us.

"What do you say to a chocolate, chocolate, and more chocolate dessert crafted by Matteo before we go home?"

"Yes!" Lilah exclaims.

Hand in hand, we walk across the cold sand to our snow globe bubble and enjoy the decadent dessert.

"You forgot one more 'prise," Lilah states.

Lachlan looks over at our daughter and wrinkles his brow. "I did?"

"Yes, you didn't tell Mommy you invited Miss Gina and Mr. Greg to my party tomorrow."

"You're right, I did."

"You talked to my parents?" The concern is evident in my voice.

"Yes, I asked for your hand in marriage and for them to join us for the party."

A rush of emotion I've been holding back falls over my cheeks.

"Don't cry, gorgeous. I would hope Lilah's partner would ask me in the future, despite the antiquity of the gesture. The same goes for us."

We thank Matteo again for his delicious meal and drive home. Lilah is sound asleep by the time we pull into the garage.

"I'll take care of Roxie while you put her to bed. Meet me in the bedroom?"

"Will you strip down to the sexy lace lingerie you have beneath that dress and your engagement ring?"

"Who says there's lingerie under this dress?"

I wink at him, and he groans and lifts Lilah out of her seat.

EPILOGUE

EVA

A few weeks have passed since a mysterious invitation to a book club arrived in the mail for me. It instructed me to pick up a novel and read it before tonight's meeting. I love a good thriller and devoured it in a few days. Since then, I've been waiting for tonight.

A book club. Sweet! It will be nice to share my thoughts about books with someone other than my fiancé.

"Lachlan, I need to leave."

"Have fun, babe."

"Bye, Mommy. See you in the mornin'."

"You too."

"We'll keep the fort up for sundaes tomorrow afternoon. Love you."

Right before six, I knock on the door at Alannah's house. It's tucked in a secluded neighborhood with a gorgeous community garden.

Alannah throws open the door as I climb the stairs. "I'm so excited you're here."

Curious phrasing, but I ignore it. When I step inside, I'm greeted by Maggie, Willa Cappelli, if I'm recalling correctly, and Carly.

"How's engaged life?" Carly inquires. "I'm sure you're glad you decided against a fling."

"Absolutely," I reply.

"When's the big day?" Maggie asks.

"We want a small, intimate wedding. It'll probably be in the late spring."

Once they're comfortable, Carly calls for everyone's attention. "Good evening, ladies. Welcome to our monthly book club meeting."

Echoes of "welcome" and "nice to have you here" surround me. We spend the next hour-plus discussing the book in detail. We share our opinions and objections to the story and the crazy twist at the end.

Carly steps before the group and states, "I would like to call this meeting to order. When we were together last, we voted to allow those who are engaged to our list of members to join us rather than waiting for them to be legally wed. With that said, I would like to welcome Eva Washington soon-to-be Hagen to our group.

"Wait, working with Lachlan was a setup from the beginning?"

Maggie grins at me. "Maybe a little."

"How could you know we would hit it off?"

"If anyone could break through the armor around his heart and daughter, it was you," Maggie replies.

"Wow! You ladies have skills." I'm not even a little upset that they saw my connection with Lilah at the party. Who knew a job interview and an invitation to a holiday party with my brother would lead to Lilah and Lachlan. I'm overjoyed.

A chorus of laughter surrounds me.

Carly asks, "Are there any motions to be heard?"

The room falls silent.

"No motions are set forth tonight. I request you consider names to be added to the new list for doctors and nurses. The same parameters would apply. There must be at least one woman included. We will vote on the inaugural members at our next meeting. I open the floor to discuss our next potential couple," Carly states.

"How do you decide who to fix up?" I ask.

Kelsey replies, "We have the potential candidates, and we work from that. If we see an avenue to assist a person on the list, we do."

I refocus on Carly.

"I will canvass the room for suggestions and set them up front. Please vote before you leave. Our next event will be the charity sports game hosted by the Gugliotti family. This year it'll be a softball game in late spring." She finishes by sharing the book for next month. "I shall read the names and adjourn our meeting for this month. The York Police Department list includes Donovan Davis, Piper Montgomery, and Esmeralda Garcia. Former honorees are William Ramirez, Grant Washington, Luca Cappelli, Santino Gugliotti, Zachary Smithson, and Callan Craven."

She continues reading aloud. "The York Fire Department list includes Bradford Collings, Alden Rhodes, Aidan Madden, Landry Reed, and Mia Arden. No former honorees to date. Lastly, the EMTs in York County include Séamus Penn, Jude Pascal, Hollis Booker, Lexington Soren, and Lacey Ransom. No former honorees to date."

We chat a little longer, and the guests leave slowly. It's amazing that these women have been successful setting up their friends and coworkers for the last six years. I'm excited to be assisting them now.

Thank you so much for reading *For Love & Cookies*!

I hope you love the matchmakers. Find out which first responder they set their sights on next coming summer 2024!

Did you love *For Love & Cookies*?

Thank you for taking the time to read it. I hope you loved it!
If you liked this book or another one of my books, please consider posting a review.
A short line or two will be perfect! It helps indie authors like me get noticed. I appreciate your support and feedback.

COMING SOON

Scala Talent and Sports Management
Moonshot

MY BOOKS

Protecting Us

Hers to Protect

MATCHMAKERS' BOOK CLUB:

For Love & Coffee

For Love & Basketball

All my books in one place: www.nicolevidal.com/books